Poetic Justice

The Faces Of Retribution

Short stories
by
Wauchope Friday Writers Group

Poetic Justice

The Faces of Retribution

All Rights Reserved

ISBN: 978-0-6459672-0-3

For information address
desleypolmear@hotmail.com

First Printing 2023

Table of Contents

Table of Contents

A Word from the Facilitator

I facilitate a writing group at the Wauchope library on a Friday. I like to help and inspire others who have an interest in writing. In 2022, I had a small group of women who produced wonderful stories and then succeeded in publishing their first lot of stories in a book. How proud I felt, and so did they.

This year, in 2023, I have facilitated a group of new writers who have all been keen to write. From day one, they put pen to paper, and by September, they had finished their stories. In addition, one member from last year's writers group attended the new group, as I continued to mentor her on her ongoing writing journey.

At 9.30, as a personal touch, we begin by writing what we've been doing over the past week before our morning coffee and biscuits. It's a way of connecting with the group. We have lots of laughs during the 3 hour writing session, which covers many subjects. It amazes me how quick they put pen to paper when I give them a subject to write about. I think they amaze themselves too. The writers all agree, that in the 3 hours, they think of nothing but writing.

In this book, 2023, I urged them to write fiction, perhaps covering a murder or a mystery. They have come up with some great stories and I am proud of them all.

In the latter part of the book, they have written shorter stories on any subject they chose.

I am blessed to have my administrator, Carolyn Williams, to help with managing our private group page on FB and to plan the flyer for advertising and the media.

This yearly book would not happen except for my friend, and publisher, Michael Davies, who puts all stops out to help with this publication. I thank you.

Desley Polmear
www.desleypolmearcreative.com

The Stalker and the Hunted

by Carolyn Williams

Chapter 1

Stalking is a dangerous and insidious crime and the impact on the victim can be devastating. The conviction rates for stalking in England and Wales are shockingly low. Only one in a thousand stalkers are convicted.
Suzy Lamplugh Trust.

According to the Australian Bureau of Statistics (ABS) about 1.6 million women and 587,000 men have been victims of the crime of stalking since they reached the age of fifteen.

* * *

The nightmare escalated after a regular Friday night out. It was one am on September fourth, 2021 when Gail Mason got home and let herself into the quiet beach house, overlooking Brighton beach, in England. The sudden burst of light from her mobile phone made her jump. The light cast a small glow in the dark room. Mum, the screen read.

'Hi Mum, I have just got through the door. Everything is fine. Thanks for dinner, it was lovely and just what I needed. I will call you tomorrow.'

'Sleep tight sweetheart and try not to worry. Call me if you need me.'

Although Gail was twenty-six and had left home at eighteen to go to university her Mum still checked up on her most nights. Gail found it equally irritating and endearing. As she slung her jacket across the back of the sofa and slipped off her shoes, she noticed a small puddle of light seeping from beneath her bedroom door. I don't remember leaving that light on, she thought, as the hair on the back of her neck bristled. She lunged for the overhead light switch and blinked rapidly as her eyes were flooded with welcome light.

'Anyone there?' she called out, as she stood with her hand on the door handle, her body tense and prepared to run. The sound of silence thundered in her ears as her heart hammered against her chest wall. She waited and waited but the silence persisted. No response to her call, no sound of activity from her bedroom. Only the sound of her own breathing disturbed the still night air.

I can't live in constant fear, Gail thought, as she picked up her old hockey stick and stormed towards the bedroom. The door crashed back against the wall as she barged through it wielding the hockey stick like a mighty sword. The room was as she had left it except the antique lamp on her bedside table was switched on, and she was certain a pink pair of sandals had been moved. Gail was meticulously tidy and her shoes were always arranged in colour order. The pink sandals sat next to the red running shoes, followed by a pair of white leather strappy sandals. The pink sandals should not be next to her yellow shoes. Her best friend, Barb Hopping, called her obsessive and maybe she had a point, but Gail could not stand clutter. She liked everything in the right place and could not relax if she was surrounded by disorder. A less meticulous person may not have noticed that the middle drawer of her chest of drawers was very slightly open, but to Gail's keen eye there was no doubt that someone, other than herself, had opened and closed the drawer. With a sinking feeling she knew without doubt that the stalker had been in the beach house.

Her immediate thought was to call the police or her mother, but she did neither. Only three months ago she had called the police to her previous flat in London. They had treated her as an over anxious female and even suggested she had perhaps watched too many Netflix horror movies. If the comment had not been so inappropriate and patronising, she would have laughed out loud. There was no point calling her mother who would only worry and insist she drive back to their family home. An hour's drive at this time of night was not to be taken lightly and the thought of getting from the house to the garage through the garden terrified her. What if he was still lurking outside? Nothing for it but to tough it out here, she thought, as she rechecked the locks on every door and window for the second time. They were all secure. How the hell did he get in here and how did he find out where I was living? She jumped as a whistle indicated the water in the kettle was boiling. She tried to control her shaking hands as she poured the water over a chamomile teabag in her favourite mug. She was shivering and would have loved a hot shower but felt far too vulnerable to take her clothes off. The movie psycho had a lot to answer for at times like these.

By the time she had finished her tea and slipped a comforting hot water bottle between the bed sheets and doona Gail was feeling less panicked. Every light in her small beach house was lit up, like Blackpool illuminations. Although it made sleep virtually impossible it was comforting. Gail lay still for many hours, her ears attuned for any unusual sounds. It was only as the sun began to peep over the horizon and reflect its morning glow on the flat, glass like ocean, that her eyelids fluttered shut and she slept. Gail had no idea how bad things would get.

Chapter 2

A loud thumping on the front door and the tuneful, how much is that doggie in the window doorbell chime, eventually pulled Gail from her slumber. She threw back the bed clothes, pulled the sweater she had worn yesterday over her pyjamas and hurried to answer the door. Her head was pounding, and the incessant banging was tantamount to a herd of noisy elephants crashing through the savanna.

'I am coming,' she yelled, as she opened her bedroom door and spotted the face of her friend Barb, peering through the front window.

'Quick, come in,' Gail said, stepping back as a blast of cold wind hit her.

'Are you okay?' Barb said, as she enclosed her in a bear hug. 'I was so worried about you when you didn't turn up for breakfast, and I could not get hold of you.

You are never late for anything. I called your Mum, and she got in a bit of a panic too I am afraid.'

Gail groaned. 'You make us some coffee while I call Mum before she drives out here or calls the police.' She noted the time as she picked up her mobile phone. It was almost eleven am. She had been due to meet Barb at eight-thirty. No wonder she got in a flap, Gail thought. Barb was right, Gail was never late. The pair had been meeting for breakfast every month for years and she had never missed one or been late.

Her Mum answered on the first ring:

'No Mum, you do not need to come over, Barb is here now. Nothing is wrong. I just didn't get to sleep until late last night and overslept this morning.'

'That is not like you, Gail. You are never late for anything. If anything, you are irritatingly early.'

'Yes, I know Mum, but there is a first time for everything. Anyway, I need to hang up, Barb has just made coffee. I will call you later.'

She reached into an overhead kitchen cupboard and pulled out a pack of paracetamol. She popped two from the blister pack and swallowed them with a glass of ice-cold water, before sitting down at her old kitchen table.

'Here's your coffee.' Barb passed her a large mug of coffee and Gail inhaled the familiar comforting aroma.

'Right, now you have dealt with your mother, you can tell me what is really going on?' She placed a reassuring hand on Gail's arm and gave her a gentle squeeze.

Gail pushed her tousled black hair back off her face and turned to look at her best friend. Her eyes glistened with unshed tears as she replied, 'He's back Barb, the stalker is back.'

'Simon, you mean?' Barb was surprised to hear this news. 'Are you sure Gail?'

'Of course, I am sure. Who else would have been sneaking around in my house? He was in my bedroom; he had moved my shoes and been through my chest of drawers.'

'How could he have found out you were in Brighton and in this beach house? Are you sure you are not imagining it?'

'Definitely not. I know he has found me. He's a stalker Barb that is what stalkers do. They follow their victims from place to place, terrifying them and making their life hell. I can't move location again. It took me months to find this beach house and a new job. This is my third move in twelve months. I don't know how he tracks me down each time. He seems to get some perverse pleasure in ruining my life.' Barb looked at her friend who now had her head bent forwards and was crying. She took the coffee cup from her shaking hands and put it in the dish washer.

'You need to report him to the police and maybe go and stay with your Mum for a couple of weeks.'

'It is pointless reporting him to the police. All the advice I've received so far has been useless and expensive. He will just deny everything and that will be the end of that. He is so charming and plausible the police believe him. He manipulates the situation to imply I am making a story up to cause trouble because he dumped me for someone else. Everyone knows that is not true. I only went out to dinner with him once, and that was as a thank you because he helped me out with the end of year reports. After that, you know he would not leave me alone. You witnessed what he was like in the office. He watched my every move and obsessed over every guy I spoke to. When management finally got rid of him, he blamed me, but he had two previous warnings involving the same behaviour with another employee. She apparently moved away to Ireland, with her husband and children but not before he almost destroyed her marriage.'

'I didn't know he had done a similar thing before.' Barb felt more than a twinge of guilt. For months she had thought Gail was exaggerating the situation. Simon seemed like such a nice guy it was hard to believe he could be a stalker. That is why he gets away with it, she thought. She regretted doubting her friend, who had been close to a breakdown before leaving London, three months ago.

Gail pushed her chair back and wiped her eyes with the sleeve of her sweater.

'I will just have a quick shower and get dressed.' Her headache was starting to subside to a dull ache.

'If you feel like going out, why don't we head down to Lucky Beach Café and get some lunch?'

'Sounds like a good idea. Crying always makes me hungry.' She was doing her best to put on a brave face, while hiding the real fear she felt.

Chapter 3

Although it was early Autumn and the wind was already cold it was a bright day and Barb's new red Audi gleamed like a ripe strawberry in the sunlight.

Just like the car's engine Gail purred with appreciation.

'Wow, it is lovely,' she said, as she cast an appraising eye over the vehicle.

'There have to be some perks for working so hard.' Barb grinned and hopped into the driver's seat. Barb was head of the human resource department in a large global technology company. She more than earned what went into her bank account each month. She was a high achiever who thrived on hard work. She had recently left a five-year relationship, which had suffered due to her poor work/life balance. With the pressure now off, Barb was looking forward to being single again.

Gail looked around at the bustle of activity along the sea front. Couples, friends, and families sat at the outdoor seating area of the café, enjoying a relaxing drink or meal. The atmosphere was carefree and happy and a great way to wind down after a week at work. The café was always busy on Saturdays. Gail felt safe when surrounded by lots of people and she felt the stress of last night begin to subside. She smiled at the young waitress who placed their meals on the table.

'Thank you, that looks delicious,' she said, looking at the well-presented food on the plate in front of her.

'I know this may not be a good time, as you have only been in your new job for three months but I wondered if you could take some annual leave or leave without pay? Jack and I had an eleven-night cruise booked for the end of September. Obviously, we will not be going as a couple now. I offered to pay Jack back his share of the holiday costs but he said he didn't need it, and suggested I take my Mum or a friend with me instead. It was a generous gesture given I had just ended the relationship. To be honest I think he was quite relieved, although I doubt, he would ever admit it. I have discounted inviting my Mum for obvious reasons, but I thought you might like to come if you can get the time off work. Given Simon is hanging around again it might be good for you to get away for a couple of weeks, and it would be fun.'

Barb looked at her friend, waiting for a response. 'It would be a free holiday, but you would need to buy your own champagne.' She smiled encouragingly. Barb had never met anyone except Gail who only ever drank champagne.

'It sounds inviting and it would be good to get away for a break. The trauma of the last twelve months has left me exhausted. I really thought it was over and Simon had given up. I would love to accept your offer if I can negotiate the time off work. I will chat to my manager on Monday to see if it is possible and then give you a call. Where is the cruise ship sailing from and where is it going?' She was already feeling a bubble of excitement.

'It leaves Southampton on 30th September and visits the Canary Islands and Portugal.'

'Sounds lovely, just what I need.' Gail raised her glass and smiled. The stalker was pushed to the back of her mind for now.

Chapter 4

The next few weeks passed slowly as Gail waited patiently for her unexpected holiday. Initially she hadn't held out much hope of getting the time off work but a work colleague, Sue Baker, offered to give up her own two weeks of leave.

'I don't have anything planned Gail so you take my two weeks. I wasn't going away so I can take my holidays anytime. Besides I would feel bad if you couldn't take up your friend's offer. I have never been on a cruise so you will have to fill me in on all the details when you get back.'

'I have never been on a cruise either. I have never really wanted to go on one. My idea of a cruise has been a bunch of people partying all night, getting blind drunk and behaving badly or a hoard of old folk on walkers or in wheelchairs, playing trivia or bingo. Barb tells me I am being ridiculous, that it's not like that at all, if you book the right type of cruise. She has been on several cruises and has always had a great time, so I will trust she knows what she is doing.' Gail had been surprised at Sue's generosity in forgoing her time off to help her out, particularly as they had only known each other for three months. She had a feeling they might become good friends, although she was closer to Barb's age of thirty, than her own age. Most Friday nights, after work, was drinks night. Gail made a mental note to shout Sue a couple of drinks as a thank you. Brighton had topped lists as the UK's best place for a night out, and having been forced to leave her London home Gail was determined to enjoy the opportunities Brighton had to offer. If only she didn't have Simon invading her life everything would be perfect. She loved her new home, her job, and the fact she was closer to her family. It had been almost eighteen months since she had a special man in her life and she was ready for a new relationship, but she knew that would not be possible while Simon was watching her every move. He had previously threatened that he would get rid of any man in her life. Gail wasn't sure exactly what he meant by that, but having seen a side of his personality that he hid so well from others, she was not willing to take any chances. Leaving the after-work drink venue on Friday nights, she had been sure she was being watched. She was also sure the multiple calls she received to her mobile phone were from Simon. It was always an unrecognised number and when she did answer, there was silence. It was time to change her number again. Max, a work colleague had given her a lift home, after a late meeting one evening, and the phone harassment had intensified. After half-hourly calls until three am Gail had turned her mobile phone off. On more than one occasion she thought someone had been in the beach house. Nothing had been disturbed but she couldn't shake the feeling. Maybe it was the lingering fragrance of her own perfume, that had been sprayed in her absence.

By the time the day arrived to join the cruise ship she was desperate to get away. Gail was constantly fatigued, unable to get a good night's sleep due to frequent nightmares. She was ever vigilant and conscious of every sound that might herald a threat. Her sense of isolation grew as others doubted the validity of her concerns. After all, Simon seemed to be such a nice guy to her friends and ex work colleagues, that had met him. He seemed an unlikely stalker and that was what frightened her the most. Getting rid of him from her life felt as impossible as trying to blow away the wind.

Chapter 5

The journey to Southampton Dock took just over two hours from Brighton, and as their bags were pulled from the boot of their cab, Gail looked towards the beautiful cruise ship that towered above them.

'Wow, that looks magnificent. I have never seen a cruise ship that close before. It is huge. Much larger than I expected.' Barb smiled at her friend's delight.

Gail was surprised at how efficiently their check-in process was and within a short space of time they had embarked and were sipping champagne at the sail away party. Barb bubbled with anticipation and Gail felt immense relief, as the expanse of grey water increased between Southampton Dock and their beautiful cruise ship. As the live band pumped out music that assaulted their ears, Barb and Gail raised and touched together their champagne glasses.

'Here's to a great holiday with lots of sun and fun,' Barb shouted, above the music. Although this was not a specific singles cruise, she was already thinking of the potential to meet a new man, from among the two thousand passengers. Top of Gail's wish list was a good night's sleep and to feel safe.

They giggled like schoolgirls as they unpacked their suitcases. The bottle of champagne and chocolates in their cabin were impressive. Gail pushed the door to their balcony open. It was almost dark and lights had started to twinkle along the coast line. Gail leant against the balcony rail and looked down at the dark water below. The gentle rhythmic hum of the ships engines was relaxing. She closed her eyes and swayed as she felt the soft vibration through the soles of her bare feet.

'I can see why you find cruising so appealing.'

'I thought you might get to like it if you gave it a try.' Barb stepped out of the shower, wrapped in a white towel. 'Get a move on, dinner is at eight-thirty,' she said, as she hunted for the hairdryer.

'I am really hungry; I hope the food will be good.'

'The food will be great, trust me, you will love it. We can hit the gym to keep off the kilos if you are worried about your weight.'

Barb was stick thin and could eat whatever she wanted. Gail had to control her weight by watching her food portion sizes and attending her local gym. She loved the regular workouts but had been virtually housebound since the return of Simon. Her world had shrunk over the last few weeks to, work, Friday night drinks and a weekly visit to her mother. She hoped if she kept a low-profile Simon would lose interest and get on with his own life.

Gail was unaware that for Simon she had become his life and his obsession. Although he gave the appearance of such a sweet and happy guy his true feelings simmered just below the surface. His childhood had been difficult, the family could at best be described as dysfunctional, at worst toxic. He had never known the love of parents and grew to adulthood still craving love and attention. Gail had been kind to him and appreciated his help at work and that had been the catalyst for the current situation. Simon was convinced that she would get to love him if she would only give him a chance and let him build a relationship with her. His swarthy good looks meant he had no trouble attracting other women but his relationships were usually short lived and ended when he became too needy and possessive. He knew it would be different with Gail. He would forgive her for getting him sacked from his job, if she would give him a chance. As he lay on his bed, watching the shadows dance across the ceiling, he fantasised about the life they would have together.

'Not long till we meet again Gail,' he said aloud, as he kissed the photograph, he had stolen from the beach house.

Chapter 6

'Rise and shine sleepy head.' Barb pulled back the curtains and early morning sunlight flooded the cabin.

'What time is it?' Gail groaned and tried to pull the sheet back over her face.

'Seven-thirty and time you were up. I have already had a walk around the deck and checked out where the gym is. Let's get breakfast and then we will have a leisurely day. Maybe hangout at the pool if it is warm enough.' The dark sky of Southampton had been replaced with a clear blue sky and the day held lots of promise.

'I had the best sleep I have had in months.' Gail pulled her unruly hair up into a loose ponytail and rubbed her face with a sweet-scented face wipe. 'I feel great, eight hours of uninterrupted sleep and no nightmares.' She almost skipped through the cabin door as they left to go to the dining room.

'Today is an at sea day so we can do whatever you want after breakfast. I'll give you a tour of all the facilities so you can see what's on offer. There seem to be lots of couples and families on board but we might spot a few other singles.' Barb laughed as Gail gave her an exasperated look.

'Just joking, I know you just want a restful holiday but it won't hurt to look. I'll check to see if they have a solo traveller meeting planned. That can be a good opportunity to meet up with other singles.'

By early afternoon they were on sun loungers pool side, sipping cocktails and enjoying the feel of warm sunshine on their skin. Gail tried to read her book but now she was so relaxed she was finding it difficult to keep her eyes open.

'Think I'll just go for a little walk,' Barb said, as she sprang off her sun-lounger. She always had difficulty sitting still for long.

'Do you mind if I don't join you? I am so comfortable and relaxed I really don't want to move.'

'Of course not, you just relax. I won't be very long.' With that she pulled a bright green, loose linen shirt on over her swimsuit. Gail couldn't help but notice what a stunning figure she made, her long legs striding out confidently as she zig-zagged around the sun-loungers and their occupants.

I wish I had half her confidence, Gail thought, as she drained the last of her champagne cocktail and picked up her book. Before long, her eyes closed and her book dropped unnoticed onto her chest.

Gail jumped with fright as her sun-lounger was rocked. She woke instantly to see Barb looking down at her.

'Are you sleeping again?' Gail checked her watch and was surprised to see she had slept for almost two hours. She was equally surprised to see that two guys were standing with Barb.

'Look who I met on my walk. Do you remember Tom Edwards? He worked in our department about five years ago before he went to work in Dubai. And this is a friend of his, Jake Morgan.' Gail shielded her eyes against the sun and smiled up at them as Barb made the introductions.

'Nice to meet you both. I think you were just leaving the company when I was joining as a new graduate Tom.' She turned to Jake as she got to her feet. 'What about you Jake, do you work with Tom?'

'No, I work in London but we have been friends since school. I'm only here because Tom and his fiancé parted company. This cruise was a wedding present from his parents. Neither of us have been on a cruise before and wouldn't have picked it as a number one choice for a holiday but perhaps it might be fun after all.' His smile was genuine and Gail noted his perfect white teeth. Such a contrast against his beautiful dark skin.

'That's a coincidence. I'm here for a similar reason. This is my first cruise too.' It wasn't long before all four were deep in conversation, as they sampled a range of cocktails and champagne and whiled away the afternoon.

'Well, that was an unexpected surprise,' Barb said, as they changed for dinner. 'How amazing to meet up with Tom again. He is such a great guy. I was shocked to hear he and Penny had called their wedding off. They had been together for years. I wonder what went wrong?'

'I am sure you will find out. You are good at getting information out of people.' Gail laughed when Barb replied, with feigned indignance, 'I'm only interested. That's quite different to being nosey. Anyway, let's change the subject. What did you think of Jake? Isn't he gorgeous? You two seemed to get on very well considering you have only just met. Do I detect a hint of romance in the air?'

'Yes, he is gorgeous but looks aren't everything.' Gail could not help but reflect on Simon's good looks. Looks could be deceiving, as she had found out. Even with an ocean between them she hated how he could invade her thoughts.

'Let's see how tomorrow goes on the trip to Porto.' Barb smiled and Gail felt her cheeks flush. Tom and Jake were joining them for the day. Having read all the Harry Potter books Gail was keen to visit the Harry Potter film location, Livraria Lello. She had been surprised when Tom and Jake asked could they join them.

'The more the merrier,' Barb replied. She was looking forward to a full day exploring Porto and enjoying Tom's company. Day 2 and a potential new man in her life, if only for the next nine days of the cruise. Life couldn't be better.

Chapter 7

Porto lived up to expectations and the day was wonderful. In the morning, Gail fulfilled her wish to see the Harry Potter location and amazed Barb and their friends with her intricate knowledge of the books, their characters, and the life of JK Rowling. For lunch they found a lovely restaurant down a tiny back street. They squashed around a small table and shared a large platter of fresh seafood, washed down with Super Bock beer and a glass of champagne for Gail.

After lunch, at Jake's request, they visited the Church of Sao Francisco. Having learnt during the morning that Jake was an architect and lover of old monuments it seemed appropriate to visit this beautiful 13th century monument. The building was declared a UNESCO World Heritage Site for its intricate goldleaf carvings and Gothic interior. Jake's face lit up with delight as he marvelled at the wonderful Baroque architecture. It was a subject Gail knew nothing about but she was spellbound as she listened to his running commentary. He seemed pleased when she asked questions and it seemed natural when he took her hand to lead her through the building. Everything about him was sophisticated.

Gail inwardly cringed remembering the morning and her juvenile delight in all things Harry Potter.

'I'll see you back in the cabin unless you fancy a swim,' Barb said, as they flashed their ID to get back on the ship.

'You go ahead. I'm going to get a coffee and change my shoes. My feet are aching after today's walking. I should have worn my old battered running shoes instead of these new trainers.' She pointed at the fluorescent pink shoes and laughed. Having spent the day with Jake she was relieved she had left her old trainers at home. He was immaculately dressed, just as she was. They had that in common. When she got out of the lift at deck six, he leant towards her and kissed her on the cheek.

'See you at dinner.' He didn't wait for her to reply, but waved and turned in the opposite direction.

Gail watched his departing figure. She was relieved he hadn't walked her back to her cabin. It could have been awkward. He seems lovely, and he did hold my hand. But perhaps I am reading too much into it, she thought. She pushed her key card into the door lock and entered the quiet cabin. The smell of her own perfume overwhelmed her. She stopped in her tracks and looked around. Superficially everything in the cabin seemed fine but an instinct, older and more compelling than any intelligence, warned her to be cautious. The monster, that was fear, threatened to engulf her. She pulled the cabin door closed behind her and raced towards the communal areas in search of people and safety.

Barb heard Gail shouting her name before she saw her friend rushing towards her, almost knocking into those standing around the pool in her haste.

'What's wrong? Is there a lion on the loose? You look like you are running for your life.' It was a while since she had seen Gail so frantic.

'He's been in our cabin and sprayed my perfume everywhere.' She grabbed Barb's arm and attempted to pull her up off the sun lounger.

'Wait until I get a towel around me for heaven's sake,' Barb said, as she collected her belongings. She was still dripping wet from her swim and not too happy about being interrupted so soon. They walked back to their cabin in silence as Gail tried to prevent a full-on panic attack.

'I can smell your perfume but I don't think it is overwhelming. It's just that our cabin has been shut up all day. I expect one of the staff had a sneaky spray or two when they came in and made the beds this morning.'

'They wouldn't do that. They are not supposed to interfere with passengers' property, are they?'

'Gail, it is just a tiny spray of perfume. There is no harm done. You need to relax.' Take a few deep breaths and try to calm down. Your imagination is getting the better of you. Simon is miles away. You are completely safe on this ship.' It was several minutes before Gail spoke.

'I'm sorry. I haven't had a panic attack like that for months, but I know why I got so frightened. The smell took me back to when he first started stalking me. He used to send me gifts of perfume and the times he got into my flat he used to spray my own brand of perfume everywhere. It was almost like a signature tune he used to let me know he had been there. He did the same in the new beach house.'

'I can't imagine how awful this experience has been for you and I'm sorry if I sounded a little snappy. Let's go and sit in the last of today's sunshine and I'll get us both a drink. You change your pink trainers for something more comfortable while I get some clothes on.' I think I have underestimated how much recent events have affected her, Barb thought, as she slipped out of her wet swim wear and reached for a fresh white towel, to dry herself.

The company at dinner later in the evening helped to dispel Gail's anxiety and fear. Tom and Jake entertained the two friends with stories of their previous holiday adventures. Mountain climbing in Nepal, trekking through North Africa, kayaking and bungee jumping in New Zealand.

'Of course, that all changed when Tom went to Dubai and met Penny,' Jake said. He glanced at Tom's face suddenly aware it may not have been wise to mention Penny. She was the one who had called off the wedding not Tom, but if he was upset, he didn't show it.

'We did have some great holidays, didn't we? I think one of the reasons Penny changed her mind about our marriage was my longing to travel and see the world whilst she wanted to settle down and have a family immediately. I wasn't ready for that, marriage yes, but children, not yet. I thought Penny would be happy to compromise and wait a few years to start a family so we could travel and see the world together but when it came to making a choice, she wasn't willing to wait and I wasn't willing to have children before I felt ready. It's a huge responsibility. I would love children one day, but in the future, not now. I just wish we had made our feelings clearer to each other sooner.' He picked up his glass and took a large mouthful of red wine.

'Well, I must say your adventure holidays sound amazing. The highest mountain I have ever climbed is Mount Snowden in North Wales and I thought that was a triumph.' Barb had restored the happy, carefree atmosphere after Tom's unexpected reveal. She had a knack of saying the right thing and putting people at ease.

'Don't forget your success in triathlete events Barb,' Gail said. 'You have always been super fit and very competitive.' Barb blushed at her friend's praise.

'I have always been the complete opposite to Barb. I am very happy to do a workout in the gym a couple of times a week but anything more strenuous is out of the question.'

Jake laughed. 'You all do more than me then. I play football once a week in winter and a bit of cricket in summer. I enjoy the social aspect and get-togethers after the games more than the exercise.' He topped up their wine glasses and poured another champagne for Gail. Thank God he is not an exercise fanatic, Gail thought. The only exercise I would enjoy with Jake would be a stroll along a moonlit beach. The thought surprised her and she made a mental note to cut back on the champagne.

Chapter 8

'It is lovely to be greeted by sunshine every morning. Look at my tan after only two days.' Gail held her golden brown arms out for Barb to inspect.

'You have an advantage over me with your sallow skin and ability to tan easily. I will still look lily white or maybe slightly pink when we leave the ship. I'll have to fall back on good old spray tan. I might get that done when we go to the spa later this morning. Remember we are booked in at eleven am for a massage and facial.'

'I'm not used to all this pampering, but I think I could get used to it.' Gail was relieved that a good night's sleep had washed yesterday's fear away. A few hours in the spa would be enjoyable, but what she was looking forward to most, was seeing Jake later in the afternoon. She had not come on this cruise looking for romance, but having met Jake she couldn't deny how attracted she was to him.

'What are Tom and Jake doing this morning?' Gail asked Barb, over breakfast.

'Hitting the gym this morning and then hanging around the pool until we are finished in the spa. I said we would catch up with them for a drink at about three pm, if that is okay with you? They both seem keen to spend time with us and I'm in no hurry to meet up with anyone else, and you look like you are enjoying Jake's company. Tom is good fun and we have quite a lot in common, not least our recent break-ups. Neither of us are looking for a serious relationship just yet, but some fun in the sun is welcome.'

'Same here. Fun in the sun with no commitment sounds good to me.' I'm not sure that is strictly true, Gail thought, as soon as the words were out of her mouth. She wasn't one for casual relationships.

'It's almost eleven am, are you ready to go?' Barb asked, as she came out of the bathroom.

'Yes, I'm ready but I am just looking for my book to take to the spa with me. Have you moved it?' Gail was throwing pillows from her bed and pulling the sheets back.

'No, I haven't moved it. Where did you last have it?'

'It was on my bedside table when we went for breakfast.'

'Well, it can't have gone far.' Barb watched in amazement as Gail got more frantic in her search, pulling the suitcases out and searching the wardrobe.

'Gail, leave it for now, we can look for it later. Probably one of the cleaning staff has moved it. If we don't leave now, we will be late.'

Gail scowled, but picked up her bag and went to the door. She wasn't convinced with Barb's explanation but decided to leave any discussion about the missing book until later. She could hear the hint of impatience in Barb's voice.

The faint hum of the engines pervaded the peaceful environment of the spa centre and the scent of multiple beautiful fragrances filled the air. The masseuse was gentle but firm and Gail sighed as her tense muscles relaxed under her experienced hands. She hovered close to sleep the words of the masseuse were far away and fleeting, like tiny dandelion heads blown around in a Spring breeze. Before long she gave in to the utter abandonment of sleep. Barb's lips twitched with a hint of a smile as she watched her friend drift off to sleep, relieved that for the moment she had forgotten about her missing book.

The matter of the missing book resurfaced at the end of the evening when they returned to their cabin.

Gail hadn't mentioned the book during the afternoon they had spent with Tom and Jake, nor during dinner or during the show they attended after dinner, but it was not far from her mind. As soon as they were back in their cabin the hunt began.

'It can't just disappear without trace,' she said, as she resumed her search. After thirty minutes of searching every available space in the cabin and on the balcony, it was obvious the book had gone. 'It must have been stolen,' she said, as she slumped down on her bed.

'We will report it tomorrow, if you think it is that important. I think if a crew member was going to steal something they would take something valuable, like your watch that you leave out of the safe, or one of my designer jackets. Why would anyone want to take a cheap paperback book? You have probably taken it out with you, and left it somewhere on the ship. We can go and check in lost property in the morning.' Barb yawned and walked to the bathroom. She did her best to close the door gently, despite her growing frustration.

She doesn't believe me, Gail thought. Familiar feelings of not being taken seriously flooded back and once again she felt alone. She lay awake long into the night as her fear was replaced with a growing sense of anger towards the stalker who was trying to destroy her life, and those who found it so hard to believe her. All her fears over the last fifteen months had resurfaced and threatened to ruin her holiday and that of her best friend's. The bonds of friendship can be fragile and she didn't want to lose her friend.

Chapter 9

'I've changed my mind about diving with the sharks,' Gail said at breakfast. A highlight of the cruise for Barb was the opportunity to swim with sharks. She had done it once before when she visited Lanzarote and was keen to do it again. Gail had agreed to do it with her but now had cold feet.

'I'm not a strong swimmer and I don't know how I would cope underwater with sharks. I know they cater for beginners, but what if I had a panic attack? I will be much happier to stay on dry land, while you, Tom and Jake enjoy the thrill of swimming with an apex predator. I'll have a wander around the shops and market and meet you back at the beach later.'

'Well, if you are sure. Will you be okay on your own for the morning?'

'Of-course I will. I don't think I will get lost and I can always ask for directions if I need too. My limited Spanish will get me by.' She pulled a dog-eared phrase book from her pocket and laughed. 'A relic of my parent's holidays in Spain. Mum insisted I bring it along!'

Barb was secretly a little relieved. She had begun to wonder if Gail was up to the dive, having seen how quickly she had panicked over her missing book. Barb had experienced the serenity of travelling alone, and thought not for the first time, that it had its advantages.

'How did your morning go?' Barb asked, when they met up in the early afternoon.

'It was lovely, I wandered around a fifteenth century castle, a music museum, and a handicraft museum. I stopped at a local café for a milkshake and pancakes and did a bit of people watching. I saw a couple of small children jumping and splashing around in a water fountain. I was tempted by their squeals of delight to join them. I also bought a few gifts to take home.' She opened two large carrier bags and Barb peeped inside. Gail didn't mention that she was certain that she had been followed.

'Anyway, enough about me, did you three enjoy your morning?'

'It was brilliant, even better than I remembered. But I am looking forward to lunch and a relaxing afternoon now. Tom and Jake walked on ahead to get a table for lunch so we better get going. Do you need help with those bags?'

'No thanks, they are quite light.' She slung the bags over her shoulder and pulled her cap down to shade her face from the harsh sunlight.

Over lunch, Gail listened with a hint of envy as Barb, Tom and Jake relived their dive experience. One day I'll give it a go, she thought. Barb got her wish of spending the afternoon on the beach, and swimming in the crystal-clear water to cool off when it got too hot. Gail lay back and let the soft white sand trickle through her fingers. She was conscious of the hot afternoon sun beating down on her skin. It was only when she felt like the breath was being sucked out of her lungs by the heat, that she made her way into the ocean. The sunlight sparkled off the salt water as she eased her shoulders under the surface of the waves and began to swim. Her stroke was smooth and graceful. It was a couple of minutes before she was aware that Jake had joined her. They swam together in silence for a couple of hundred metres before Gail gestured towards the beach. The swim back to the beach was made harder by the pull of the outgoing tide. The smooth water was deceptive and Gail was relieved to have Jake by her side. As she felt the reassurance of the sand beneath her feet she smiled at Jake. He smiled back as she took his hand.

'Is everything alright? You seem unusually quiet this afternoon.'

'I'm fine. Just winding down and enjoying the beautiful beach after walking through the old cobbled streets this morning. It was quite tiring. I think maybe I have had a bit too much sun.' She did consider telling Jake what was really on her mind but decided against it. She didn't want to risk their new friendship with talk of a stalker. With his arm around her shoulders, she felt blanketed in security and when he unexpectedly kissed her, all thoughts of the stalker evaporated.

When they returned to the ship, much later in the afternoon, Gail called into Guest Services to ask about her missing book. She expected it would be a waste of time, so was taken by complete surprise when the guest service officer pulled it from a box and held it up.

'Is this it?' she asked, as she handed it to Gail.

'Yes, it is. Do you know where it was found?' She opened it to the front page and there was her name and message from her Mum. There was no doubt the book was hers.

'Sorry, I don't know where it was found or who handed it in. It must have been handed in on my day off, but we get so much property handed in there's no guarantee I would remember even if I had been on duty.' Gail was about to ask if they kept a register of information but was deterred by the queue that had formed behind her, and an older man who was audibly sighing with impatience. She walked away, happy to have her book back but disgruntled that the mystery of who had taken the book was still unsolved.

Barb spotted the book as soon as Gail entered their cabin.

'Oh, you found your book. Where was it?'

'I've no idea. Someone must have handed it in to guest services.'

'Well, now you have it back you can stop worrying about it.'

Gail didn't reply, Barb wouldn't understand. Of course, she was glad to have the book back, but it didn't explain how it came to be removed from their cabin in the first place. Maybe a crew member had taken it to read, she thought. She couldn't bear to think of the alternative.

Chapter 10

With her book back in her possession and no anonymous phone calls in the last twenty-four hours Gail relaxed and threw herself into the fun of the holiday. A day in Santa Cruz, admiring the beautiful architecture, lunching on traditional tapas and walking on golden sand beaches, was followed by a day in Las Palmas, Gran Canaria. All four joined a hike to the epic Bandama Caldera volcanic crater. The views from the viewing platform were spectacular. Gail surprised herself by agreeing to hike down into the crater itself. It was an experience she would never forget. She felt a real sense of achievement. She reflected on how good that felt. Being stalked had infected all parts of her life, fear and chronic anxiety had plagued her since the stalking began, and her confidence had been destroyed. Having Jake by her side made her feel safe and she would like nothing more than a relationship with him, but was it fair to take their friendship further while the threat of her stalker was still present?

The Stalker and the Hunted

A quiet day at sea gave her plenty of time to think about her future. Spending time with Jake had given her a window of what her life could be like again. She had become distrustful of men, even though rationally she knew not all men were stalkers. But she had been so wrong about Simon she now doubted her own judgement. She had to start trusting her own instincts again and perhaps that should begin with Jake. Over the course of the afternoon, they had shared details of their families, their jobs, their friends and their hopes and dreams for the future. Despite how close they were becoming Gail did not disclose that she had been and still was being stalked. Maybe tomorrow, she thought. Barb and Tom had gone to the gym and then disappeared to Tom's cabin with a bottle of champagne.

'I'll give Tom a call before I head back to change for dinner, I would hate to interrupt anything special.' Jake grinned and Gail couldn't help but smile.

'Good idea.' She blushed as he took her face in his hands and kissed her.

As Gail walked back to her cabin, she could still feel the flush of heat from her face. Is Jake wishing we were in a cabin drinking champagne? she thought. She could see how he looked at her.

Gail was not the only one who recognised how Jake looked at her. From a safe distance Simon watched as Jake kissed Gail. He squeezed the drinking glass in his hand so tight that the glass shattered, showering the carpet in shards of broken glass. Crimson blood oozed through his clenched fingers and dripped to the floor. He didn't feel the pain. It was obliterated by the rage which threatened to erupt and spoil his plans.

'I have to stop this before it goes any further,' he said, through gritted teeth. He could not stand by and watch another man take the woman who should be his. He was tired of hiding and biding his time, waiting for Gail to realise they should be together. Eight days of following her around this ship and into every port was exhausting. He hated the heat. He would have to make it clear to Gail there would be no more holidays in the sun when they were together. Simon had sunk to the bottom of his reserve in terms of capacity to cope. He recognised he could not go on like this. He had to have Gail in his life. As he watched his own blood pour from the lacerations in his hand he came to a decision. He would give her one more chance, one more day. If he couldn't have her no-one would. He wrapped the bottom of his tee shirt around his hand and fighting waves of nausea he hurried back to his cabin. He pulled a clean white towel from the bathroom, removed his bloody tee shirt, and wrapped the towel around his injured hand. He lay on his bed, a full bottle of whisky by his side. His hand now throbbed with each beat of his heart. He curled up on his side. His rage now spent had given way to silent tears that drenched the pillow beneath his head. He was weeping for his dream, which was hanging on by a thread as fine as a spider's web. Without Gail there would be a desert of nothingness ahead of him. He could not let that happen. If we can't live together, we will die together was his last thought, as he fell asleep letting the near empty whisky bottle drop to the floor.

The full moon hung like a large silver ball in the dark night sky, casting speckles of light that reflected on the ocean. The heat of the day had been replaced by a crisp night time air. Gail felt the gentle breeze ruffle her hair as she sat in silence, on the balcony, waiting for Barb to return from her after dinner walk with Tom. The sound of the cabin door opening made her jump with fright. Her every sense was heightened as she fought to control her fight or flight response.

'Thank God, it's you. Lock the door behind you.' Gail almost collided with her friend as she tried to get to the door.

'Why, what's happened now?' Barb's calm, matter of fact question was lost on Gail. She was doing her best to control the fear that threatened to overtake her.

'Look at this.' She snatched her previously missing book off her bed and opened it at the back page. Get rid of the boyfriend or I will get rid of him for you!!!!! The ugly red letters filled the page.

'Simon must have written this when he took my book, but I didn't see it until this evening. I recognise his writing.' She slumped down on her bed. 'He might be dangerous Barb. What am I going to do?' The desperation in her voice was obvious and for the first time Barb began to worry that Gail's fears were justified. Could charming, charismatic Simon really be dangerous and was it possible he was on the ship with them?

Chapter 11

The security officer listened as Gail explained her situation and her fear that her stalker was a passenger on the ship. She opened her book and showed him the threatening message she had found the night before. After giving the information Gail watched as he completed an incident form.

'Are you sure this message wasn't already in this book before you boarded the ship?' Gail had to stop and think. Was it possible the message had been left in the book when Simon had been in her beach house?

'Well, I can't be a hundred percent sure, but I think I would have noticed it, and I didn't have a boyfriend before I boarded the ship.' She hated that she was now doubting herself. A knowing look passed between the security officer and Barb. Gail felt her heart sink. They weren't going to take her fears seriously. She felt close to tears but fought to stay calm.

'Simon may have thought you were seeing one of your work colleagues. You did think you had been followed from your Friday night drinks venue,' Barb said.

'Worst case scenario Simon is on this ship, so what can you do to protect Jake from harm, given he has been threatened?' Gail spoke with as much authority as she could muster.

'I can advise him to be careful and I can check if

Simon Foster is a passenger. In the interim make sure you securely close your cabin door when you leave and make sure your balcony door is firmly closed at night. Try and avoid being on your own in isolated places until we get this sorted out.'

'Come on let's get off the ship and leave him to do his job while we explore Lisbon. Tom and Jake will be waiting for us.'

The thought of sightseeing in Lisbon was far from Gail's mind but she did need to have a conversation with Jake and explain the situation before the security officer approached him.

Simon felt the effects of last night's whisky binge as he waited for Gail and Barb to leave the ship. The cold shower had done little to ease his thumping headache and he inwardly raged at the thought of another day in the sweltering sun. He watched as Gail and Jake exited the ship deep in conversation, Jake pulling her close as she rested her head on his chest. Their intimacy cut through him far more than yesterday's kiss. He had warned her, he had given her a choice to end it with the boyfriend, but she had ignored him so far. He maintained a slither of hope that she may change her mind by the end of the day. If only she would love me like I love her, he thought, as he pushed thoughts of revenge to the back of his mind for now. He could wait another day. He knew with absolute conviction that he could not and would not live without her.

Chapter 12

'I'm sorry I didn't tell you about the stalker earlier but I thought I had escaped him by coming on this cruise with Barb. It seems I may now have put you in danger.' Jake wrapped his arm around Gail's shoulders as she rested her head against his chest.

'Don't worry about me. I can take care of myself. Just start at the beginning and tell me the whole story.'

By the time they had wandered hand in hand around the castle in the charming town of Sintra, Gail had left nothing unsaid. She felt like a dark cloud had been lifted from her shoulders when Jake listened without interruption, and didn't attempt to dismiss her fears.

'No wonder you have been so frightened, this Simon seems intent on being part of your life.'

'I can't believe this all happened because I invited him to dinner as a thank you for helping with some reports. He obviously got the wrong impression. I suppose it's my fault in a way.'

'No, that's crazy. Work colleagues interact regularly. It doesn't mean they are or ever will become romantically involved. When you told him you weren't interested, he should have respected that and left you alone.'

'He must be using an alias as the security officer told me that there is no passenger listed as Simon Foster. I don't know what to do next. Do I leave the ship and get a flight home or hope security can locate him on the ship?'

'Why don't we check in when we get back to the ship and then you can decide? If you want to fly home, I can come with you if you would like me to.'

Gail was taken aback by his generous offer to fly back to the UK with her. Before she could consider leaving the ship, she would have to contact her mother and ask if she could cover the cost of the air-fare. Moving house three times in twelve months, to escape her stalker had depleted all Gail's savings. All she had left was a couple of hundred dollars and an almost maxed out credit card. She felt trapped. But now Jake had been threatened she had more than herself to think about. Perhaps the safest thing would be to end her developing relationship with Jake. Gail felt the anger surface. The stalker was dictating her every move but she couldn't risk Jake becoming a target. The first man she had wanted in her life and she might have to give him up for his own safety.

Once again, neither noticed the angry young man watching from a safe distance. His rage enflamed by their increasing closeness, threatened to end their lives by the end of their holiday.

It was late afternoon when they arrived back at the ship. It came as no surprise that the ship's security officer did not have good news. They had been unable to locate Simon and without lining up every male passenger for an identity parade there was no way of finding him.

'Only two more days and we will be back in Southampton, then I suggest you make another report to the local police. I am responsible for alerting the authorities on shore of any reportable marine incident but apart from the threatening message in your book there is really nothing to report. The message could have been left before you boarded the ship and your stalker may not be on board. As a precaution, I suggest you both avoid isolated areas of the ship. If you see your stalker, feel unsafe or an incident does occur, dial reception on speed dial or alert a crew member immediately.'

Gail looked crestfallen but thanked the security officer.

'I suppose like so many other women I will have to wait until he becomes physically violent before any action will be taken to stop him.' Jake took her hand as they walked back to her cabin. She felt relief that he was by her side.

'Do you want to get off the ship? We could stay in Lisbon tonight and look at flight options tomorrow.'

'No Jake. It is only two more days, and he will find me where-ever I am so there is little point.' A sense of resignation snuffed out the optimism she had felt with Jake by her side.

Gail's mother had helped her so much financially over the last eighteen months she decided it would be unfair to ask her for money. If she left the ship her stalker would have succeeded in ruining her holiday and that of her friends. She was not prepared to let that happen.

'If you are sure that's what you want let's try and enjoy our last couple of days. Tomorrow, we visit Vigo. It has some great ancient architecture that I want to show you and if we have time, we could get the ferry to Cie Islands. The beaches are meant to be some of the best.' Jake was doing his best to lift her spirits and reassure her that all would be well. Gail wished she had his degree of certainty. She thought back to how confident and carefree she had been before Simon began to stalk her and wondered where that young woman had gone. Little by little her world had shrunk. It would have been easier if he had been violent towards her. At least the police may have taken some action and she wouldn't have this terrible feeling that most people, even her closest friends didn't believe her, or thought she was exaggerating the situation. Living with a permanent knot of anxiety was impacting her physical and mental health with each passing day.

Chapter 13

After a night of little sleep Gail woke with another headache. Her neck and shoulders were stiff and sore due to the constant muscle tension. She resolved to book in for a massage later in the day. The cabin was quiet. Barb had already left for her morning walk around the ship's decks and a gym session. She was a bundle of energy and enjoying every aspect of her holiday and the cruise ship facilities. Gail smiled as she read the note stuck to the mirror, BACK SOON, two thumbs up and a smiley face. She stretched her arms and swung her legs out of bed. The blue sky beckoned as she opened the balcony doors and listened to the applause of the sea breeze. It was going to be another day of perfect weather.

Gail was tempted to go to breakfast early as she was hungry, having eaten little at dinner the previous evening. She was also eager to meet Jake for their last day of sightseeing. However, the warning from Alan Frost, the ships security officer could not be ignored. At this time of the morning the corridors to the lift were often quiet and it was possible that you would not encounter other passengers until you reached the more populated communal areas of the ship.

Jake had made it clear last night that he wanted to continue with their budding relationship once they left the ship, and they had already planned the first weekend they could get together. Although Jake worked in London the trip to Brighton would only be a one-and-a-half-hour drive and Gail could go up to London on her week day flexi days. Distance would not be an impediment. Ripples of joy alternated with acute anxiety when Gail considered the way forward. A relationship with Jake filled her heart with hope but the physical risk to any man in her life could not be ignored. Simon was dangerous, even if she was the only one who believed it.

In his own cabin on deck eight Simon was putting the final details of his plan together. He had hoped his warning to Gail would have been enough for her to stop seeing the new man in her life. It was obvious to him now that they were more than just friends. He shed tears for the life he should have had with her, but he would not accept her rejection. If he could not have her in this life, he would have her in the next. He was not sure if he really believed in an afterlife where they could be together for eternity but if not, he would accept endless oblivion rather than continue his life as it was, without her. He pushed his dark hair back from his face and looked intently at his reflection in the mirror. His face was symmetrical and angular, his skin flawless and his body fit and strong. He was aware he was a good-looking man and he had no problem attracting women. Maybe his mother had been correct when she said he always wanted what he couldn't have. He had to endure one last day of this oppressive heat and pain and then it would be over. Leaving his cabin in a rush he almost collided with the linen trolley on the corridor outside his door.

'Sorry, Mr. Mackie,' the young woman said, as she moved the trolley out of his way. He bit back on the spark of anger as he gripped the knife in his pocket. The fleeting thought of using the knife on this careless crew member left as quickly as it had surfaced. His target was Jake and he smiled as he fantasised about how he would end his life. He would not use the knife on Gail; her skin was so perfect he didn't want her marked. Surely, she would realise that, when the time came.

Chapter 14

Barb and Tom were taking the local ferry to Cie Islands and Gail and Jake planned to meet them later, so they had most of the day to themselves. As they had done on previous days they wandered hand in hand through the city, Jake providing a running commentary on the ancient architecture. To any interested observer they were just another young couple in love, with their whole life ahead of them. Gail thought back to their first day together, when her only wish was to visit the Harry Potter location. How things had changed in such a short time, she thought.

'Let's go and taste the local seafood, it's meant to be the best you will ever taste.'

'Great idea, I'm famished. I think it's all the walking we have done.'

'I've picked out one of the local restaurants based on a friend's recommendation, but if you would rather go somewhere else just say so.' Gail loved the way he researched and planned everything. She quite liked having activities planned for her, if she retained free choice. She had experience with two previous boyfriends who expected her to arrange everything and another two who were extremely controlling. It was not an attractive feature. Jake did not fit into that category. He was organised and consultative and she liked that about him. As she watched his smiling face, she decided she would not walk away from him, and let her stalker rob her of her freedom. Jake was right, the seafood was some of the best she had ever tasted. She giggled as champagne bubbles went up her nose.

'To us,' Jake said, as he refilled her glass.

'Yes, to us.' She felt tears of happiness threaten to spill over and dabbed at her eyes with a spare napkin.

'I didn't know great seafood and champagne made you cry. I will have to remember that.' He smiled, reached over, and took her hand.

I am falling in love with this man, Gail thought. She felt certain he was feeling the same way about her.

Pushing all thoughts of her stalker aside, she had never felt happier. Last night had been a turning point for her relationship with Jake and she couldn't wait to catch up with Barb and tell her she and Jake were now officially a couple. As they sailed away from Vigo later in the day Gail felt a pang of regret. The day had been special and wonderful and she didn't want it to end.

'We will have to come back one day,' Jake said, as if reading her thoughts. He pulled her closer and kissed the top of her head. Both recognised that Vigo would always be a special place for them.

Later, that evening as they finished dinner Barb whispered, 'Would you like our cabin to yourself tonight? I am sure Tom will be happy for me to spend the whole night with him. It would be a nice change to wake up with him.' Gail laughed. Barb and Tom often disappeared to his cabin for what they euphemistically referred to as a late afternoon rest.

'Maybe, I think Jake would like that and I know I would. It has been difficult to keep our hands off each other all day.' She blushed, her neck and cheeks turning a bright pink. Her conservative Methodist upbringing was never far from the surface when sex was mentioned. Barb gave a less than subtle thumbs up to Tom and Gail felt her flush deepen. They had obviously discussed the suggestion earlier. If Jake had been aware of the arrangement, he gave no sign of it. He seemed oblivious to the interaction between Barb and Tom until Tom turned and said, 'Any chance you can make yourself scarce for our last couple of nights Jake?' His discomfort was evident and Gail felt compelled to rescue him.

'You can share with me,' she said, as quickly as she could and looked away from Jake's face.

'You don't need to agree to this,' he said, later in the evening, as they walked to the theatre for the evening show. I know you have single beds in your cabin but Barb and Tom shouldn't have put you on the spot like that. I can spend the night in one of the lounges, we don't need to share.' His concern for her feelings made her feel cherished in a way she hadn't experienced before.

'I don't want you to feel pressured either, but I would love to spend the night with you if that's what you want too.' Gail felt the familiar blush. There was no need for Jake to answer her question his kiss told her all she needed to know. The four friends gathered for a last drink in the piano bar after the show. Gail was not a fan of classical music but nothing could deflate her buoyant mood tonight.

'I'll go and collect a couple of things from our cabin,' Jake said, as he pushed his chair back. 'You finish your drink and I'll see you in about fifteen minutes.' Gail watched him walk away. She watched other women turn his way as he passed and she inwardly gloated. He's all mine, she thought, with smug satisfaction.

'Fancy a nightcap?' Tom asked, as he drained his beer glass.

'Not for me thanks, I've had enough champagne for one day.' Gail checked her watch. It must be at least fifteen minutes, maybe more since Jake had left them.

'I'll head off, Jake must gave gone straight to our cabin,' Gail said, as she looked at Barb.

'Do you want us to walk with you?' Barb went to stand up.

'No need, there are lots of people milling around tonight. I'll be fine. You finish your drinks.' Her buoyant mood had made her complacent.

'Okay then, see you in the morning, but not too early I hope.' Barb laughed and winked at her best friend, who hurried away her face flaming. Gail's courage started to desert her as she hurried from the lift and along the corridor towards her cabin. The silence unnerved her and she repeatedly looked behind her. She sighed with relief as she slid her key card in the door lock. She flicked the light on expecting to see Jake but the cabin was empty. She put the strong smell of perfume down to anxiety. For a fleeting moment she wondered why Jake wasn't there until she realised he didn't have a key card to the cabin. Unless Barb had given him her card, she thought. Unlikely, he would have told me. She slipped off her shoes and sat on her bed. Should she wait for his knock on the door or should she call him? She checked her watch again. It was almost fourty minutes since he had gone to his cabin. He should be here by now. As she tapped in his number, she tried to control her increasing sense of panic. Where was he? Had he changed his mind about spending the night with her? His mobile finally went to message bank. She tried a second time, then left a brief message, 'Where are you?' All the fear she had suppressed throughout the past couple of days returned with a vengeance. Unable to shake off the fear she was unable to leave the cabin to look for Jake. With shaking hands, it took two attempts to punch in Barb's mobile number.

'Pick up, pick up,' she screamed at her mobile, before Barb answered.

'Jake's not here, did you give him your key?' Her voice was shaking as she fought to maintain control.

'No, I still have my key. We'll go back to his cabin and see if he is still there. Try and stay calm and stay where you are until I get back to you. I'm sure there will be a reasonable explanation.' She ended the call and began to run. A multitude of possibilities crowded her thoughts. None of them were good.

Chapter 15

Jake had not heard his attacker approaching, only becoming aware he was not alone when the cold steel of the knife blade sliced into his side. Even as he clutched his wound and fell forwards, he could not see his attacker clearly. He did hear him laugh and scream with satisfaction just before his head smashed into the metal door frame of his cabin and he lost consciousness.

Back in her cabin Gail took deep breaths, gulping in air to stay calm. The cabin becoming claustrophobic so she flung the balcony doors open to let more air in. Within seconds she was grabbed from behind and held in a vicelike grip. Gail tried to scream but a hand was clamped across her mouth. As she was twisted around to face her attacker she looked into the eyes of a madman. He bore little resemblance to the Simon she remembered. His eyes were wide and wild; his face was contorted with rage and only centimetres from her face as he screamed at her.

'This is all your fault. I warned you what would happen.' Gail fought to swallow the bile that filled her mouth as his hot breath and spittle covered her face. With one foot on an outdoor chair and the other on the balcony safety rail Simon dragged her closer to him. Gail knew instantly that he intended to kill her as he tried to lift her over the balcony safety rail. From his elevated height she was little match for him but she struggled and fought with all her strength. The metallic smell of blood on his shirt drove her on. The blood was not her blood and with a clarity that life or death situations can sometimes evoke, she realised that Jake was probably already dead. Her vision began to blur. Her airway became obstructed as her attacker's arm tightened around her neck. His other hand gripped the fabric of her shirt as he tried to lift her. The fabric ripped but she could still not get free. She was getting weaker with each second that passed. I'm going to die, she thought, as distorted visions of her parents floated before her.

Another scream, not Gail's filled the cabin. Barb felt Gail's fear before she heard her strangled cries. As Gail fought to keep her right foot anchored around the leg of the outdoor table, she watched her friend charge towards her and her attacker. She felt her attacker's grip on her neck loosen as Barb's body slammed into them with such force, she felt her body lift off the ground and fall backwards onto the balcony. The force of the impact which had facilitated her release, caused Simon to lose his balance and as he toppled over the balcony safety rail he grabbed hold of Barb, taking her with him into the churning black water below. Gail tried to stand but her legs gave way and she rested on her hands and knees gasping for breath. She tried to shout for help but no sound came out. The cabin was filling with both fellow passengers and crew members who had been alerted by the screams. Gail pointed and managed a hoarse sounding, 'Over,' before she lost consciousness.

A crew member activated the person overboard procedure and as the emergency medical response team transferred Gail to the ship's hospital facility, she was aware the ships engines had slowed and the ship was turning. Tears cascaded down her face and dripped from the oxygen mask that was strapped across her nose and mouth. Her best friend had saved her life but may have lost her own in the process.

'Gail, can you hear me?' The voice sounded far away but she recognised it was Jake. Her eyelids felt heavy and she struggled to focus on his face. He was in a wheelchair and had a white dressing around his head and one arm was in a sling, but he was alive. Tom sat beside him.

'You're alive,' she whispered, as she struggled to sit upright. With sickening realisation she remembered what had happened.

'Have they found Barb?' The familiar feeling of panic caused the heart monitor to reflect the erratic rate and rhythm and set off the alarm.

'Not yet, they are still searching,' Tom said. His face was the colour of fresh white snow and he fought to hold back tears. Gail looked at the long black hands of the large clock on the wall. It was just passed two am. Barb had been in the water for over two hours. Could she still be alive? she thought.

'Come on back to bed now. You have concussion and need to rest.' The nurse was kind but firm as she spoke to Jake. The knife which had pierced his side had bounced off a rib so had not damaged any vital organs but had required sutures to repair the tissue damage. Of bigger concern was his head injury. As he had fallen forward after the knife attack, he had hit his head against the metal door frame. He was unconscious when Barb and Tom had found him just outside their cabin. It was several minutes before he regained consciousness. The laceration to his forehead had been sutured and a dark bruise was appearing across the bridge of his nose and left eye.

'I won't be far away,' he said, as he was wheeled back to his bed.

'You need to rest as well,' the same nurse said, when she had settled Jake. 'You will have a very sore throat for a few days and you will develop more bruising around the front of your neck and upper body. You are very lucky to be alive.' She adjusted the heart monitor and dimmed the light above Gail's bed.

'I know I'm lucky to be alive. I really thought I was going to die, but my friend.' Gail couldn't finish the sentence as sobs caught in her swollen throat.

'Don't give up hope the ships are still searching for her.' The nurse was trying to reassure her distressed patient but Gail sensed that her words were hollow. She didn't believe her friend would be found alive. As the hands of the clock ticked around hope began to fade. When the sedative Gail had been given took effect, she could no longer keep her eyes open and she gave in to sleep. The lengthy search and rescue operation continued while Gail and Jake slept. Only Tom kept vigil. Few passengers slept as word of the incident spread. Later they spoke in hushed whispers as they learnt that a body had been retrieved from the ocean and taken to the ship's morgue.

Chapter 16

Tom sat with his head in his hands and waited. Each minute resembled an hour. His elation when he had been told the body pulled from the ocean was male was only momentary. Barb was still missing. He realised her chances of survival diminished with each passing second but he tried to stay positive. If anyone could survive, she could. She was extremely fit, a successful triathlete and a strong swimmer. But even with her abilities she was no match for the Atlantic Ocean. The waning moon was still bright and strips of light reflected off the water, which resembled a mill pond. Not too far from the ship Tom could still see the light of the man overboard marker. The lights from the ship's rescue boat mingled with the lights of other ships that had come to assist in the search. A sudden surge of activity on the water alerted Tom to a change. Within minutes the ship's rescue boat was returning to the cruise ship.

'She's alive,' the crew member called out as he hurried towards Tom. 'I don't know anything about her condition but they are bringing her aboard now.'

The sun had risen when Gail woke to learn her dearest friend had been found alive, clinging to a piece of buoyant debris. She was dangerously hypothermic and after initial emergency care she had been flown by rescue helicopter to the closest major hospital for ongoing treatment.

'It's unbelievable that she survived,' Tom said to Jake, when he sat by his bedside later in the morning. It appears the momentum of the fall over the safety rail threw her clear of the ship so she avoided potentially fatal injuries. Her left ankle is fractured and will need surgery at some point but for now she will stay in the intensive care unit for rewarming and breathing support. Her condition is critical but stable. Her parents have been told and are on their way from their home in Scotland to be with her. I will join them as soon as we dock in Southampton.'

'What a nightmare. Why don't you go and get some sleep? You look exhausted.'

'I will, but I just wanted to give you and Gail an update on Barb's condition, and see how you were both doing.'

'I have a headache and sore side but other than that I feel fine. Apparently, I will need head injury observations during today and be transferred to Southampton General Hospital Emergency Department to be checked out tomorrow when we dock. The same for Gail. Sick bay until we dock and then the hospital. The staff had a hectic night but we slept through it, thanks to my bump on the head and the sedative Gail was given. Sorry you had to wait for news of Barb by yourself.'

'That's okay. I am just so relieved all three of you are alive. I had no idea a random stalker could be so dangerous. I thought he was just a nuisance who would eventually move on.'

'You've only got to look at domestic violence incidents to realise how serious stalking is and how tragic the consequences can be.' Jake was surprised at his friend's naivety but he was not without blame himself. I should have been more cautious about my own safety and that of Gail, he thought. He didn't believe a stalker would do anything risky on a cruise ship, where it would be impossible to escape their crime. He didn't understand the relentless neurotic behaviour of Gail's stalker. It's comforting to think we can spot a stalker but we can't. It's easy to imagine the sleezy looking guy in a trench coat or a shadowy figure in an alley way as a stalker but in most cases, they look the same as everyone else. They have families, work places and social settings. We may mingle with them in our daily life and be completely unaware of their behaviour and its impact on their innocent victims. There was no doubt in Jake's mind now that if Barb hadn't intervened the stalker would have plunged to his death taking Gail with him.

'Do you feel up to providing a statement?' the official looking crew member asked Jake.

'I've given mine.' Tom patted his friend's arm. 'I'll leave you to it and catch you later.' He stood up to leave. The room started to spin. 'I really do need to get some sleep,' he said aloud, as he left the room, his hand leaning on the wall for support. First, he must message his parents. He had two missed calls from them. Last night's incident had made the UK TV news and they would be worried. Jake had spoken to Gail's mother, June Mason, a couple of hours ago and the ship's doctor had reassured her that Gail would make a full recovery. She was made aware they would go from the ship to the hospital to be assessed, as soon as they docked in the morning. June would be at the hospital to meet them. She would not feel better until she saw her daughter with her own eyes.

As the news spread amongst Barb and Gail's many friends and colleagues, they were equally horrified and surprised by the news. Simon had seemed like such a nice easy-going guy; as far removed as he could be from a stalker in the minds of most people. They were finding it difficult to comprehend that he could be so violent. Even his own small group of friends were shocked. One or two knew that he was still pursuing Gail in the hope of a relationship but did not consider him a stalker. Evidence that in our culture stalking is often normalised, minimised, and even romanticised. Only Gail and Bernadette O'Brien, the woman who had relocated to Ireland to escape from Simon, had seen his darker side and recognised the danger. Even in death he had left his mark. Neither woman felt regret for his untimely death, their relief was too great.

Epilogue

The lights from the Christmas tree cast sparkling rainbow shadows across the ceiling as Gail looked into the dancing flames of the wood burning stove, and reflected on her life as a wife and new mother. It had been over two years since the near tragedy on their cruise holiday but the memory was still sharp and able to generate the old fear. Despite her wonderful new life, she had been left with a feeling of being unsafe. It was a feeling that ebbed and flowed but had not disappeared. Going for a walk, answering the phone, even opening an email could feel risky on a bad day. She no longer wore her old favourite perfume. It provoked too many bad memories. Even the smell of it on others could cause her heart to race and her hands shake. Her stalker was dead but the fear he subjected her to, had not left her, and maybe it never would. She was not alone the experience of being stalked could remain with victims indefinitely. It could have a lasting impact.

'No time to dwell on the past,' she said aloud, to the pink teddy she held in her hands. She resumed wrapping Christmas presents. She inhaled the smell of pine from the tree. Mixed with the fragrance of cinnamon and nutmeg, for Gail it was the smell of Christmas. Tomorrow would be Christmas Day and it would be the first time the four friends and their families would celebrate Christmas together.

Jake and Gail had been married for just over a year. Barb and Tom were still single although marriage had been mentioned, but for now they were happily working and travelling the world. Almost losing her life had changed Barb's perspective. Months of recovery had given her plenty of time to think. Success at work was no longer her number one priority. She intended to live life to the full and enjoy every minute of every day. Memories of struggling in the dark waters of the Atlantic had not left her and she was in no hurry to board another cruise ship. She was fortunate that the ocean was like a mill pond on that fateful night and that she was a strong swimmer, but even so she had been aware her chances of survival were slim. She had begun to hallucinate as she got colder and weaker and had little memory of her actual rescue. She owed her life to a discarded old oil drum that she had clung to as she watched the sweep of the search lights in the distance.

Jake walked into the lounge room with the baby cradled in his arms. A four-centimetre scar on his forehead the only visible evidence of the injury he had received from the stalker.

'Is she asleep?' Gail whispered.

'Almost.' He pushed the pink woollen blanket away from her tiny face and Gail gazed with wonder at their beautiful two-week-old daughter. She had her father's perfect dark skin and long eyelashes, and that beautiful intoxicating smell that only new babies possess. Her name was Barbara Nyssa: Barbara, in recognition of the woman who had saved her mother's life and Nyssa from the Greek for new beginning.

It was going to be a wonderful Christmas, full of love and gratitude.

In Australia if you or someone you know is being stalked you can contact;

1800 RESPECT on 1800 737 732 or through the online chat.

In the UK you can contact;

The National Stalking Helpline

0808 802 0300

The Love of Family

by Janette R Cook

Dedicated to my husband John.

Without his love of our country, and our travels, this story would not be able to describe the wonderful outback.

Chapter 1

Sydney 1973

'Well Ted, we are finally home mate,' Lance Corporal Michael Fleming shouted to Corporal Edward Harrison over the noise of the RAAF DC3 Transport bringing them into Sydney Airport.

It didn't seem strange at the time how neither of them had spoken about catching up sometime in the future. But real life takes no heed to the plans we make.

Three days later, both men, twenty-two years of age, had been demobbed. They had handed in their uniforms, boots, kitbags and any other Army issue. They walked out of Holsworthy barracks, shook hands, and with a casual good luck, went their separate ways to restart their lives and enjoy the rest of 1973 on civvy street.

Ted and Mick felt comfortable returning to using their old familiar names. Much better than the formal Edward and Michael their officers had called them during the past two years at several army camps in South Vietnam. Mick had been the A Company cook with intermittent participation in actual military action. Ted, however, had been on more operations into the jungles than he would ever talk about.

When he said, 'I don't want to ever relive how hard it was to remain on constant alert for tunnels, bamboo traps and ambushes.' It was his way of putting the last two years behind him.

'Not sure how I will resume my previous life,' Mick replied. On the mind of each of them, were struggles and troubled thoughts of whether it would be possible to fit back into their previous, young and free way of life. In the intervening almost three years, they had lived a whole lifetime, and as sure as Australia stops for the Melbourne Cup, they definitely felt older than their twenty-two years of life.

Prior to his conscription, Mick had been in his second year of an Accounting and Marketing degree at Sydney University, as well as working in the family firm; a plan in the making since his birth. He would have to accept being called Michael again, as Mick didn't live up to the image the firm required for a future partner.

A family farm life outside Moree was waiting for Ted, and this life would be like chalk and cheese in comparison to his Vietnam experience. He had already decided he wouldn't divulge much about the horrors of jungle warfare he had witnessed or lived through.

For now, the only item on the agenda was catching up with their own families and re-joining drinking mates at the pub.

Chapter 2
Ted at Home

Settling back into a country way of life at Warrawee, just ten kilometres west of Cloverdale, went better than Ted had expected. Some of the other blokes who had left Vietnam before him, had written back to comrades still patrolling in the stinking tropical jungles. In those brief letters, they told of being booed and having things thrown at them as they marched last ANZAC day. Being a returning soldier from Vietnam didn't have the same prestige as if they were from the Korean or WW11 conflicts. No one could see anything changing in that Communist country, whether Australian soldiers were there or not.

Ted looked at his reflection in the mirror before he ventured into town on the first day. He noticed lines around his wary eyes, and how muscled his arms and legs were. Those muscles were the result of tramping through swamps, vine covered enemy territory and digging into the tunnels that honeycombed the jungles.

The older men in town stopped Ted in the street, and slapped him on the back, saying, 'Good to see you've come back safely, young fella. Next time you're in the pub I'll shout you a beer or two.' No one criticised his participation in the conflict. It was just bad luck that his number came out in the conscription birthday ballot.

The mates of his pre-war youth took a bit longer than he had expected before they treated him the same as the rest of the ones he used to drink with. They were the lucky buggers who had stayed at home because their numbers weren't drawn out of the barrel.

Ted hoped he understood how they felt. Hardly any of them had been out of the state, let alone out of the country, and they certainly had not been put into a situation of kill or be killed. The only killing any of these blokes ever did was to cull the mobs of kangaroos and wild pigs that caused havoc and devastation in the wheat and cotton paddocks. They had often killed a few beer cans on fence posts down at the local dam late on a Saturday night after a long binge.

Still, it wasn't too long before the horrors of Vietnam army life had lessened and Ted got back to farm life. Work hard, play hard. And life went on, with no hint of what the future would bring.

Chapter 3
Mick

In Sydney, Mick asked his family to give him a little breathing space. He needed to acclimatise to civilian life in the city, before he recommenced his studies at Uni. He wanted to share some fun with his mates, find out what their lives were like now, and if they were happy with their chosen career paths. It was unfortunate that he didn't seem to be able to slot back in to the young life he used to live.

In quiet moments, some niggling thoughts would invade his subconscious, and suggest that accounting in a big office and constantly worrying about the bottom line, would be a slow death for him. Answering to his father and uncles until it came time for him to step up and take a place on the board of Fleming, Fleming and Ashcott. Chartered Accountants may not be his vocation after all. That seemed to be the insistent and unwelcome thought on most nights. He broached the subject with his father, Michael Fleming Senior. 'Michael, it just seems hard because you have had two years of a life without boundaries. You will soon settle down. If your dear mother was still alive, she would tell you the same.' He patted his son on the back as they walked from the office.

After having his concerns brushed away so easily, Mick understood that his family did not have any idea of what jungle warfare with an enemy, indistinguishable from a friend was like, or the stresses this brought every minute of every day and night. He knew that his mother would have been more understanding than his father. She would have known a little of the call of the vast countryside. Having come from Bourke, she still had a little country girl heart even though she had lived in the city, and it's why she had asked to be buried at the Burke cemetery, alongside her parents.

Mick Fleming also knew that he would never try to explain his past. The memories were too raw, so he continued with the pretence of working towards his predestined life, until the one day he just didn't turn up for work.

Chapter 4
Mick, the next few years

Watching the disappearing city in his rear-view mirror, and the wide welcoming plains of the country on the other side of the Three Sisters and Katoomba, Mick felt a peace flow through his heart and all of his body.

'Thanks Dad, for giving me the Belmont for my 17th birthday. It will be my home now that I am free of your expectations,' he shouted out loud to the opening vista of the outback.

With no set destination or plan in mind, Mick had thrown some clothes, a swag and some miscellaneous cooking and eating utensils in the back. He felt he was now on a searching mission to find out all he could about the real Mick. He had decided that he would stop in any little country town on the road west, which may offer a temporary job to supplement his meagre bank balance and the small inheritance from his Mum's father. That seemed enough of a plan for now.

Army life had helped Mick develop a well-toned body, and with his handsome face and blonde hair he felt confident that his looks and demeanour would help him find gainful employment. He knew he didn't have many civilian skills, but was a bit of a handy man willing to have a go at anything. He could also turn his hand at serving a basic meal if any place had a reasonable pantry and freezers. There seemed to be an increasing number of roadhouses springing up on the highways these days, as more and more people took to the road in the affluent and carefree days of the 70's. He was sure they would all appreciate a good hearty meal.

Over the next few years, his survival habits increased, and his ability to talk to the right prospects, gave him all the employment and cash he needed to live a good life. Most places would even give him somewhere to sleep as well as a job, which meant he didn't have to use his travelling bedroom all the time. Mick and his trusty van crossed Australia both ways, travelled from Port Augusta up the centre to Katherine, over to Broome and back, and up to the Gulf.

One memorable time came when he slept under the stars along the Nullarbor and a wonderful serenity came over him, which enabled him to sleep without dreams for the first time in years. He had paddled in the emerald ocean lapping the unbelievably white sand on an Esperance beach and walked through the Bungle Bungles and felt entranced by the red of the Pilbara landscape. These memories kept him happy and sane. At times, the nightmares would come out of the blue, but he learned how to recall the good times to banish the bad.

As the drought tortured the far western cattle stations in 1978, Mick found himself traveling on a TSR (travelling stock route) on the Outback Highway north of Tibooburra. After driving on what seemed an endless ribbon of red dirt, saltbush and spinifex, he came across a small mob of cattle with a drover and about ten working dogs. The drover had an old truck with the back partially closed in, and the remaining portion had several cages for the dogs. His caravan was parked under some white Cypress trees. This was where his wife kept a fire going and where the tucker was prepared. There was a black billy constantly on the boil for when her man would stop for a cuppa. There were another ten or so dogs on chains under the trees, resting. Mick had learned these were the night dogs. They were trained to bark out loud if the cattle would stray from the holding area that was erected each day. The day dogs were trained to go quietly around any straying cattle and bring them back to the herd and off the road when vehicles were going past. A little further away from the camp was a large horse trailer, a battered 4WD and a string of three extra horses. These were used in rotation to rest which ever one had been ridden the previous day.

When Mick slowed down, and stopped his van, he decided he may as well get out and talk to the rider. He surmised that a chat to break the monotony of life in the long paddock would help break the daily grind.

'G'day, name's Mick. I can see you have a mob to control, but your blue heelers all look like they are doin' a great job,' he said to the rugged man, with skin of tanned leather.

'Yeah, had this string of dogs for a few years and wouldn't trade 'em for quids. The name's Johnno. The lady over there is me missus, Rosie. She's a bloody good mate to have on the road. Good cook and never whinges when the goin' gets tough.'

Mick could tell that Johnno was hungry for a new face and audience to hear his thoughts. He would surely have lots of ideas and opinions that came after being on the road and away from home for long periods of time.

Over the next few days Mick stayed with Rosie and Johnno, and shared stories of their different lives, and their thoughts on many subjects. They spoke of government, dole bludgers, and the best cattle to run in times of prolonged drought. Johnno said that this lot was a mix of Brahman and Droughtmaster cross bred steers, and they did okay in tough years. He didn't have any females in this mob, because after they had calves, they were too much worry if water or feed was scarce. Whenever the drought was over, Johnno said they would return to the station before turning the cattle out onto the Channel Country to fatten up for sale.

Mick and Rosie shared a few tips for cooking and Johnno showed him how to ride among the cattle and keep them calm. This was necessary when impatient drivers didn't want to wait, or blew their horns and tried to drive through the mob.

When it came time for Mick to leave, Rosie said, 'You should go and see our bosses, Larry and Karen Grainger, at Crossroads Station. We will be back there when it rains and the grass regrows, but for now the TSR will be our home.'

She told Mick that all the family would appreciate another cook when Karen was busy home schooling the two children. 'I reckon that after some of the things you have cooked for me and Johnno, you will fill the bill real good.'

Chapter 5
Mick '77

Acceptance of this suggestion seemed like a no brainer. Somewhere in his mind, Mick had lately been having thoughts about settling down in one place for a while. He turned west at Windorah, and travelled along the Diamantina Development Road (DDR) with Bedourie as his first stop. In the little town, the first priority was to ease his tired body from the bone shaking corrugated road over the last three hundred kilometres. After half an hour in the Council artesian bore pool, the next stop was the pub for a few coldies. Next stop was the local store to stock up on a few provisions before the big luxury of a night in a motel in the main and only street. The town had Birdsville to the south and Boulia and Mt Isa to the north.

Next day, Mick continued west on the still deeply corrugated road. Behind him were giant clouds of dust, swirling up in waves, blanking out all his journey so far. It was going to be another bone-shuddering day, but that didn't worry him anymore. Every day was an adventure to embrace and enjoy. It was a motto that Mick repeated every time he travelled a different road. He slowed down and read the rusty sign, with paint peeling and the almost mandatory bullet holes in it, stating that he was at the front boundary of Crossroads Station.

It was another forty minutes before the large and sprawling homestead and out-buildings came into sight. Peppercorn trees and colourful Bougainvillea ringed the main house, providing shade and cool areas to sit with a beer on hot afternoons after a hard day's work was over. It seemed to be an oasis with vibrant colours of hope in a desert of despair. Sprinklers pumping artesian water on to the lawn made the whole homestead look very inviting. But any hint of greenery stopped at the fence surrounding the house. From there, and as far as the eye could see, it was red dust, sparse saltbush and a few stunted trees, struggling to stay alive. The normally large areas of saltbush were showing the effects of being harvested for a little sustenance to the few breeders not on agistment or with Mick and Rosie. Most station managers tried to hang on to the breeders to start re-building the stock when the rains came again. Saltbush and whatever hay they could source, or afford were sometimes the last chance to get by a little longer, and keep the Bank at bay.

Getting a little closer to the homestead, Mick could see someone in a large sunhat busily unpegging clothes off the overloaded long washing line. He slowed down to ease the likelihood of his dust enveloping the lady and her clean washing. To make sure she could see who was approaching, Mick had driven his battered wagon up to the fence, just outside of where the lady was standing. She was a pretty woman, perhaps mid-twenties, with light brown hair. Her attire was shorts and T-shirt. He could see her quite shapely tanned legs.

He smiled while lifting his dusty Akubra and said, 'Hello, you must be Mrs Grainger. I guess I should explain the reason for my visit so far off the beaten track.'

He told her that Johnno and Rosie suggested he should visit. A slight tension eased on her face as she folded the last of the laundry.

He stretched out his arm for a handshake. 'Name's Mick Fleming and I spent a few days with Johnno and Rosie a week or so back, and they said it wouldn't hurt to drive out here for a visit.' This was enough information for her to not feel threatened by having a stranger calling in unannounced so far off the main roads. 'Hello, my name is Karen. My husband Larry will be home soon. We own this money-eating place, along with our bank. Would you like a cuppa to wash the dust from your throat?' Karen said. 'Kettle's on.'

'That would be most welcome, Karen. Sorry to call in with no warning, but Johnno said it wouldn't be a problem. He just drew me a mud-map to show how to find the station.'

Over a refreshing brew in the spacious homely kitchen, and a serving of a large slab of boiled fruit cake, Mick told Karen that this was just like being a kid again. He had always loved visiting Nanna Olsen in Bourke whenever his Mum could get away from the city to visit her parents. Then he revealed the reason he had ventured out this far. How he had been a cook in the army, and in heaps of roadhouses and little cafes in towns anywhere between Broken Hill,

Perth, Cobar and Lightning Ridge, with several others along the way.

'In some places, I also picked up a lot of knowledge in fixing stuff and I now consider myself to be a reasonably good handyman and I'm looking for a job. So that is my verbal CV. Not that impressive, I know. But I will turn my hand to most things and that is my reason for being here. With a bit of luck, we can help each other for a while.'

'You sure don't mess around with small talk, do you? Slow down and relax a little. We don't rush things out here these days. I would suggest you smell the roses, but they have sadly gone to the big compost bin in the sky, as well as just about every other plant that used to make me smile when I gardened. Only the Bougainvillea and the native peppercorn trees are left to brighten my life, I'm afraid.'

Around five o'clock, a dusty stockman rode up and dismounted. He appeared tired and dispirited as he stretched his long body, standing on the dusty, red earth. He had unsaddled, fed and watered his horse. Karen made the introductions. The three of them settled into the homemade squatter's chairs on the wide veranda to enjoy a beer or two. Karen left the men after a drink to check on the little monsters, as she called their two children, Troy and Bec.

Larry understood that Mick wanted to have a base for a while. He didn't say that over the last few years, he had met a few Vietnam Vets passing through. They couldn't settle into the old lives and had taken to the track, just as Mick was doing.

So, he offered this troubled man a place to sleep in return for a bit of station work, or even some house duties while Karen managed the School of the Air classes for their two children.

'Our finances are stretched to the limit, and there won't be any pay to start, but all food and personal needs will be supplied. We can talk money when it rains whatever century that may occur,' chuckled Larry.

The offered conditions seemed as good as he could have hoped for, and Mick was enjoying their company and the isolation. He hoped he could help them at least as much as they were offering to help him.

Chapter 6

Crossroads Station

The drought dragged on for another year, and Mick stayed on too. He helped them in any way he could, and over time, became one of the family. The kids, Troy and Rebecca, started calling him Uncle Mick, except when he would stand in for their Mum as their teacher. Then they cheekily called him Mr Fleming, until the lessons were over.

Finally, the rains came, and everyone had beaming smiles. Now they could talk of the future and make plans to restock and welcome Johnno and Rosie back to the station. Johnno had sent a message saying they were heading home with most of the steers in reasonable shape, under the circumstances. Unfortunately, there were less head than when they took to the road. They had slaughtered some for their own use and sold others to pay for the provisions that they needed for survival. A few had also met a sad fate with the road trains that traversed the country.

Larry hoped they could find a sale for some of the heaviest steers to lower the overdraft a bit. He said a little prayer that the breeding stock could start a new herd rebuilding the viability of the station and their livelihood. He knew that buying new stock would be both too expensive and hard to locate. With a promise of a good season ahead, everyone was eager to start restocking.

Chapter 7
Ted '73 to '78

Edward Harrison had once again become known as Ted and had really taken to the country life with the freedom to make changes on the farm. His Dad and Mum had given him free rein to change some planting regimes and choices of fertilisers with less non-organic residue remaining in the soil, as this was becoming a research worry for all producers.

He diligently read The Land newspaper, which was a weekly farmer's bible. He devoured any scientific information discovered that would improve cropping, pastures and farming techniques' enrolled in a TAFE course, provided by the National Farmers Federation (NFF) studying new ways of irrigating the cotton crops. Currently large dams that were going in on every station using broadacre farming, would be a major cost saver and help the bottom line. It was realised that open channels to direct the water allocation to each grower were losing at least thirty percent to evaporation in the hot western sun. But this water still had to be paid for. Any solution for the costly evaporation was never far from Ted's mind, along with the other ways to make the farm more profitable;. at least profitable enough to support two families. Finding solutions to these problems were always on his mind, while he went about his farming and cropping work.

Ted had started courting Lois Green from Cloverdale where she was renting a small house. Since coming to the area, Lois had attracted the attention of several young bachelors around Cloverdale and Moree. It wasn't every day a gorgeous red-haired girl with big green eyes came into the area to stay for more than a week. Ted felt quite proud that Lois was just as attracted to him, as he was to her, and in no time they were a couple. Every Saturday night, whenever harvest or planting didn't require his presence, he and Lois would go to the dances at every little town hall or School of Arts building within a hundred kilometres.

Sometimes, they would just have a BBQ in someone's back yard or down by the river. But it all added to the enjoyment of the young crowd, along with youthful freedom.

Lois had been in the town for a few years now, after graduating as a Registered Nurse at a Queensland hospital on the Gold Coast. Shortly after completing her training, she gladly accepted a position at Moree Hospital, where she loved working.

In a quiet moment away from the crowd, Ted confided in Lois. 'I had struggled to settle back into my previous life in Australia. After Vietnam, I really worked at covering up all of the confusion I felt in the life I am living now. I am so grateful that Mum and Dad have been one hundred percent understanding and patient when any unexplained sombre moodiness comes over me.'

Lois had seen some of the same worries and attitudes at the city hospital during her training.

'I have seen many returned men who entered hospital with self-inflicted injuries, unexplained illnesses or binge drinkers. Although I can't possibly feel the same as you do, I know that love and understanding really helps with troubled minds.'

She promised him that she would always be his confidante when he wanted to vent, or to just sit quietly until he felt ready to come back to his life now.

Previous experience and a natural caring personality were perfect in a partner for Ted, making

Lois someone to complement him, and provide any reassurance he would need. Her farming background as a child was an added bonus. She understood the need for hard and long days in the planting and harvesting seasons, along with the added security of an off-farm income in the hard times.

February 1979 saw a large family wedding for Lois and Ted. They had a casual wedding breakfast, then a seven-day honeymoon on the Gold Coast, before returning to start the next planting season.

Over the previous Christmas the young couple had worked hard, but enthusiastically, cleaning out and remodelling the vacant manager's accommodation ready for them to start their married life together.

During the past few years, after the end of the Vietnam conflict, information was revealed of illnesses in babies fathered by returned men. In addition, rare cancers among the men were being blamed on the defoliant Agent Orange. The poison had been sprayed over large areas of the jungles where the soldiers were patrolling. At times they were drenched in the solution with little or no care taken to protect them. Because of this information, and even though they were young, Ted and Lois made a conscious decision to not have any children of their own. Instead, they would adopt a child or two in the early years of their marriage. They knew they may have to wait for any adoption to happen, but with their busy lives and their age, they were prepared to wait for a family. They would start the process later in the year.

Life was good and busy, and they were happy with the current situation and their decision to adopt.

Chapter 8

Crossroads '78 - '79

As Mick, Larry and Johnno dismounted from their dusty horses and walked toward the house, Karen came to meet them with a concerned look on her pretty face.

'I thought I would talk to you out here, away from the kids. Dad called just after you all left this morning, and said that Mum has cancer and he wants me to come down to Tamworth for a while. I have been trying to organise the household to cope while I am away. I rang Julie to see if she could supervise the schoolwork in my place. Luckily, she agreed in a heartbeat and will be here as soon as she can.'

'Julie Harris is Karen's best friend, and she has just gone through a very long period off work, recovering from both whooping cough and a very serious case of rheumatic fever,' Larry said.

'She has been looking for a new position as a nurse. In the meantime, it seems she is quite open to spending some recuperative time at Crossroads. With no family of her own, Julie would love to be accepted as part of this family,' Karen said.

Arrangements were made in a whirlwind, and within two days, Karen would hitch a ride with the Royal Flying Doctor Service (RFDS) plane to Longreach, where she would catch a scheduled flight to Brisbane and then on to Tamworth to her family.

Chapter 9
Julie

At her home in Tugun in south-east Queensland, Julie was determined to prove her ability and resilience for the tough solitary drive out to Crossroads. Firstly, she gifted her indoor plants to neighbours, and secondly, she placed her unit in the hands of an estate agent to rent out for at least six months. Then she began the long drive from her home. She headed out to the other side of this massive state to help out her best friends.

Julie had been there before but had forgotten just how far from civilisation the homestead really was. Being given the chance to help others after recently needing care herself, was a humbling experience.

After eight tiring days of driving, she pulled into the front yard at Crossroads. Immediately, two excited children came rushing out to her. Their big gap-toothed smiles only made them look more adorable and huggable. Aunty Julie was going to be a welcome asset to this family unit, Larry thought.

In no time at all, Troy and Rebecca were hugging Aunty Julie and opening the Lego and sweets she had brought. She knew little gifts would bring joy to the kids, who would surely be missing their Mum.

Larry introduced Mick to Julie and immediately they were relaxed with each other. As so often happens in nature, they felt a subconscious awareness of attractive qualities acceptable to both of them for any future relationship. This was only natural, as Julie and Karen were so much alike. They had shared five years boarding together at a girls' school in Armidale. To keep the family unit functioning and happy until Karen returned was not going to be difficult.

Station life soon settled into a new but familiar pace. Johnno and Rosie carried on as the Jackeroos made sure the remaining stock were grazing wherever the saltbush had regenerated after the life-giving rain. Rosie actually enjoyed outside work much more than around the house, especially since she had experienced nearly three years on the road with only basic house duties. Johnno felt it was natural to have Rosie by his side while he rode amongst the cattle or checked the bores and water tanks.

Now that his two station hands were back, it allowed Larry time to spend repairing some of the old tractors and a bulldozer. These would be needed to clean the bore drains and clear the fast-growing stubble. Mick and Larry worked side by side, servicing the motor bikes, the station Landcruiser, the electricity-providing generators and Mick's precious wagon. They also had to check on the windmills which brought the water from the underground Great Artesian Basin to the surface, before it flowed into the channels that replenished the cattle water troughs. These same windmills also supplied better water pressure to the house.

Mick took to tending the few plants in the house garden, as though he had been doing this all his life.

In no time at all, it seemed the bougainvillea was blooming again, and the big straggly Peppercorn trees flourished with the welcome moisture. He had even dug up some red earth in one corner of the house-yard and planted some lettuce, carrots and spinach seeds, which were soon poking their first leaves through the softened ground. A couple of stunted rose bushes missed by Karen, started to show signs of life, and sprouted buds. A delighted Julie told Mick, 'It is great to have time for us to chat out here without the kids around.'

Chapter 10
Julie's story – 50's to 70's

Julie told Mick about her upbringing in a few foster homes after her parents were killed in a head-on car and truck accident while she was at school. She was nearly six at that time.

'After much searching, no relatives could be found to take care of me. The only alternative was for me to become a foster child. Mostly, my life was stable with good foster families. The third family who fostered me generously paid for my schooling until I turned eighteen years of age. Reg and Nancy Wilson were older than most for fostering children. They had been doing it for years, so they were still on the approved list. This offer included my tuition and boarding fees at a very well respected school for girls in Armidale. Apart from paying for my schooling, the lovely old couple always expressed a wish to give me a real start after graduation.'

She told Mick how shocked she was when Gordon White, the Wilson family lawyer, came to see her at the school.

'It seemed unbelievable that his clients had been involved in a car crash and killed instantly. Just like Mum and Dad. How unfair was life that the four people who had loved me most, my parents and the Wilsons, should die in almost identical circumstances was the overriding thought that stayed in my mind,' Julie said.

This shocked young schoolgirl sat on a straight-backed chair in front of the lawyer, unable to take in all that he was telling her. Once more alone was all she could think. Twice an orphan, sort of.

After giving her some time to take in all this shattering news, and while the school counsellor sat with her arm around Julie's shoulders, the lawyer went on with more information.

"Reg and Nancy had no children of their own, but belonged to a large family of siblings and most of their possessions and money were bequeathed to them. They had a small unit on the Gold Coast which they have left to you, so that you will always have a home base after your school days are finished. There is also a cash bequest to help with your living expenses while you study to become a Registered Nurse."

'There wasn't a huge amount of money to support me while I studied, but I was lucky enough to find Lois, another student nurse. We hit it off straight away, sharing the unit and expenses and had a really fun life for the next three years. I confess, my recent solitary life then became more gregarious, even a little outrageous, after Lois moved in. We bonded in much the same way as Karen and I had been drawn together while at boarding school. Karen and I roomed together at the school. We were both feeling a little lost being so far away from familiar places, and we were drawn towards each other as thirteen-year-olds are likely to do. In no time at all we were bosom buddies and swore we would be friends for life.'

After this disclosure from Julie, Mick opened up too. 'Although I have a father in Sydney, I really was the black sheep and a failure to the family. I have always felt that I was alone in the world too.'

'We are two peas in a pod.'

Over time, Larry could see a close relationship blossoming between Mick and Julie. When Karen returned, she jokingly called him a natural match-maker and a hopeless romantic at heart. All of them celebrated the good news about Karen's Mum now being in remission from her breast cancer.

Chapter 11
Cupid and Plans '80

The old married couple, as Julie called Karen and Larry, were secretly planning for her and Mick to drive to Longreach on the premise of replenishing the household pantry and the stock supplies. They would have to arrange a carrier to truck all the purchased feed and machinery parts back to the station.

'You two deserve a break from your unpaid work. Stay for a week or so to enjoy a few of the sights around Longreach. Maybe you should even drive to Winton to see the historic little town,' said Larry.

It seemed an offer too good to refuse. Although their love was still very new, both of them thought it would be great to share time together.

As they were preparing to leave Crossroads on the restocking trip, Larry told them there would be no problem if they wanted to stay away for longer than a week.

'Just make sure you both come back as we're used to having you around. The kids would miss you terribly, and Karen and I would too.'

'We love having both of you here with us.'

Julie and Mick were overcome by these disclosures from their friends, and they returned the compliment. 'The four of you are more family than we have ever known, and we will be forever grateful,' Julie added as Mick nodded in agreement.

Until now they had shared some kisses and hugs, but had chosen to go slowly with anything more physical. Both of them were quiet until Mick tried to lighten the slightly tense atmosphere in the vehicle.

'I will admit that I'm looking forward to buying some new 'Y' fronts and toiletries, and cleaning up my scruffy appearance.'

'I understand, 'cos I'm looking forward to shopping in Longreach, too.'

After a hearty counter meal of steak and chips, stewed apples and rice for sweets, they went to their room and were silently relieved to see twin beds.

After showering down the hallway, they returned to the room to be overcome with a sudden shyness. Feeling unsure of the next step, they whispered Goodnight across the space, and then both spent a night of broken sleep.

While heading to their next stop, each attempted to address the elephant in the room. Slowly and hesitantly, they each expressed hopes of deepening their relationship.

'I don't know why I have turned shy,' Mick said. 'I think it is because I have never felt so strong about any woman before, and I don't want to make the wrong move and lose you. Julie, you are my best friend, and I know how good I feel whenever you are with me. I have to say I really want to make love to you and be with you forever. I worry that if I do or say something that changes our relationship, and you don't feel the same about me, I would be devastated.' This all came out in a quiet, tremulous voice while he drove, keeping his eyes straight ahead, afraid to look at her.

'I am relieved that you have spoken exactly what I have been feeling and thinking too. Don't even contemplate losing me. Just like you, I want us to be together forever. We should start the next part of exploring this new love tonight. Because your parents weren't happy, I have worried that you may never have wanted to be married.'

'This love is real, not a marriage of convenience or status the way my parents' marriage appeared to me,' he assured her.

On the way from Jundah to Longreach, Mick gently assured Julie. 'Our love will overcome any doubts I used to have before you came into my life.'

It was a happier entry into town, knowing they both had expressed their thoughts, desires and fears so openly.

The early part of the afternoon was spent diligently purchasing all items on the lists from Larry and Karen and arranging a local bloke to transport it to the station. Then it was a fun time with Mick replacing his old underwear, deodorant, and razor blades and a much-needed haircut. Julie enjoyed shopping for shorts and tops, a sexy bra and a new pair of sandals.

After enjoying the overdue shopping spree, they dined at a small Chinese restaurant, just a short walk from the motel.

They sipped their wine, and ate by the light of the dim candles. 'I think I fell in love with you the moment I first saw you,' said Mick. 'I love the way you are so gentle with Troy and Bec, and how you always know what to say to them. I remember when you made some sandwiches and cordial and took the kids down to the dry dam and had a picnic. You pretended all of you were in town with a river running through a park. Everyone laughed for a long time after that. I think you will make a great mother one day.'

'I saw how excited you were the first time you discovered the new bud on Karen's rosebush and couldn't wait to tell her,' Julie replied.

'Or how you made us all laugh when you told us stories of things you and Karen got up to in the boarding school. You and Lois certainly enjoyed a great single life whenever you weren't working, too. So, good for you! Youth passes too quickly sometimes, with not one memory worth holding on to,' Mick replied with an air of sorrow in his voice.

This friendly back and forth conversation continued until the meal had ended and the last of the wine had been sipped.

Mick's gentle but hard-working hand was on the small of her back as they left the restaurant. They walked hand in hand in the warm moonlit night to their motel room. Along the way Julie spoke, 'We are in Swan Street now. I wonder who had decided to call all of the streets in Longreach after Australian birds!'

Feeling relaxed, but excited, they entered the motel room to see the large queen-sized bed strewn with pink and white flowers from the bougainvillea bush outside their room.

Mick had secretly asked the manager to do this when he had registered that afternoon.

Julie had tears in her eyes. 'You are making this night so special for me, and for us.'

This was the night they were now ready to consummate their love. Both were eager to give their hearts and bodies to each other.

'Mind if I remove this light shawl from around your gorgeous body?' Mick kissed her shoulders and neck and murmured, 'You look beautiful tonight.'

'Thank you,' she whispered.

Julie unbuttoned his shirt, and slipped her hands into the space to feel his heart beating just a little faster than normal.

He leant in close. Their kiss was a slow burn, building to a release of any doubts they may have had this morning. 'I feel this night has set us free from the past, and making love to you is the most wonderful way to start a new and beautiful life together.'

He fell with her on to the bed, where he started to take off her little T-shirt and bra. His lips brushed so gently across her aroused nipples, before he lightly nibbled each one in turn. Their arms became entangled as Julie was also attempting to remove the new clothes that Mick had bought today.

'I'll take care of that,' Mick said, as he rose from the bed, unzipped his pants, and stepped out of his briefs. Julie was doing the same with her jeans. Mick re-joined her among the petals, gazing at her lovely naked body, eagerly waiting for his return.

He entered her slowly, pushing into her depths over and over again. After climaxing together, Mick relaxed beside Julie while their breathing slowed.

'I love you so much,' they said simultaneously. Later, they lay wrapped in a loving tangle of arms and legs, and drifted off to a contented dreamless sleep.

Through the night, Julie woke to feel Mick's arm around her, holding her close. Never had she felt so loved and secure in her whole life. Having lived all these years with no parents of her own and no real family in her background, it had always seemed impossible to be more than an honorary member of Larry and Karen's family.

From now on she could dream of being a couple with Mick, and maybe children one day too. With a quiet, contented sigh, she snuggled up a little closer to Mick with their bodies fitting perfectly together.

When they woke later, they made love again, exploring their bodies in a more gentle but sensual way. This new and wonderful love they had found together became more exciting and perfect with each arousal.

The night before, Mick had ordered breakfast to be delivered to their room at eight o'clock. When it arrived in the breakfast hutch, he called from under the tangled sheets, 'Are we able to book in for another two nights? Now doesn't seem the right time to hurry through this new life.'

The new lovers spent the remainder of the morning in their motel room. After lunch they walked around the town seeing the historical sights, before driving out to the Thomson River to watch the sunset. Time was immaterial to them at the moment, in the bubble of their first real love.

Never before has someone made me dream of a future filled with love. When they returned to their room that night, Julie laid her head on his chest and whispered, 'I can't believe I could feel this happy.'

'I will do all in my power to make you happy,' Mick answered. 'When we get back to Crossroads, we'll tell Larry and Karen that we want to start planning for a future instead of just drifting through life. Oh, and one more thing. Before we go any further, and even though I should have asked you before we made love, will you marry me?'

Julie turned to face him, their lips almost touching, and with tears in her eyes she whispered, 'Nothing would make me happier than to be your wife.'

After leaving Longreach they headed north to Winton, and camped at the billabong, just to the west of the town. It was the same billabong where almost 100 years before, a young, inspired Banjo Paterson had written the lyrics to Waltzing Matilda.

Further west they stopped at the historic Middleton Pub. The publican said, 'This is the only remaining staging post of the nine that were originally along this road to Boulia. The Cobb and Co coaches would stop here, change the horses, the passengers would have a comfort stop, a meal and a drink. Every coach was for both mail and passengers, so they would pick up and drop off any letters or parcels for the stations in the district.'

He also gave them a little more information of the area. 'If you camp out at night anywhere between here and Boulia, you may even be fortunate or unfortunate, to witness the Min Min Light. This brochure will tell you the history about it and life beyond the black stump.'

Mick and Julie enjoyed a drink and a meal at dusk, before snuggling into their swags in their bedroom on wheels.

The following day they continued travelling west and reached Boulia in the mid-afternoon. They booked a room at the pub for three nights, plus dinner and breakfast.

The stay was full of fun, laughter and talking to the locals. They gained a better understanding about living in the far west of the state, which demonstrated a different but challenging lifestyle. Three days later it was time to leave Boulia and drive back to Crossroads to start planning their future.

During the trip back to the station, Julie confessed, 'Mick, there is something I need you to know before we marry.'

Hearing the seriousness in her voice sent chills to his heart. Mick tried to lighten the sombre mood. 'There is nothing you can say that will change my mind, unless you admit to being an axe murderer.'

Julie laughed a little at that, but confessed, 'No, I'm not an axe murderer, but my information does need you to seriously consider what I am telling you. You know that I had a serious bout of rheumatic fever last year. My doctor, as well as my own nursing training, tells me that my heart will have been compromised.'

'What could that mean to your future health? Will it cause any problems, and would you need to take precautions every day?' Mick quietly asked.

'I believe that if I carry on just as I'm doing now, and as long as there are no extended periods of stress, there shouldn't be any worry.'

Mick said, 'When the RFDS plane comes to the station next time, we will get the doc to give you a complete examination. He can tell us both what's needed to keep you in good health.'

With that plan in place for the future, the conversation turned to more exciting questions. They pondered little problems, such as where Mick could buy an engagement ring fit for his future wife, where

Julie would buy her wedding gown, where would they be married and who would perform the service? They spent lots of happy travel times planning it all.

Both said they really had little or no desire to be wasteful with some of these unnecessary extravagances. 'We should agree that as long as we both wear wedding rings to show our love and commitment, no engagement ring is necessary.'

Mick thought when the visiting padre came for his three-monthly visit to the station, they could arrange the wedding. 'We'll call him on the pedal wireless and tell him of our plans.'

'If I adjust a sundress that I brought with me but haven't worn yet, it could easily be my perfect wedding gown,' was how Julie solved one more problem.

It didn't seem possible that all the wedding needs were solved so quickly. Agreeing that it was really because they were so compatible, Mick stated, 'At this rate we can possibly also solve all the problems of the world before the next stop.'

Travelling down the dusty, but scenic road, Julie commented, 'This trip is just like a show I watched on TV each week at home. It was called, Ask the Leyland Brothers. The program showed us animals like the bustards, the emus and the camels that are around us now. But seeing them in real life is so much better.'

Chapter 13
Exciting News

Their vehicle pulled up at the fence, and the screen door burst open as two happy kids came rushing towards them. 'You're back, you're back,' they shouted.

Laughter seemed to be everywhere as the four of them embraced and danced around in the red dust. The younger two of the group were glad to have them back and secretly expected gifts from town, but the travellers were experiencing a new but unfamiliar feeling of homecoming.

Larry and Karen also stepped down from the veranda to welcome the couple back. Nudging each other and noting immediately how Mick and Julie were standing together holding hands. Karen smiled at them. 'I think you two may have some news for us. You look like cats that got the cream.'

Julie answered with a cheeky grin. 'It is all your fault. We left as friends. And, now look at us. We are back, totally in love, and busting to get married. I never knew what I wanted in life until now. I've learned that Mick is the perfect answer to my prayers.'

'Same here,' Mick said. 'My happy future is now secure in the love that we have found with each other.'

'Congratulations, you two, but it is no surprise to us at all. We saw it ages ago.'

'Why do you think we sent you both on a shopping trip?' Larry chimed in, as they all hugged.

'You had better come up to the house and have a drink to celebrate. You can tell us all about it, while we have some tucker,' said Karen.

Back on the shaded veranda, Bec hugged and talked to her new doll while Troy played with his new Matchbox truck. Both were overjoyed knowing that the Roald Dahl and Dr Seuss books they had openly wished for, were in their bedrooms. Going to bed to read them tonight was going to be great fun, the two children reckoned.

The adults sat around the big weathered timber kitchen table, having a beer or three to celebrate the happy couple and their great news. The excited and animated couple kept revealing all of the plans they had formulated in the van for the last three hundred kilometres or so. Both said they didn't want a fuss or a big wedding. However, there were a few things they needed Karen and Larry to consider.

'We would like the padre who visits here every three months to marry us, and we want you both to be our witnesses. As a special family touch, will you allow Troy and Bec to be our page boy and flower girl?' Karen agreed to that request immediately.

'There is one more favour. I have two guests we would like to invite. Lois was my great friend while I was nursing back on the Gold Coast, and she is married now. I would love the two most special women in my life to meet each other. I assumed you would agree, so I sent a letter to her, before we left Bedourie, asking her and hubby to come.'

At this moment, Mick took over the conversation. 'So, that's everything except for the biggest favour of all. We would appreciate living here at the start. Then we intend making plans to head back east and get some employment. Probably only to Longreach, where Julie could return to nursing and I could look for any job around town. I'm willing to try my hand at anything, as you both know. I just hope it won't take too long.'

'Wow, you really have made a lot of decisions in such a short time,' said Karen.

Chapter 14
Wedding Plans '80

Over the next nine weeks many plans were put in place for a Crossroads wedding.

Mick and Julie drove back to town and arranged for the only general storekeeper, Terry Olafsen, to order two wedding rings from Brisbane. They used the novel idea of metal washers to approximate their finger sizes. Terry promised to send the washers to achieve the correct fit. Mick bought a new sports shirt for the big day from the limited range. 'I will send a message with the outback mail truck when the rings arrive,' Terry promised.

At the homestead everyone was busy moving furniture into the spare rooms. This area was now jokingly called, the honeymoon suite.

There was a small sink already set up from years ago, and a very small gas camping stove they would use. Or, if they preferred, they could still share the kitchen with the whole Grainger family.

'This will be a perfect kitchen for us,' smiled Julie, as she dreamed of her life here with Mick. This home was already making such great memories for them.

The young lovers seemed to take any possible inconvenience in their stride, with the plans going ahead over the next two months.

The padre had advised them that he was currently on holidays and would be about six weeks later than his normal schedule of visiting the Grainger's. However, he said he could still make all the necessary arrangements for the planned nuptials, pick up the rings, and even bring flowers for the bride's bouquet and the gorgeous and excited flower girl.

The situation was almost the same for the Flying Doctor. 'Naturally, I would be there in a heartbeat if there was an emergency, but to fly in for a simple medical check is a bit harder to arrange. Hopefully my Estimated Time of Arrival (ETA) will probably be late August.'

Those dates satisfied everyone and life went on as before, including the highly anticipated arrival of Lois and her husband a week before the wedding day, set down for 10th October 1980.

Chapter 15
Disturbing news

On a mid-September morning, the RFDS plane landed on the little air strip five hundred metres from the homestead. As the doctor and the pilot alighted from the Cessna, Mick stood waiting to help carry any equipment they had brought with them to the pick-up truck.

'Hi Andy, good to see you again. Good flight?' Mick asked, as he shook the pilot's hand.

'Morning, Mick. Yeah, good trip, great scenery after the rain in the channels. The Cooper is running towards Lake Eyre. The pelicans have already moved in, ready to nest and mate'.

Doctor Rolf Cardew joined in the conversation. 'I had heard about them somehow knowing when to head to the remote middle of Australia, even if it hadn't rained for ten years or more. But I've never witnessed it until today. It was both magnificent and amazing.'

'You're right doc. Nature is unbelievable. It never fails to fascinate me.'

'I can't wait to introduce you to my lovely lady, Julie, so we had better get a move on, just in case you get called away.'

With the paddock-basher truck loaded with Rolf's medical equipment and an esky, the three men climbed into the cabin for the bumpy trip back to the ladies, Larry and the kids.

There was a pot of tea, a large plate of sandwiches and a chocolate cake waiting out on a bench on the bougainvillea-shaded side of the house.

Firstly, they took about forty minutes, and a refill of the tea in all the mugs, to catch up on the news from town, and the usual comments on the weather. Everyone was worried about the lack of readily available stock to replace beasts sold two years ago, when drought gripped the land.

Rolf then stood. 'This is an opportune time to give all of you a brief three-monthly medical check before I commence the full examination Julie has requested.'

As expected, Troy and Bec had no health problems to worry the parents.

'Don't forget to always wear large hats and keep the zinc on your noses when out in the sun.' He also gave them their next vaccination for measles, mumps and tetanus, and reminded them to clean their teeth twice a day. Karen and Larry were also passed as A1 with no follow up needed.

'So that only leaves you two, and then we can all relax and have a longer chat.' Rolf smiled.

Mick and Julie went into their makeshift lounge room. 'We have a few questions needing answers. Julie had rheumatic fever about a year ago and doesn't feel that she has fully recovered. Would that affect her living a normal life from now on?'

'Yes, Julie probably has a weakened heart from that. I will check on that later. You were in good health last time I visited, and I presume you have been in reasonable health since. I will check your BP, sugar, cholesterol, and urine, to exclude any possible problems. Once I've completed that we'll know more.'

At that point, Mick left the room and waited down the hall until they emerged thirty minutes later.

It was evident that there was a change in Julie's demeanour. She looked as though she didn't know whether to laugh or cry.

Mick rushed to her side first and demanded, 'What the hell has happened?'

'If you recall, I said that Julie shouldn't have too much worry if she doesn't get pregnant for a while to let her body recover a bit longer. Well, it is a little late for that now. It looks like Julie is about eleven weeks pregnant. So, we will have to be more aware of any changes in the health of her or the baby, over the next six months. It shouldn't present a big problem, with regular checks. You should think about moving into town before the due date though,' Rolf explained. 'Just to be on the safe side,' he added.

'For now, just enjoy that you are both about to become parents. Congratulations!'

The two stunned lovers hugged and kissed and smiled at the thought of becoming a family of three. They turned to Rolf, 'We will think about moving after the wedding, but not now.'

'That seems a sensible way to go about it. I will check you now, Mick. Then we can go out and give the good news to the others.'

Julie took the hint and left the room to sit in their little kitchen and wait for the two men to emerge.

Mick took off his shirt, exposing his sun-tanned torso and sat while Rolf placed his stethoscope on his chest and took his blood pressure.

'Mmmm, have you had a cold or a cough lately?'

'No, no cold or flu, but I have noticed that I have been coughing a bit lately. I just assumed it was from the dust coming out of these unused rooms and bed mattress we are sleeping on. Why, what do you think is going on?'

'You seem to have a murmur in your heart, and your lungs didn't seem to be fully inflated or deflated when you were breathing in and out for me. You look as though you have lost a bit of weight since I last visited, but I guess your current active love life could have a bit to do with that.' Rolf grinned.

'Still, I need to ask a few questions. Is there any history of heart or lung disease in your family? Was any problem detected when you had your army medical?'

'No, the Army Medic said I was a strong as a Mallee bull, and I have been. About six months ago I started to feel a bit breathless and tired, and I do experience a little chest pain after doing any hard work.'

'Did you ever come into contact with any poisonous herbicides or defoliants like Agent Orange or DDT, while you were in Vietnam?'

'Yeah, sometimes when we were on operations in the jungle, the planes would shower us in Agent Orange. Probably didn't even know we were there. What do you think is the problem?'

'I don't want to worry you too much, but I will take a sputum sample and some blood back with me. I would like to rule out lung cancer or any other serious cause. Relax for now until we know a bit more.'

'Well, let's not tell Julie at the moment. We would

like to share the good news of the baby with our friends. I'll follow it up with you later.' The news had shocked Mick, but he'd keep quiet about it for now.

Mick and Rolf walked back to Julie. As she stood, Mick noticed the beaming smile on her beautiful face. 'All good here,' Mick assured her. 'Now let's go out and share this special news with our family.'

The screen door opened with its usual squeak, and everyone on the veranda turned as they emerged.

It was more than impossible to contain their happiness, so they both declared together, 'We're going to have a baby.'

Shrieks of joy and hugs from Karen, giggles from the kids and backslaps and handshakes all round went on for a few minutes from Larry and Andy.

'How far along are you?' queried Karen.

'Rolf says about eleven weeks, which I guess means about the time we went to Longreach,' Julie answered, while her smile just got bigger.

'Well, just as well the marriage is arranged, otherwise I'd have to get out the old shotgun, eh Mick,' Larry threatened jokingly.

Andy apologised while interrupting the excited crowd to tell Rolf that they had another call to make about an hour away.

Larry quickly brought the truck around and reloaded all the gear. Andy and Rolf climbed in, and he took them back to the plane to attend what would turn out to be a broken leg of a stockman outside Boulia.

Back at the house when the excitement had died down a little, Julie and Karen went inside to start cooking their night meal. 'This pregnancy will probably put a strain on my heart, and Mick and I should move to Longreach. Probably no later than the start of my third trimester,' Julie said.

'We will worry about that in the coming months. Let's just enjoy our lives here for now.' She ended any more conversation about leaving and began peeling the potatoes.

After the news had settled down a little, life was busy preparing for the wedding.

Chapter 16
Reunion

On 30th September, in the early afternoon, a dusty jeep pulled up at the front fence, and two smiling people emerged from the cabin. Julie ran out to hug

Lois. Mick just stood with his mouth agape as he looked at Lois' husband.

Before any introduction could be made by the two hugging women, they heard exclamations of, 'I'll be buggered.'

'I can't believe it.'

'What are you doing here?'

'Are you the future husband?'

And the only part of those phrases that made any sense to the girls came when the two men spoke. 'Bloody great to see you again after all this time.'

While the two men hugged each other, a few eyes started to tear-up at this very happy sight.

Introductions were unnecessary when it became increasingly evident these men were well known to each other. It was a seemingly impossible scenario that Julie's best friend from nursing days was married to the man who had been the best friend of Mick during their days in Vietnam.

Their catch-up conversation went on for a few hours that night and every day until the wedding.

On these quiet nights, Mick and Ted would sit around the fire pit sharing stories of their lives over the past few years. Both agreed that meeting Lois and Julie had been the best things that had happened to them. The impending birth of their baby brought an even greater happiness, Mick said.

One night Ted brought up the upcoming birth and wished them happiness for a long and exciting life with their baby. He confided to Mick, 'Lois and I have decided that we would put in to adopt a baby fairly soon. We're not prepared to take a risk of complications with the health of a baby, or me. There has been a lot of data coming out about returned Australian soldiers suffering many cancers, and fathering disabled children. It is being blamed on exposure to Agent Orange, in that damn jungle.'

Mick looked around to make sure they were alone. 'Ted, my doctor is testing me for possible lung cancer symptoms. He asked if I had been exposed to any poisons in Vietnam. I haven't told Julie about it yet, because she has enough possible worries with her heart and her pregnancy. I thought it was best to wait until after the wedding when I receive some confirmation from the tests currently being carried out.'

After sharing this news, both sat in silence for a while. 'I hope this never ever occurs but if the worst does happen to both Julie and me, I would be so happy and relieved if I could know that you and Lois would take care of our baby. Raise her or him as your own, but always tell how proud we were to have been the parents, and how we chose you to raise our special child,' Mick said.

'We would be so proud and willing to raise your baby. We would certainly give the baby the best life possible, if it ever comes to that. But, let's put all that out of our minds for now. You two will be around for years raising a big family, and you can all visit Warrawee anytime you want.'

On the morning of the big day, Larry taxied the padre from the air strip to the house, along with the flowers and the wedding rings, ready for the ceremony.

First came the pre-wedding consultation with the bride and groom, giving a little home-spun advice on how to have a happy marriage. 'Never go to bed still angry with each other after a spat.'

With those formalities out of the way, Julie changed into her wedding dress, which was now adjusted to allow for her expanding waistline.

Karen gave the two young wedding attendants a reminder of how they had to walk down the garden path to the shaded corner of the yard where the ceremony would be performed.

The wedding guests comprised of the pilot, Karen, Rosie and Johnno. Each smiled at a nervous Mick, and beamed at the beautiful bride as Larry escorted her down to the makeshift altar. The path was strewn with saltbush and applejack leaves, in lieu of flowers, but so fitting for this station wedding.

After the vows were exchanged, the bride and groom kissed and the marriage certificate was signed. Everyone congratulated them and took photos before moving back to the house for the wedding feast.

Not so much a feast as a good old Aussie BBQ, with meat from a station beast, followed by a jelly trifle all washed down with enough drinks to ensure that everyone was fully hydrated.

A little after midnight, Julie stifled a yawn and suggested it was past her bedtime. Mick rose to scoop her up in his arms and carried her to their quarters. Cheers could be heard from those lounging on chairs in the yard.

Over the next week everyone shared laughter and memories. They made promises to keep in touch more often than they had done in the past.

There were bittersweet emotions when it came time to say goodbye. Lois and Ted took their leave, after saying, 'It's necessary to be home in time for the annual wheat harvest due to start by the middle of the month.'

Chapter 17
Sadness Revealed

Life continued in a less active manner than before the wedding. Julie was quite often exhausted after a morning of light housework. She slept for an hour or more most afternoons.

Mick received a letter from Doctor Rolf Cardew, which had confirmed the worst, and he'd suggested that the soon-to-be parents should move into Longreach by the New Year. Rolf wanted to start treatment for Mick ASAP, which, hopefully, would slow down the cancer.

One afternoon, while working in the machinery shed, Mick confided to Larry all of his bad news, before seeking any suggestion of how to disclose this to Julie without causing excessive stress.

Larry answered, 'I can't think of any words that would lessen the sadness and worry for Julie. Just sit quietly with her, remind her that you love her and you will move Heaven and Earth to beat this for as long as possible. Karen and I will do all we can to help you both move to town and set up a home there.'

Following dinner, when they had gone to their bedroom, Mick put his arms around Julie. 'My darling, nothing can make what I am going to say ease my heartache for you, and for us. The doc has sent me a report confirming his suspicions from when he examined me on his visit before the wedding. I have lung cancer and he said we should soon move to Longreach. We both need to be closer to any urgent medical help that could become necessary from now on.'

Julie sat in stunned silence while rivers of tears flowed down her flushed cheeks. She dropped her clenched hands into her lap. 'Oh, Mick, .I can't bear the thought of losing you. To think I have waited all my life for a love like ours, and now it is going to be stolen from us so soon. I love you more than words can ever say and our baby will love you too. We must do all we can to stay healthy and together and fight like hell to beat this.'

The night was spent clinging to each other as they confirmed their love over and over. They spoke of finding ways they could beat their insidious life sentences.

Breakfast in the morning was a subdued gathering, knowing that Larry had told Karen all about it.

Karen tried to bring up the subject of moving away. 'Larry knows someone in town who has a separate empty house at the back of his block. He reckons you will be able to rent it at a peppercorn rate until you get on your feet.'

Larry told them, "I will contact my mate to enquire. In the meantime, we should work on having a great Christmas next week, and any move could be planned for the New Year."

There were small smiles from the sad couple. The mention of Christmas brought interest from Troy and Bec straight away. Troy said, 'We sent letters to Santa, but don't know if he will find us so far away from town.'

'You needn't worry. Santa has found this place every year before, and this Chrissy won't be any different.' With assurance from Dad, they raced off to get out the old plastic Christmas tree and baubles. They wanted to make the house pretty for Santa.

Even though sadness and worry overshadowed the festive season, all the adults worked at making Christmas Eve and Christmas Day a time of laughter. Everyone contributed with home-made bon-bons, chocolate crackles, jokes and crepe paper crowns to wear at the table.

Lunch was a mix of hot meat dishes served with vegetables and salad. Mick had a big smile on his face as he boasted, 'I have an unfamiliar feeling of accomplishment, knowing I have supplied the vegies from the station garden. This has never happened to me before.'

Next day, Larry's mate in town sent a message. 'The house is vacant and has most furniture in it, except a bed and a fridge. I understand their financial situation, and as long as the power bill is paid, and the house is maintained, I won't ask for rent until they're back on their feet.'

Relieved looks on their faces showed how much this gesture had meant to them both. Now they could begin packing their meagre personal belongings ready for their move. Julie packed all their clothes in suitcases lent to them by Karen, and kitchen utensils and cutlery were packed in a box from the shed.

Neither had brought much with them besides clothes when they came to the homestead, and therefore had little to pack and take away.

The one thing they would never have to leave behind was the love everyone in the household shared in abundance.

Chapter 18
A New Home

A cavalcade of vehicles left Crossroads early January 1981. Mick and Julie led the way in Mick's very old panel van, packed with their personal belongings. Next came Karen with Bec in Julie's little car. It was planned they sell it for a bit of ready cash. Larry and Troy in the station jeep were the last. Their vehicle was loaded with all the spare furniture, the packed boxes and some linen to use at the new home.

Not wishing to tire Julie too much, they decided to stay at the Windorah pub for the night to both break the journey, and, just possibly, to prolong the inevitable goodbyes.

The three hundred kilometres to Longreach seemed to both fly by and to drag at the same time, with mostly treeless plains all around them as they traversed the dusty road.

Julie and Mick were trying to prepare for whatever would be the next step in their medical care and setting up their first home together. They knew they were losing the companionship, but not the love of people who had become the only real family they felt they had ever known.

With everyone helping, the furniture was carried

in and placed where it seemed to be the right place, but would probably be moved around later. Julie and Karen made the bed that had been delivered from a merchant in town.

After dinner, every one of the Graingers rolled out their swags, ready to sleep in the lounge room for a couple of nights. 'We are not looking forward to returning to the station without a precious part of our family,' was the way Karen explained their short stay.

The next day was to be their last full day together, when Larry and family would leave, so it was a good time to drive out to Muttaburra. It was an educational, but a fun trip. They showed the children the dinosaur remains, of what would be called the Muttaburrasaurus after the fossilised bones were uncovered in 1963. The awestruck kids issued several 'oohs, aahs and wow, look at the size of it.'

Too soon, it was time for the long drive back to town for a BBQ on the banks of the Thomson River. During recollections and reminiscing on every great time they'd had together, they watched the fiery red sun dropping below the stunted, twisted trees behind the blue hills in the distance.

Chapter 19
Life Changes '81

'Oh, Mick, I should be happy, expecting our baby, being married to the love of my life, and having a place of our own, but, instead, I worry all the time. Since Karen, Larry, Troy and Bec have returned to Crossroads, I have lost my confidante. You are wonderful, but it was lovely having Karen with me, 'cos she knows about being pregnant and how the hormones and pregnancy effect a woman. I should know that from being a nurse, but everything I ever learned has gone out of my foggy brain.'

'We had better follow up on some medical appointments now that we have settled in. If we go to the hospital tomorrow, we can ask about the best doctor for expectant mothers and one for my problem,' Mick suggested. He had hoped the process of appointments would help Julie dispel some concerns, and give her something else to contemplate. She was about twenty-eight weeks into her pregnancy and was definitely showing the baby bump on her usual trim figure. They both loved feeling the strong kick whenever they touched her swollen belly.

Mick had noticed that she was now becoming breathless after small bouts of housework or walking around town.

He was also suffering increasing pain and breathing difficulty from what he assumed was his cancer progressing. This worried him more than he would ever let on to Julie. He was determined above all else to stay strong, and to be there for the birth of their baby. Looking forward to seeing and nursing their baby was the one bright highlight in their otherwise worried lives and bleak future.

Julie's GP, Dr Medcalf was taking great care of her, but was still concerned. He scheduled weekly visits, allowing him to keep a close eye on both Mum and child. Her blood pressure was a little too high and her ankles would appear swollen whenever she arrived for her check-up.

Mick's doctor was also concerned about his patient, with the pain and breathlessness increasing, and his continued weight loss becoming more troubling.

On Valentine's Day, Mick rose early and walked around the garden behind their home, picking flowers randomly to decorate the breakfast tray he planned to take into Julie. Coming through the door, he heard moaning from the bedroom and raced in to find Julie curled into the foetal position with pain etched on her face. Pulling the sheet back to help her roll over, he was dismayed to see the mattress covered in blood. Immediately scooping her up in his arms, Mick carried her to their panel van, where he lay her down on the bench seat, before driving to the hospital with the horn blaring as he stopped at the front entrance.

It was fortunate Doctor Medcalf was actually at the hospital, doing his morning rounds and took over immediately.

While the nurses wheeled Julie away on a bed, another tried to reassure Mick that his wife was in the right place. 'We'll take good care of them both.'

'As soon as Dr. Medcalf says you can see her, we will let you know. Perhaps you could have a coffee while we are waiting for the arrival. It will help you calm a little.'

Mick ran his fingers through his uncombed hair. He was indecisive. Should he leave the ward, or go to have a coffee to calm his nerves?

'And, if you don't mind me saying, you don't look like you are doing too well either,' the nurse said to Mick.

'I have lung cancer and I am fighting it as well as

I can. I need to be strong for Julie and I only have concerns right now for my wife and our baby.' At that moment a nurse appeared at the door of the waiting room and said, 'Mr Fleming, would you come with me please? Your wife is asking for you.'

Mick hurried down the corridor with the nurse, to the Delivery Room. Pushing the door open, he hurried to her bedside. There was a tube in her arm and another in her nose, while two nurses were by her side, and the doctor had his stethoscope on her belly.

Doctor Medcalf turned to face Mick. 'I am afraid Julie has lost a lot of blood and the baby is distressed. We need to carry out a caesarean section straight away. I have called another doctor to assist and we should be ready to go in half an hour. You should sit with her now, as this may calm both of you. It is a serious situation, especially with the heart, but we will take every care with your special lady.' He put his hand on Mick's shoulder and left the room.

For the next twenty minutes they spoke of their love for each other and possible names for their baby before finally settling on Oscar for a son, and Rachel for a daughter.

'If anything happens to me, please tell our child every chance you get, how much I would have wanted to live and be the best mother ever.'

Mick knew it was now time to tell Julie of the conversation he had with his mate, Ted, before the wedding.

Although Julie was shocked that Mick hadn't told her before, she agreed, 'If our baby is going to be an orphan, just as I was, I can't think of a better outcome for our child than to be adopted by our good friends.'

As Julie was wheeled into the operating theatre, Mick fell to his knees in the little hospital chapel and prayed as never before. He just asked for God to look after Julie and the baby, and please let them live. A prayer he kept repeating over and over, until the doctor emerged an hour later. It was immediately obvious, from his slumped shoulders that the news was not going to be good.

'I'm so sorry to have to tell you that we couldn't save Julie. The loss of so much blood and her compromised heart was just too much for her. She was awake and able to hold her baby daughter before she passed away.' Mick covered his face with his hands and let out a loud scream. 'No, this can't be happening. Why my Julie?'

Dr Medcalf rested his hand on Mick's back. 'Things happen in life which are inexplicable to us,' he whispered.

'You said we have a little girl,' Mick said, after receiving this devastating news.

'Yes, you have a healthy little girl but she is a few weeks premature, so we have placed her in a humidicrib to stabilise her.'

Mick slumped down again in the chair with his head in his hands. After some minutes of sobbing quietly, he asked, 'Can I see her now please?'

A caring nurse walked Mick down to the ICU where little Rachel lay in her crib, her tiny legs curled up to her chest, wearing mittens and a napkin which seemed about twice the size of her little body.

Mick was shown how to put his hand through a little aperture to touch her. Rachel instinctively curled her tiny fingers around his index finger, bringing another bout of tears.

After leaving Rachel, the nurse took him to say goodbye to Julie. She stayed in the background while Mick told his wife how proud he was of her fight, how beautiful their baby girl was, and how much he loved them both. 'Rachel has your colouring, and your little round face. I will always tell her how brave you were.'

Chapter 20
Plans for the Future

Within four days, the Grainger and Harrison families had arrived in Longreach to be with Mick, and help make arrangements for Julie's funeral and the future care of Rachel. They were all shocked at Mick's weight loss and inability to carry out much work, before tiring and needing to rest.

While the two children played outside, following the service and burial, the five adults sat around the tiny kitchen table and spoke of the future. Karen and Larry expressed surprise and happiness to Lois and Ted. 'We are so glad that Julie agreed with Mick's plan for the future, and we know that you two will do everything you can for him and Rachel in a home full of love.'

Later, there was a mountain of paperwork to be processed and certified at the local Court House.

'Although I've never submitted a claim like this before, I have followed the instructions and legislation to the letter, and as far as I can ascertain, it will only be a matter of time before you are notified that it is finalised,' said the clerk.

There was so much sadness through all of the proceedings. Mick was completing papers to formally allow the adoption of his precious daughter, Rachel. Ted and Lois would then become her legal parents. Rachel's birth certificates would always show that he and Julie were her parents first, and the amended one would show the details of her adoptive parents.

It was decided that Rachel would, originally, be registered as Rachel Fleming. Her adopted name would then be Rachel Fleming-Harrison.

'Rachel will always know everything about Julie and you, and the fight you both endured with your health, to bring her into the world. She will know that you chose us as her new parents to love her, just as much as you and Julie would have,' said Lois.

After those formalities, Mick said, 'I will stay in Longreach until Rachel is discharged, and I feel confident to care for her on the long drive to Warrawee.'

A few days later, Mick's landlady, Linda Reynolds, dropped by to see how he was getting on.

He explained the plan for Rachel and himself to live with friends near Moree. 'I could drive you both to your new home if you would like, and help with all baby duties,' Linda offered. Mick immediately accepted the offer. 'A woman's company and experience with a new baby will be much appreciated on the long drive. If you would do that for us, you can drive the vehicle back here, sell it and keep whatever you recoup to help pay any outstanding bills we may have left behind.'

Chapter 21
Warrawee

On 23 April, 1981 Mick passed away, and his body was returned to Longreach to lay beside his beloved Julie.

For the next seventeen years, Lois, Ted and Rachel always believed they lived a life blessed with happiness and sunshine.

Rachel often talked about her biological parents. While she was sad that she had never really known them, she was totally happy with her second Mum and Dad.

On a warm September afternoon while Rachel was in her room preparing for the Higher School Certificate exams, Ted and Lois were sharing a drink on the front steps. Ted turned to Lois and said, 'By the look of those dust swirls near the mailbox, we could be having a visitor very soon'.

A dust covered BMW pulled up at the house fence and a tall, elderly man got out.

He introduced himself as Michael Fleming Senior from Sydney. 'It took me a little while to find this place. I trust I am speaking to Edward and Lois Harrison?'

'Yes, this is my wife Lois, and I am Ted Harrison. How can we help you?'

'I had my lawyer trace the whereabouts of my son, Michael, who I hadn't seen since 1973. I was bereft when I learned that Michael had passed away almost eighteen years ago. Records also disclosed he had been married and had lost his wife in childbirth. Through more investigations they found out that Michael's child, my only grandchild had been adopted by Ted and Lois Harrison, and I presume you are those lucky people?'

Through tears and apologies, he admitted, 'My pride and stubbornness prevented me from reaching out to my only child. I should have told Michael that after seeking psychological help to gain some understanding, I learned it was a regular problem. In many cases, the returning soldiers found it almost impossible to settle back to the life they had lived prior to conscription. I deeply regret not having the chance to apologise to my only son for my failings and weaknesses.'

'It is far too late for apologies now. But you need to know that Mick had a full and happy life. He found his real self, and a wonderful wife and friends who understood and accepted him. I served with him in Vietnam, and I was lucky too. Lois is a loving and understanding wife, just as Julie was for Mick.' Ted reached out and put an arm around Lois so that Michael Senior could recognise a loving family when he saw one.

Rachel emerged from the front door and waited to be introduced to the visitor.

'This man is your grandfather, Michael Fleming Senior, from Sydney. He has been searching for his son, your Dad. During this process, he learned that your Dad had passed away, but his search led him to you.'

'Hello,' she said, as she held out her hand.

The family politely invited their guest in for afternoon tea. During this awkward time, Mick's father divulged the full reason for his investigation and visit. 'My doctor has informed me that my heart is in a bad way, and he has told me to get all my affairs in order. I know you do not know me, but I came here to meet you, and tell you that although I cannot atone for the past, you will have a secure future as far as money is concerned. It is obvious you already have a good life with loving parents. I won't intrude in your life, but as long as I live, I will always be there to help if ever you need financial assistance. And when I die, you will receive the inheritance that rightfully belonged to your father.'

With nothing more to be said, he stood, placed his business card on the table, and thanked them for their hospitality, and walked to his car.

Rachel followed. 'It has been good to meet you, and thank you for your financial offer. I may be in touch sometime, but no promises.'

'That would be nice,' he said, before starting the engine and driving away.

For the Fleming family, life went on as before at Warrawee.

The Power of Resilience
by Monica Hales

Chapter 1.
Woodstock

Emily Phillips was back at her childhood home. It had been twenty-eight years since she had been in Woodstock. The memories flooding back. Her father, Bill Thompson had passed away six weeks ago and the farm needed to be sold. Her three older brothers, James, Ben and Charlie, their partners and Emily's husband, Andrew, had come together to tackle the almighty mission of clearing the house, and vacating the junk from the sheds and paddocks.

Emily tried to see the farm when she came up for the funeral. She had slid away from the wake to have time on her own. She drove the twenty-five kilometres from Ben's place in Cowra to Woodstock, past the old water silo, the soccer fields, the church and the small line of shops in the main street. Taking the final curve toward the property, there in the distance was the letterbox. The makeshift box was the same, though weathered over the years. Her father had made it from left over cladding and two small sheets of galvanised steel formed the roof pitch. It was to resemble a miniature version of the farmhouse.

147

James, her eldest brother, was given the task of painting it. He had coloured the box white and the 204 was a bright red. Yet now, the structure had endured the test of time. The numbers were now a dull brown, the wood chipped and the paint all but peeled away. *Had it really been twenty-eight years?* She tried to remember the farm, but was it a distant memory, or was it a memory gained from looking at photos. Emily was lost in thought as she sat in the car. Tears welled in her eyes as her mother came to mind. Suddenly a car drove past tooting the horn and it broke her concentration. She glanced over at the letterbox again, reversed onto the road and looked at the driveway in the rear-view mirror, then drove away.

She had returned from Woodstock to Ben's place, no one even noticing she had gone. Andrew, Ben and Charlie were in an intense argument about the farm. Obviously, this feud had been going for a while, as most of the people had already walked out to the front lawn, offering their condolences to James and his wife, Kira. Emily walked down the hallway, voices loud reverberating from the kitchen.

'You can afford it. You would make a motza as a doctor. Don't be such a tight arse,' Ben implied.

'How much do you make a week, huh?' Charlie was berating Andrew.

'Em hasn't been there for years. Why should we help?' Andrew was trying to make a point when Emily walked in.

'What would you know about running a farm and the costs involved? It's not just a house block like your fancy five-bedroom suburban monstrosity.' Ben was riled up. 'We need to get it fixed up so we can sell. You have plenty of money. I've been helping Dad for years at my expense. It's time you coughed up.'

Ben had met Julie in the final year of school. They married at the registry office the following year, as Julie was pregnant and was starting to show. He did an apprenticeship in construction and then built their home on acreage, five kilometres south of Cowra, just off the Olympic Highway. Building work was scarce, which meant he travelled a lot to Canberra and then topped up his income from agistments on the property. Money was always tight. Now that his three children had left home, the farm needed a lot of attention, prompting the need to hire help. Unfortunately, Ben's commitment in assisting his father at his property, especially in recent years, resulted in him neglecting his own place. He was tired.

He had aged a lot since Emily last saw him at her own wedding, four years previously.

'Stop yelling! People can hear you from the road. Everyone is leaving.' Emily tried to talk above the commotion and pull Andrew away. 'This is not the time.' She glared at Ben.

'This is the time, Em. We need to sort the place out. You need to get back here and help us. When can you come?' Ben demanded.

'I don't know, Ben. I must apply for leave. Andrew needs to get a locum. It's not that easy.' Coming back and clearing the house was the last thing she wanted to do. Nothing in the house belonged to her. She hadn't been there since she was four years old. The mere thought of returning to Woodstock filled her with anxiety. Although she had resolved her feelings of anger and abandonment years ago, she had no desire to revisit those memories.

'What do you need me for anyway? There's nothing here for me,' she said, as she dragged Andrew out to the front.

'It's about family Em,' Ben yelled after her.

Six weeks later, Emily had returned to the farm. She decided to come up on her own, yet here she was in the car with Andrew driving. Travelling west from Sydney, the trip had been a quiet one. Emily gazed out the window, deliberating the events only hours before.

The evening began pleasantly, with polite, boring conversations.

How was your day? What was the traffic like, any interesting cases?

Emily had already downed two glasses of wine before Andrew had even come through the door. She was anxious about the evening ahead. She needed to face Andrew about leaving for Cowra in the morning. He was adamant that she shouldn't go. The argument had escalated.

'You don't need to go. I'm more important than them. Who looked after you the past month? I did. Did they care? No! Now, you should be here for me. Why be with them? How quickly you forget that they all abandoned you years ago. They sent you away. You were only four. And now you go running to that stupid place, back to them.'

'Please Andrew let me go up, the boys need me.'

'They need my money you mean. That's what they want. Not you. Listen to me. You don't need to go.'

Words were spoken that should not have been. Emily had provoked him and when he got angry, the verbal abuse would start, followed by the physical violence. He dragged her in front of the tall cheval mirror in the bedroom.

'Look at yourself. You are lucky to have me. Who has looked after you? Not them. I have given you everything. Is that not enough? Stay here with me.' He then started the baby talk. 'Please Em, don't go. Forget that place. I'm the one who cares about you. Stay here with me.'

He began the groping, kissing her neck, caressing her breasts and rolling her nipples, telling her how much he loved her. She tried to move away and stumbled to the floor. He was on top of her. She had nowhere to move. 'Oh, Em, you smell so good. Your skin so soft. You always make me hard. I love you, Em.' He was whispering and blowing in her ear. His words meant nothing. She gave in and zoned out.

It'll be quick. Hang in there.

'See, baby, how great is this? We have each other. That's what counts. You may even be pregnant tonight.' Andrew went to have a shower. Once Emily heard the water running, she quickly got up and went to the other bathroom to clean up. Feeling the soreness in her upper arms from his grip, there were no signs of a bruise. She peered at herself in the mirror. She was inquisitive. He never leaves a mark on me; never a bruise. Her head hurt. She brushed out the matted mess, tidied her face, went to the fridge, and gulped a glass of wine. How did I end up like this. I was to be a doctor. Where has that dream gone? All he wants is a baby. I'm no baby machine. She shook her head and pointed to the ceiling. Little do you know, Andrew, I'm on the pill. Huh! And I have no intentions on stopping it. I'm going to be a doctor. You'll see.

She was surprised and angry when Andrew had packed a bag and joined her in the car.

'I thought you couldn't get away?'

'Darling, I couldn't let you drive all that way on your own. Whilst out riding this morning, I asked Richard if he could cover my surgeries tomorrow. He was free and I was able to lock in a locum for the next two weeks. Jane is cancelling my appointments as I speak. So, you see, it's all sorted.'

Emily was confused. 'You didn't even want me going. So why are you coming?' Once more, he acted like nothing had happened. Mr nice guy, the loving husband. Emily felt the seatbelt rub against her arm and she flinched. What were his vows? She remembered him standing there, looking incredibly handsome in a slim-fit navy suit. I promise to respect, trust, and care for you. I will cherish you. 'Total bullshit,' she said.

'What did you say Em?' She had not realised she had spoken aloud. 'We're a team, Em. Those boys cannot do this without us, particularly for financial support. They need my money. Let's face it.' He had his hand on her knee and gave it a firm squeeze. It made her cringe. 'While your brothers seek assistance, they'll get it, but on my terms.'

Three hours later, they pulled up in the drive and the letterbox had gone. A large copper plate sign hung from the fence with 204 etched on it, catching the sun's rays. It was one of Charlie's pieces. He was a carpenter by trade and yet his love was making art, from pottery to woodturning and now metalwork. She felt a sense of sadness not to see the old, dishevelled box there anymore. The tyres rumbled over the cattle grid as they continued their journey along the lengthy, level, dirt road toward the house. As they rounded the final bend, there it was. The rustic yet picturesque home with wide verandas standing high on a small rise, overlooking the creek with the untouched, natural beauty of Mount McDonald in the distance.

'The house doesn't look too bad. I thought you said it was a mess,' Andrew stated.

'Well, from what the boys said. They must have done a lot of work already.' Charlie had stayed on after the funeral to give Ben a hand. They had replaced the old roof with new Colourbond sheeting and the weatherboard cladding had a fresh coat of paint. Wooden beams, enclosing the veranda, were now freshly stained with oil. It looked amazing. The lawns were freshly mowed gardens mulched and new plantings finished the look beautifully.

As they pulled up in front, two lively border collies warmly greeted them, eagerly vying for attention. They licked their newly found friends with affection. While Emily was patting the dogs, she heard Charlie's voice calling from behind.

'Daisy, Bosco. Get away. Come here?' He walked up to Emily and gave her a tight hug. 'Glad you came. The others are all inside.'

As Emily walked over to the front steps, the concrete path that led to the old, hills-hoist clothes line caught her eye. A sudden feeling of pang of loss came over her. She started to sob, an intense grief enveloped her. Crumbling to the ground, she sank to her knees, her head buried in her hands. Andrew was trying to pick her up, but her legs were like jelly.

'Em. Emily. Emily! Come on, get up?' he yelled.

'Leave her be,' piped Charlie. James and Ben had now come from the house and knelt next to her. 'It's okay Em. We are all here for you.'

Andrew was unsure what to do or say. He thought she was being ridiculous and was embarrassed by her behaviour. Emily, with her brothers, just sat there on the dirt driveway, all lost in thought. Lost in their own memories. Time stood still. Andrew walked back to the car and retrieved their bags. Kira greeted him on the porch.

'Hi Andrew, we weren't sure if you were coming. Em said you had to work. But it is nice to see you. Come on in.'

'What's that all about?' he said, as he flipped his head in the direction of the four siblings.

'I'm not sure Andrew. It has been a long time since Em has been here. There are a lot of memories to process. She needs time with her brothers.'

Andrew just huffed and walked past her into the house. On entering, he was surprised at the simplicity yet vastness of the interior. To his right stood an expansive living room, decorated with a variety of chair designs and lounges. Although mismatched, they exuded a sense of warmth. Four, distinct armchairs, were arranged in front of the open fireplace, whilst others were strategically positioned near floor-to-ceiling windows, offering the occupant the view of the surrounding paddocks. Directly ahead was an archway, serving as an entrance to a corridor that undoubtedly led to bedrooms. A spacious, traditional kitchen was on his left. Wooden cupboards lined one wall, each door fitted with glass panels. A charming, white, apron sink stood beneath a bi-fold window that opened to the veranda. A lengthy countertop housed six stools, completing the look.

'Hi Andrew, would you like a cuppa?' Julie, Ben's wife, sat at a long wooden dining table, it's surface ingrained with imprints of pencils and crayons. It comfortably accommodated eight chairs.

'Thanks. But do you have any wine?'

'Um … sure … red or white?'

'Do you want to put those bags away first?' Kira interrupted. 'I'll show you where you can put them.'

'Okay, I'll do that now.'

Andrew returned to the kitchen, just as the siblings walked in. Emily was still sniffling and sat down in front of the window.

Julie handed her a box of tissues. 'Do you want anything? Cuppa, wine.'

'I think we all need a drink,' Andrew bellowed. 'I happened to bring a selection of bottles from my cellar. I'll go get them from the car.' Looking smug, he reappeared with a box of wine. Pulling out a bottle of red wine, he noticed Emily and the boys all had beers. 'I didn't know you liked beer, Em,' he pronounced. She did not respond.

Emily was looking at James and Kira. 'I might go and freshen up. Am I in my old room?'

'We thought you would like the back room that looks out over the paddocks,' Kira replied. 'Is that okay?'

'That will be fine. Just give me a few minutes.' Andrew followed her into the bedroom.

'What was that display out there? You just left me standing there looking like an idiot. Get yourself together.' He left the room. Emily started to cry again and lay down. She was not sure how long she had been there, but she must have fallen asleep. Woken by voices outside, she looked out the window. Andrew and the boys were down in the sheds. She got up and wandered down to meet them.

'Hey Em. How are you feeling?' Charlie came up and gave her a kiss.

'Better now, thanks Charlie. It was just the shock of being here. I'll be okay.'

The boys had already culled a lot of rubbish, broken furniture, and farm equipment. The sheds were the last to clear. Emily started to cough.

All three boys jokingly made a sign of the cross. 'That sounds nasty, Em.'

'This is better than it was, don't you think Andrew?' Rolling his eyes, Andrew responded with a dismissive gesture and nod. Emily continued, 'I picked up the flu after Dad's funeral, leaving me bedridden for a week. Finally, antibiotics got on top of it. This cough is persistent though. And no, it's not Covid,' she gave a smirk.

'Julie and Kira have cleared the cupboards and wardrobes in the house,' Ben informed her. 'There is kitchen stuff to go through, but this is the last big job.'

They all agreed to start in the morning. 'Let's just rest and have a great dinner,' suggested James.

Surprisingly, Andrew thoroughly enjoyed the night. The boys proved to be great company, sharing stories about the farm, their schooling, and the mischievous adventures they got up to. Meanwhile, Emily remained silent, seemingly lost in her thoughts.

On waking the next morning, the house was quiet. The girls had gone to Canberra to do some shopping, and the men had already started loading their ute, cars and trailers with junk and were heading to the tip. Now the huge task of rummaging through boxes in the garage had come. Emily deciphered that no one had moved them for years. Her fingers easily left imprints in the layers of dust on their surface. One box was now buckling at its seams from years of weighted cartons on top. It started to collapse as she dragged it from the upper shelf. She pulled back the packing tape and gripped the cardboard folds, the waft of dust making her cough. As she prised open the flaps, faces of her parents, three brothers, and herself came into view. Her hand flew to her mouth, suppressing an involuntary gasp. Tears streamed down her face. There they all were, her family standing on the front veranda. She turned the photo over. A sticker on the back showed Camera House 1994 Thompson family. Overwhelmed with emotion, Emily made her way toward the corner of the shed. She spotted her father's favourite armchair. It must have been moved out many years ago. The once rich purple velvet, now thin, and in some places down to nothing. Taking a seat, she smelt the lingering scent of tobacco entrenched in the fabric from years of his smoking habit. She studied the photo, ran her finger over her mother standing proudly behind Charlie and herself. She was smiling and her long auburn hair was tied in a bun, a few stray strands blowing over her face. Emily remembered this day well. It was the thirtieth of June 1994, her fourth birthday. All her nine cousins joined the party with Mum's sisters, Molly and Jill, and her grandmother May. She closed her eyes and tried to recall the moment of the photo. Lily-May, her mother, had been summoned by her father from the kitchen. Jill, who was employed in the camera industry, had borrowed a fancy new Canon camera. Having spent the entire day experimenting with it, the time had arrived to capture the family group photos. Mum was in her usual attire consisting of an ironed striped apron, its fabric stretched by the growing bulge of her twin pregnancy. Without giving her a moment to remove it, Jill snapped the shot.

Emily settled into the old, battered armchair, her gaze fixated on the open space which stretched ahead. Occasionally, she glanced at the photo, triggering memories. How life changes a once close family, torn apart by tragedy.

'Why do I have to leave?' she remembers asking when her grandmother drove out the driveway and headed towards Melbourne.

Chapter 2
1994

Emily loved living on a farm. It was simple, though lively, with five horses, countless goats, cows, six ducks, two guinea pigs, numerous chickens and three kelpies. The smells of the animals, her mother baking in the kitchen and even the whiffs of fertiliser carried by the wind would make her feel homely. The best thing was the freedom to run amok with her three older brothers. Though James, now fourteen, worked after school at the local servo, he'd still join his siblings on weekends. Ben was twelve, and Charlie ten. They all adored their sister and she cherished them. By taking Emily under their wing, they ventured into the woods, forever building jumps for their bikes, climbing trees, and making huts out of twigs. They loved every moment spent together. The July school holidays were fast approaching. Emily could then enjoy being out all day with her brothers. Each holiday, their mother, Lily-May would send them out with water bottles and a packet of biscuits to share. They often lost track of the time and missed lunch altogether.

The day had come; Emily's birthday. She was turning four and she was so excited about having a party just for her. The brothers had the job of blowing up balloons but had more fun making "farting" noises with them. The cousins, neighbours and even people from church came. She wore a lovely pink dress with tufts of tulle. She kept twirling in front of her mother's long mirror then she collapsed into the delicate, weblike fabric.

Her grandmother May, watched from the doorway. She was enjoying the moment. 'You look beautiful.'

'Thanks for my dress, grandma.' Emily skipped down the hallway and went to find the boys. The day was spent playing games, sprinting down to the creek, hiding in haystacks, and having fun. Aunty Jill kept taking photos throughout the day with her new camera. Families gathered on the veranda, kids pulling faces and all so that her aunt could practice. Aunty Molly and Grandma were in the kitchen helping Lily-

May. Emily made numerous attempts to sneak into the kitchen to see her cake, but her aunt spotted her.

'Out you get young lady.'

May, Molly and Jill were worried about Lily-May. She wouldn't rest. Her ankles began to swell and her calves showed lumpy varicose veins. Day by day, the bulging veins turned a deep shade of purple.

Lily-May was nearing six months, or twenty-three weeks by the midwives' terminology. An early ultrasound showed twins and subsequent scans revealed girls, due October 29th. Bill, her husband, was excited. 'We will have our own Brady Bunch, Lil, three of each.'

Even though her doctor tried to get her to rest, Lily-May wouldn't. 'How can I doc? I have a family to take care of. Bill can't do it. He has his job and the farm to run.' No-one could convince her. She loved being pregnant especially with two bundles of joy to look forward to. She had started to wash the baby clothes that had been stored in a big wooden chest in the attic. The cot had been returned from her friend, Anne, whose boy was now two. She closed her eyes picturing them wrapped and cosy in baby blankets and smiled. Bill was going to give the cot a fresh coat of paint before it was back in the house.

"It's on the list," Bill would say when Lily-May asked if it was ready.

'Sit down, Lily-May,' her mother and sisters kept saying repeatedly.

'I'm okay. It's not that I haven't been pregnant before,' she replied.

'Yes but not with twins.'

They all gathered around the huge, wooden dining table and sang 'Happy Birthday.' Emily's eyes exploded when she saw the cake. It was a Barbie Doll cake. The dress made with layers of white, pink and purple frosting. There were small, coloured flowers and sugar pearls sprinkled over the skirt. The doll even had long white gloves on. It was perfect. Emily started to cry when Aunty Molly cut the cake.

'Don't be a sook. We all just want a piece of cake, don't you want a piece?' she asked Emily.

Her tears soon stopped when her brothers brought in her birthday present. 'My own bike,' she squealed.

'Come on Em, let's take it outside,' the boys said in unison.

Emily leapt on it and with the help of the training-wheels she was off riding and doing loops around the cars. She kept screeching the tyres in excitement. 'Look Ben, I can do wheelies like you.'

She rode the bike every day all around the veranda. Once the holidays began though, she was back out with her brothers exploring. Her Mum would be cooking or doing the laundry, happy to have the kids out of her hair.

Chapter 3
Tragedy Hits

It was a glorious, warm, winter's day and Lily-May chose to do extra loads of washing, determined to have all the school jumpers and uniforms washed and ready for the upcoming term. The kids had disappeared and she was grateful for the peace. Stepping out backwards from the laundry, she turned and ventured out into the backyard. She descended the three steps to the concrete path that led to the hills-hoist clothesline. The sizeable load of washing concealed her view. She failed to see Emily's bike. Her shoe caught on the edge of one of the training-wheels and she fell straight onto the edge of the handlebars, landing face down in the dirt. She laid there cursing the bike and the fact that the washing was now splayed out all over the ground. A sharp stabbing pain caught her off guard. It made her gasp and wail, the pain becoming intense. No break, just constant. She tried to call out, yet she knew the kids would be far from the house and the neighbours too far away. With waves of nausea, she clambered up the steps, crawled her way to the phone and rang the ambulance. The bleeding started to gush down her legs as she collapsed to the floor.

Lily-May woke in the hospital bed, Bill by her side. He grabbed her hand. 'Oh Lil, I'm so sorry I wasn't there. What happened?'

'I tripped over Emily's bike. I didn't see it. The next thing I knew I had a mouth full of dirt.' She felt her stomach, the memory of the torment now a reality. 'The twins!' she screamed to Bill.

Bill started to cry. 'No Lil, we lost them and we nearly lost you too. When the ambulance arrived, you were holding the twins and barely conscious. They flew you here to Canberra.'

Lily-May spent the next three days in hospital before returning home. The first thing she saw was Emily's bike on the veranda. She glared at it and started to cry. The tears just kept coming.

'I'll get rid of it Lil,' Bill stated, and with that, the bike was gone.

'Where's my bike?' Emily asked the next morning.

'The bike is gone. Forget about it. If you had taken better care of it, things would be different.' Her father was angry at her, yet she did not know why.

What does my bike have to do with Mum in hospital? 'But it's mine!' she squawked, as she stamped her foot.

'Not anymore. Go to your room!' Emily ran down the hall, slammed the bedroom door and climbed under the covers. She started to sob, trying to be quiet so her father would not yell at her again and call her a sook.

She spent the day in her room playing with her Barbie doll and her blocks. The boys had disappeared early to avoid doing chores. Her mother never came in to check on her. She did not even bring her lunch. Emily crept out of her room and spotted her mother sitting on the lounge, staring out the window. Small, pink, knitted booties were in her hands and she was twiddling with the ribbon.

'Mum.' Emily waited for her Mum to look at her. 'Mum.' Still no response. Moving closer, Emily touched her mother's hand. 'Mum.' Lily-May flinched. 'Mum,' she said more forcibly.

The front door slammed, startling Emily. 'What are you doing? Leave your mother alone. Who said you could come out of your room.' Her father grabbed her arm and dragged her down the hall and back to the bedroom. Emily glanced over her shoulder, wondering why there was no reaction from her mother. Playing with the ribbon, Lily-May continued to stare out the window, completely oblivious of the commotion.

For the days that followed, there were lots of people coming and going. Lily-May would acknowledge them with few words. There was no laughter, no lengthy conversation and lots of whispering then grandma May came to stay.

Emily and May would sit out on the veranda and look at books. 'Grandma, what's wrong with Mum?'

She's grieving Emily. Your sisters died, and she is sad.' May gave her a big hug.

'Dad took away my bike.'

'I know, Emily. You can get another one later. We'll just wait a while.' May pulled her in close and almost smothered her.

...

Seated in the front row of the church, Bill held Lily-May tightly. She sobbed uncontrollably. Two small, white boxes with pink roses on top were placed on stands before them. The pews were filled to capacity, with additional mourners standing at the back of the church. Everyone was sad. Emily could hear noses being blown, quiet weeping and even hushed whispers. She sat close to her grandmother and avoided looking at her father. The priest came over to Lily-May and touched her hands. Bill and three friends then carried the coffins out to the cemetery. Out of nowhere, a deafening scream filled the air. The sound was ear-piercing. Emily covered her ears. It was coming from her mother. Lily-May started wailing. Bill and May tried to offer comfort, but the noise did not stop. The situation left people in a state of shock, unsure how to react. Lily-May was completely enshrouded by grief.

More people came and went over the next week. Grandma May stayed for a month to help get the boys back into the school routine. Emily spent a lot of time with her. 'Let's give your Mum some space.'

Lily-May withdrew from nightly routines. Now it was either Ben or James who would read to her instead. Every night she would give her Mum a kiss on the cheek and say goodnight, yet Lily-May was nonresponsive. She simply held the booties, lost in her own world.

After several weeks, Lily-May channelled her attention to the house. Like clockwork, in the morning, she cleaned and did the laundry, then the afternoon was spent baking and preparing the evening meal, each day the same routine. No talking. No singing - nothing. She was like a robot, absent of emotion or connection. Emily was left to her own devices, spending hours in her room playing with blocks and her dolls. When her brothers were home from school, she would be outside laughing and having fun. However, the evenings were silent. Conversations were non-existent. Finishing dinner, completing homework and preparing for bedtime became the focus.

Months went by before Bill convinced Lily-May to see Dr Jones, their G.P. Anti-depressants were prescribed, and he also suggested she go to grief counselling, yet she kept saying she was "*fine.*" Emily would often catch her mother staring out the kitchen window, her hand tucked into the pocket of her apron. She knew the booties were kept there, as she once entered the kitchen unnoticed. 'Mum.' Lily-May was startled and in a split second, she withdrew her hand quickly and dropped the booties. Emily went to pick them up for her, but her mother smacked her hand away. 'No.' Then she scooped the booties up and carefully placed them back in the safety of the pocket.

One morning, late in October, Emily had been playing in her room and she was hungry. She searched for her mother, looking in the kitchen, the laundry and outside at the clothesline. She kept calling out 'Mum.' She was frantic and ran down to the sheds. There was her mother, sitting on the ground, next to the cot, holding the precious booties.

'Mum, Mum.' Emily touched her and she was like ice. 'Mum, Mum!' Emily was screaming now and started to shake her. 'Mum, wake up!'

She ran to the neighbours. 'Come quick. Mum won't wake up.' The ambulance came, then the police. People came from everywhere. The boys came home early from school. Her father was crying, shaking his head.

'What's happened?' Emily asked Aunty Jill.

'Your mother has died Emily.'

'No, she's not. She was asleep.' Emily ran off and hid in her bedroom closet.

'No, no, no, no,' she cried over and over. Aunty Jill opened the closet door and sat down with her. Tearfully, Emily asked a question. 'Why did Mummy die?' Aunty Jill comforted her and gently explained that her mother was still mourning the death of the twins and this day marked the day they were due to be born.

Grandma May stayed on after the funeral. Emily would be woken to conversations between her grandmother and father. Her name mentioned numerous times.

'What am I going to do May? Why didn't she talk to me? I made her get those pills. I thought she was getting better. Why didn't I see the signs? I can't stay home and look after Emily. I can't give up my job. Why did she have to die? Who will look after Emily? That stupid bike! I can't be home, you must take Emily, I must work to cover the mortgage. I look at Emily with hostility. May, you must help me.' Her father was distraught.

Sitting on the veranda in the swing seat, Emily and May looked at books and talked. One day, May turned to Emily. 'Would you like to come to Melbourne and live with me for a while?'

'Am I going on a holiday? Will the boys come too?' She was excited about going to Melbourne, a big city.

'No, Emily, just you.'

'How long will I be gone?' Tears welled up in May's eyes. 'What's wrong Grandma?'

'Nothing, I must have some dirt in my eyes.' She got up and went to her room. The following Tuesday, May was heading back home. She took Emily's suitcase to the car. The three brothers surrounded their little sister, giving her a collective hug. Ben started to cry.

'Don't be silly, Ben. I'm only going on a holiday, aren't I Grandma?' Emily was nodding confidently as she spoke. However, May did not respond.

Inside on the backseat, May had purchased a booster seat allowing Emily a clear view out the window. She was playing with her Barbie doll, moving the doll's arm to give a wave. As the car pulled out of the driveway, Emily realised that her father had not come to say goodbye to her. He had already left for work. She was disappointed and it made her wonder.

'Why do I have to leave today Grandma? Can't we leave on Sunday? Then I can watch Ben and Charlie play soccer. The finals are coming up.'

'No darling. I need to get back. It's time I went home.'

Emily took a final look out the window and noticed the dogs were spooking the cows. She was laughing. 'Look grandma, Tilly, Ned and Coby are with the cows. Dad won't be happy when he gets home.'

Chapter 4
New Beginnings

Melbourne was a whole new world for Emily. She had never seen so many people, cars and buildings. Staring out the window, her mind was in overload, taking in all the strange and unfamiliar sights. She had a million questions, and May was having an arduous task answering them all.

'Do you live in one of those tall buildings, grandma? What is that for? Why does that lady wear that long dress? Why does she cover her face? She must be really cold. That man looks funny. Why are people running over the road? What is that? What are the metal tracks for? Why does everyone beep their horn? At home, it's because someone goes by and you know them. They must know a lot of people.' May pulled up by a large metal fence. She pressed a button and magically the gate opened. 'Wow, that's cool.' They headed to a lift. Once inside, Emily then pressed all the buttons.

A tall well-dressed man was already in the lift. 'Hi May. Who is this? She's a lively one.'

'Oh, hi Fred. This is my granddaughter, Emily. She is staying with me for a while.' She bent over, and pointed her finger at Emily. 'Now, young lady, don't do that again. Only press one number, and mine is number four.' May turned and faced Fred. 'Sorry about that. It's her first visit to Melbourne.'

As she entered apartment twelve, Emily's mouth was wide open. 'Wow, Grandma, this house is funny. It's in the sky.' She ran over to a long, tall window overlooking a park opposite. A young girl was riding a bike like the one she used to have. 'I wish I still had my bike,' she sighed.

May watched her run from one room to another, checking out cupboards, drawers and jumping on the beds and lounge.

'This bed is super comfy. Can I sleep here?'

'No darling,' May laughed. 'This is my room.' She led her down the hallway to the other bedroom. 'This can be your room.'

Emily loved it instantly. The view from the window also looked out over the park. She spotted train tracks. 'Look it's a train.'

'Actually, sweetie, it's called a tram. We'll have a ride on it tomorrow when I need to go to the library. Alright, let's unpack and head for the shops before they close.' They ventured outside and started to walk down the path.

'Can we walk to the shop, Grandma? How can we carry everything if we don't use the car?'

'I have this.' May showed Emily her portable shopping trolley. 'I can put a lot in here. Would you like to pull it?' Emily was having fun and laughing. The big swivel wheels spinning in all directions. 'Be careful with it. It's not a toy.'

Over time, Emily became used to the unfamiliar noises. Occasionally, she would scream at night, only to be comforted and reassured by May. As the weeks passed by, she visited lots of places. Her favourite was catching the tram into the city to the State Library. May was a volunteer there on Wednesdays and Emily loved listening to the librarians at story time. Whilst May worked, Emily would immerse herself in the world of books. She was even allowed to borrow five books a week and they would read them each night. In addition to the books, her brothers sent letters to Emily which May read repeatedly. The occasional letter also held photos. In time, she gave up asking to go back to the farm. Melbourne became her home, her home with Grandma May.

By the time Emily started school in 1996, she was reading fluently. Learning about anything and everything excited Emily. May recognised her passion for non-fiction books, especially on subjects like anatomy, biology, and physiology. She was fascinated by the human body. It did not surprise May or her teachers when Emily announced she wanted to be a doctor. Determined to do well, she studied hard. By the time she was fourteen, she had a job after school at a local pharmacy. Mrs Slocum, the owner, taught her about different medicines, diseases and cures for all types of ailments. She weighed the babies for the mothers and got to know them well. Most nights, May listened to Emily babble about her day.

'Do you like the babies, Em? You could be an obstetrician or paediatrician?'

'I'm not sure Grandma, maybe an obstetrician. That way I won't have to have a baby myself.'

'But Em, you might meet a handsome man and want a family of your own one day.'

May was shocked at how quickly she responded, a mixture of surprise and concern. Emily was adamant.

'No way, Grandma, I don't ever want to be a mother. I just want to be a doctor.'

Emily was in her final year at school and doing the Victorian Certificate of Education or VCE as most students called it. To get this qualification, Emily needed to complete Year Eleven and Twelve successfully, allowing her to pursue university. Not only did she work after school at the pharmacy, but she would then exhaust herself by staying up late to study, sacrificing sleep and social time. Emily avoided going out with friends and continually found reasons to excuse herself, saying, "I must finish my assignment. I need to study. I have to work. I want to save for uni." In the final weeks of Year Twelve, she was not eating well and getting very tired. Her weight had dropped significantly, and she complained of headaches daily. Concerned about her health, May took her to see Dr Meldrum. Unfortunately, he didn't help and proved to be a waste of time. 'Come on May, stress is a part of life so why should Emily be free of it. When she goes to university, the pressures of deadlines will be greater. The VCE is good practice for what is to come next.'

'Poppycock!' May was so annoyed at the doctor she stormed out of the surgery.

'He's right Grandma.' Emily tried to calm her down in the car. 'Uni will be harder, I'm okay.'

May went to see the Year Twelve Coordinator, Miss Linda Peters. 'I'm concerned about Emily. She is pushing herself too hard. Is there a way to reduce her workload?'

Linda tried to allay May's fears. 'Emily is a good student and just wants to do well. She chose subjects with high demands. Physics, specialist mathematics and chemistry are three of the most difficult courses to do. However, they will scale high to maximise her ATAR score. To do medicine, she needs to excel. I believe she will. Don't you?'

'Of course I do,' May retorted. 'I just don't want her to burn out before even doing the exams.'

'I have every faith that will not happen. September twenty sixth, the last day of term, is just around the corner. Then she will have a few weeks off before the exams begin. Take her out. Make sure she gets some exercise. I would not worry about Emily.' Linda showed her out.

May was unconvinced. She kept a watchful eye on Emily, concerned when she would spend many hours locked away in her room. She encouraged her to exercise like Miss Peters suggested. However, Emily remained steadfast, ate very little and continued to hibernate in her room. Study took precedence over her own health.

Before the end of term, an opportunity was presented to Emily by Mrs Slocum. Megan, the pharmacy technician was going on maternity leave and she offered Emily extra hours. She was so grateful and snapped it up. Her plan was to work for a year to earn the desired money and qualify for the Student Allowance. Once the term was over, she started working fulltime, even putting in hours on weekends. After long hours, Emily would come home and seclude herself in her room to study, often staying up till the early hours of the morning. May worried even more. Emily lost more weight and became very tired. It was obvious to May that Emily was struggling, yet Emily refused to acknowledge it.

'Don't worry so much, Grandma. It'll be worth it. Once the exams are over, I promise to take time out then. Mrs Slocum said I could have two weeks off in November. I might even head up to Sydney and see James and Kira.'

Chapter 5
The Wedding 2004

James, Emily's brother, was now twenty-seven and was married to Kira. They met at Sydney University in 1999. He was doing a double degree in law and Kira was studying media and communication. Emily and May had met them both when they visited at Christmas time in 2003. Ben and Julie also came down with their two children, three-year-old Emily and two-year-old Matthew. Julie was expecting again and was about to pop. Since leaving school, Charlie had been travelling around Australia. He picked up carpentry work where he could. Although he missed Christmas Day, he arrived two days later. Emily was so happy to be reunited with her brothers after such a long time. The week that followed was filled with endless fun and laughter, creating one of Emily's most treasured memories. Whilst altogether, James and Kira announced their engagement. Amongst all the excitement, Kira turned to Emily, 'Will you be one of my bridesmaids?'

Emily beamed with delight. 'How exciting, I'd love to.'

The wedding took place in Sydney on September nineteenth, 2004. It was held in a gorgeous old church in Hunters Hill. Two limousines were used for the wedding party. Emily, accompanied with Kira's two sisters, arrived first. Whilst eagerly awaiting the arrival of the bride, Emily spotted her brothers. She smiled and waved. James looked extremely nervous and he was pacing. Her attention shifted when she caught sight of an elderly man shuffling toward the boys. Looking a second time, she realised with a jolt, that the man was none other than her own father. As per usual, he was smoking. Emily stared at him in bewilderment. It was the first time Emily had seen him since leaving the farm ten years previously. Bill's once fit and muscular physique had changed considerably. His hair was thinning and the presence of a round, paunch belly became obvious beneath his tight-fitting shirt. His skin was thin, red, and flaky from years of steroid medication. Emily hardly recognised him. 'Hi Dad,' she said sheepishly. Bill stood next to James, waiting for the cue from the wedding planner to enter the church. He turned his head to look at her, when a woman interrupted him.

'Okay men, you can come in now and take your positions. The photographer will snap away so walk in slowly like this.' As she gave a demonstration, Ben elbowed James and sniggered. Following suit, Charlie proceeded to mimic the lady, causing them all to erupt in laughter. Their father proceeded to follow the planner into the church, without any acknowledgment of Emily. She felt completely ignored.

Later at the reception, May and Bill were standing on the balcony engrossed in deep conversation. 'You have done a great job, May.' Bill was watching James spin Emily around on the dancefloor. 'How is she? What does she remember? Does she speak about Lil or me?'

'Emily had a tough time adjusting once she realised it was not a holiday and it was permanent. She missed her brothers. It was very cruel of you to send her away.'

'You make it sound like I tossed her away.'

'She was hurting too, Bill. For goodness sake, she had lost her mother too. Losing her was hard enough without losing her brothers as well. She felt abandoned. It was hard on her and me. You never even said goodbye to her.'

'I couldn't May. I was sad, angry and miserable. Lil had shut me out for months. I lost the twins too, but she didn't want to talk about it. When Lil died, I was shattered. It was hard for me to live on without her.

Lil was my world. I lost my best friend. Let's face it I was in no fit state to care for Em anyway. She was much better off with you.' He turned away avoiding eye contact. 'I would have messed it up. The years are a blur. The boys practically reared themselves.'

May pulled him back to look at him. 'You are her father. She should have been with family. She was grieving too and had no understanding about what had happened; the bike, the deaths of the twins and her mother! She thought it was her fault. Please Bill, talk to her.'

'Where would I even begin May? She probably despises me.'

'No, she doesn't. Em was, and still is, confused.' May tried edging Bill closer to Emily when he stopped in his tracks. 'Damn it, Bill. Go to her. Em needs an explanation. Only you can set this right. Imagine moving to a city you've never seen and being taken away from home, and family. She was four. Only four Bill! You blamed her for Lily-May's death. That was absurd and unreasonable. You did toss her away.' Bill had heard enough. With his head held low, he left through the side door.

The night was drawing to a close. James and Kira were saying their goodbyes. As they reached the two brothers, James scanned the room for his father.

'Has anyone seen Dad?'

Ben and Charlie shrugged their shoulders. Julie cut in. 'I remember seeing May with him earlier on the balcony, but I haven't seen him since then.'

James took his grandmother aside. 'What happened with Dad? No one has seen him.'

'Sorry, James, but he left. We were talking about Em and I may have overstepped the line. For years, I have bottled things up, and tonight, well, tonight I just let it all out. He needed to know how leaving the farm had impacted Em all those years. Not seeing you and your brothers crushed her. Being separated from it all was truly unfair on her.'

'It's alright Grandma. Perhaps it was finally time to say something. Us boys never understood why Em left. Every time one of us tried to talk to Dad, he would shut us down and simply walk away. We weren't even allowed to mention Em's name. We are her brothers and she is our sister. It was wrong on every level. How did he react about it all?'

'He didn't say much. I did most of the talking. Once I started though, I couldn't stop. I shouldn't have pushed the issue. Yet, I do believe he recognises his mistake. He is struggling as well and possibly doesn't know how to make amends.' May's eyes welled up. 'He forgets that your mother was my daughter too. It was hard on all of us.' James pulled her in for a deep embrace.

Through tears, May was apologetic. 'This is supposed to be a special day and now I feel I have ruined it.'

'No Grandma, nothing has been spoilt. It has been a magical day for Kira and I. Things just needed to be said. After all, family is family.'

'You are one special boy, James. Now, let's put things aside for now. You need to be with your wife.'

Chapter 6
Setbacks

Year Twelve had finished and Emily consistently worked long hours at the pharmacy, followed by evenings spent studying. Besides being tired, her body ached and the headaches got worse. No matter how many times May urged Emily to take a break, Emily pushed harder. "Short term pain for long term gain, grandma," she would say.

May was thankful when the school farewell dinner arrived. Emily downed tools and had the weekend off work. Meeting up with her close friends, Shelby, Rose and Ella, they all spent the morning at the hairdressers for hair and make-up, followed with a visit to the nail salon. Being discreet, Rose cleverly disguised champagne in water bottles. When May picked them up, she could tell that they were quite tipsy.

'Best I give you all some food before you head off tonight. Pizza anyone,' May announced when they got into the car.

'Yes please,' they said, in unison and the giggling started.

As the excitement of the afternoon built, the giggles and banter elevated to squeals and shrieks. May breathed a sigh of relief when she watched them finally leave in a taxi to the dinner, hours later. She was pleased to finally have peace.

A call came through from Shelby, not even an hour later. 'It's Em. She keeps vomiting, and we can't get her up. We don't know what to do.'

May headed over straight away. Em was sitting in the toilet cubicle hugging the bowl. The hours of doing make-up, now wasted. Black lines streaming from her eyes, lipstick smudged and the hair now

covered in vomit. 'Well, young lady, I believe your
night has come to an end. Come on, it's time to get
home.' May struggled to keep Em upright. Once
home, she attempted to wash some of the muck from
her hair and decided to plait it instead. 'That can be
tomorrow's problem.'

Em did not surface till late afternoon. She looked
wrecked. Her face pale, her eyes dark and sunken.
'Well, it's about time sleepyhead,' May said, when
Emily walked out onto the balcony. She put down the
Sunday Herald that she had been reading. 'You need
water and food.'

'Thanks Grandma, just water.' She crossed her
legs in a yoga-like position as she sat on the chair,
resting her head in her hands. 'Wow. I feel like shit.
How did I get home?' She started prising her hair
strands apart. 'What is all this?'

'Ah, vomit,' May disclosed as she put a large glass
in front of her. The liquid inside was bubbling.
'What's in here?' she asked, as she put it to her lips.

'It's something to settle your stomach. Go and
have a long shower and scrub that hair. You never
know what you will find in it.'

'Yuck, Grandma.'

Emily had disappeared for over an hour. Later, May found her lying on her bed, wrapped in a towel and fast asleep. She pulled the covers up and decided to call Mrs Slocum.

'Hi, Pat. Its May, Emily's grandmother. Em had a tad too much to drink last night at the dinner. She is worse for wear today and I feel she will need at least another day to get over it.'

'Oh dear, thanks for letting me know. Does she need anything? I can drop by later once my relief comes in.'

'No thank you Pat, I believe Em just needs sleep.' May checked on Emily several times finding her in the exact same position. She was still unwell the following day, drinking little water and eating no food. 'Em, you have to eat something.' May kept pestering her. 'Eat some toast, come on, and drink that water down.'

Emily tried nibbling on the toast and sipping the water, yet she felt terrible. 'I feel so wasted Grandma. I have no energy at all. My throat is killing me. I can't go to work. I can't even keep my head up long enough to even read.'

'I have already rung Mrs Slocum. She has covered your shift, but I think I will ring her again and say you won't be in for the rest of the week. You need a break anyway. You've been overdoing it. Your body is telling you to slow down.'

'The exams are next week Grandma. I'm not ready.'

'Poppycock! You've been burning the candle at both ends for months, wearing yourself out. Don't be so hard on yourself. Your body needs to rest. Eat up and we will go for a walk. The fresh air will do you good.'

After walking for five minutes, Emily was exhausted. 'Why am I so tired? My body just aches. The air is making my throat worse. Can we go back? I think I really need to lie down again.'

As Emily slept, May rang Dr Meldrum's surgery. Despite her persistent efforts, she could not get an appointment till the following day.

'She has final exams next week. It's crucial we find out what's wrong.'

The receptionist, Lucy Wilson, was apologetic for the lack of availability. 'I'll squeeze her in at twelve tomorrow. If I get a cancellation, I'll be sure to ring you.'

May was unsure what to do. She decided to ring Miss Peters, the Year Twelve Coordinator again.

'I heard several girls overdid it last Saturday night,' Miss Peters skited. 'A few days more rest and she will be fighting fit.'

'What if she's not?' May asked. 'What happens to her exams?'

Linda tried to calm her. 'Let's not jump to conclusions just yet. It is only Wednesday. When do you see the doctor?'

'Tomorrow.'

As Linda listened, she could tell May was getting more agitated and upset. 'I understand how worried you are. There are provisions in place if things happen to students sitting exams. We can apply for dispensations if need be. Let's just see what happens in the next twenty-four hours,' she reassured her.

May's fears came true. Blood test results diagnosed glandular fever.

Chapter 7
Challenges

Emily suffered terribly with glandular fever. She had the severe sore throat, swollen lymph glands, on and off fevers with night sweats and generalised fatigue. Tracking back, Emily realised she may have contracted the disease during the Year Twelve retreat, which had taken place six weeks earlier.

'You're right, Em.' May agreed. 'Let's be honest, the retreat was about activities, like swimming, rock climbing and bush walking. Taking extra precautions like proper dishwashing of cups and utensils would not have been high on anyone's priority list.'

'Shelby calls glandular fever the kissing disease. I certainly haven't kissed anyone, that's for sure.' Emily was adamant about making sure her grandmother knew that. May encouraged her to have plenty of rest and ensured visits from her girlfriends were kept short.

Concerned about Emily's extreme fatigue, May reached out to Miss Peters again. She needed her opinion. Linda took the call.

'Hi May, how can I help?' May shared the news of Emily's diagnosis of glandular fever, informing her that Emily had possibly been suffering from it for the past six weeks and the consumption of excess alcohol at the dinner, no doubt exacerbated the condition.

'The English paper is scheduled for Monday,' explained May. 'What should Emily do if she can't sit through it? What if she can't sit through any of the exams?'

'As I said earlier this week, there are measures we can take to support Emily. It's beneficial for her to sit all the exams and complete them as best she can. If she feels her performance may be affected, she can appeal.'

Linda's advice aimed to reassure her. However, May was still apprehensive and tentatively asked, 'Linda, will that be enough for Emily to attain an achievable ATAR score for medicine?'

'Let's get the exams finished first of all,' Linda said.

May hung up the phone, took a deep sigh and went and sat on Emily's bed, relaying the conversation she just had with Miss Peters. Emily started to cry. 'All this time I've wanted to be a doctor. Now I'd be lucky to get into uni at all.'

'Now, now, you don't know that. Miss Peters suggests sitting the exams. It's a matter of turning up and doing them. You know the work it's just about being present. Look how hard you have worked these two years. If you're not happy with the results, Miss Peters said you can appeal.' Listening, May found it difficult to believe her own words. How could she expect Emily to have faith in them either. She would tread carefully over the weekend and try to keep

Emily calm. They went for short walks in the morning, followed by breakfast at nearby cafés. The afternoons were spent relaxing. Emily would intermittently read through her work then have a sleep.

Driving Emily to school on the Monday, they were both quiet. May broke the silence in the car. 'I'll pick you up at twelve. We can then get lunch, if you're up to it.'

'Thanks Grandma. I just hope I have enough energy to finish it.'

Emily's face was sombre when May picked her up. 'Can we just go home please? I'm not up to food right now.'

'Should I ask how it went?'

'No. I just want to go home.'

May respected Emily's request and they headed home. Emily spent the rest of the day in her room. Every now and then, May overheard her on the phone presumably going over the exam with her girlfriends. Emily finally surfaced around six pm. May was in the kitchen. 'You need food, tasty food. I've cooked your favourite.'

Emily appreciated the gesture. 'It smells amazing, Grandma. I'm not sure if I'll eat much, but I'll give it a try.' Although Emily ate a small amount, May was grateful to see her eat something. Without mentioning the exam, May felt that Emily would share when she was ready, if at all.

The next three weeks flew by. Her exam timetable was complete, leaving Emily both apprehensive and relieved. Understanding the potential impact of Emily's illness on her performance in the exams, Miss Peters suggested Emily go ahead and appeal to the board of studies. Together with letters from the doctor, her teachers, as well as Miss Peters, Emily submitted the relevant forms. All Emily could do now, was patiently wait for her results.

'Complete rest is the key. Don't overdo it or the disease might linger,' the doctor said at a follow up appointment.

'Poppycock!' May dismissed the doctor's words, believing that Emily needed to regain her strength. Slowly building up her stamina doing four hours at the pharmacy on Mondays, Wednesdays and Fridays and occasionally a Sunday, her energy gradually increased. After spending two weeks with James and Kira, in November, Emily began to feel more like her old self again.

Chapter 8
A Fork in The Road

The ATAR results were being released on the Monday, so Emily, Shelby, Rose and Ella spent the weekend together. Emily was fidgety. In spite of the three girls attempting to distract her by watching movies, playing games, running amok in the park, or going for walks, Emily remained anxious and she couldn't shake off the nausea.

Judgement day came. They all woke early, gathered around the computer and individually logged on to the website. Emily wanted to go last. The other girls were both surprised and happy with their results, each calling their parents with the news. Emily though, was mortified. Not only did she not get the desired ATAR to get into medicine at Monash University, but she wouldn't even be eligible for any medical degree at any university. May heard the commotion. Emily was screaming, 'All I wanted was to be a doctor. What am I going to do now? I didn't get enough.' The girls tried their best to settle her down. May tried, but all their efforts were futile. Emily was uncontrollable. 'Miss Peters said the appeal would improve my derived score, that it potentially would be higher. Obviously, that was bullshit.'

'Look, let's calm down first. No point screaming. We can reach out to Miss Peters for her advice and discuss the possible strategies moving forward.' May tried calling the Coordinator, yet the phone just went to message bank. I'm sure she would be inundated with calls today. She decided that being stuck indoors stewing over marks and scores was not helping. 'Right, ladies let's get out. I'll pack up a basket and we'll head off to St. Kilda. Time in the sun will do the trick.'

After several attempts and leaving continual messages, Miss Peters finally returned the calls and spoke to Emily. 'I know you are upset and disappointed, Emily. Keep in mind, there are other avenues. It's not all doom and gloom. Come in and see me on Thursday and we can explore alternative options. Remember, setbacks in one area can often lead to new opportunities. Stay positive and I'll see you Thursday. Your grandmother is also welcome to come.'

Emily's high hopes for the appeal were shattered when she realised that the board of studies had not considered her illness. With no adjustments, Emily's ATAR was lower than the requirement to study medicine. Miss Peters offered some advice. She suggested that Emily contemplate enrolling in a bachelor's degree, then transfer to medicine as a graduate student. You will need to do the Graduate Medical School Admissions Test, or GAMSAT, they call it. It is an aptitude test used to select students for graduate-entry medical degrees. I'm sure you will blitz that. Emily wasn't convinced, but she was listening to what Miss Peters suggested. 'Why not pursue nursing? It would provide a solid grounding for medicine. Plus, doctors with a nursing background tend to have more empathy and compassion than most doctors. Striving for top grades, which we all know you're capable of, will give you a greater chance to enter medicine as a graduate student. Going down this path would only require four more years instead of the six as an undergraduate. Overall, you would be just one year behind where you originally aimed to be.'

After days of deliberation, Emily decided to apply for the Bachelor of Nursing Degree at Monash University, starting the next year, rather than having a gap year. She continued to work at the pharmacy but reduced her hours to fit in with university. Much to her surprise, she found herself enjoying the course. Subjects like biology and anatomy came natural to her. She excelled and built a strong rapport with her tutors, who admired her dedication and enthusiasm.

During her nursing placements, Emily consistently received high praise from nursing staff. However, it was during a maternity placement in her final year that she realised she had found her passion. One of the midwives suggested she study midwifery. 'Do you know anyone in Sydney? Westmead Hospital offers a Mid-Start Program. Instead of another three years at uni, you can qualify as a midwife in a year.'

'Grandma, do you think James and Kira will let me live with them for a year? There's a program offered at Westmead Hospital where I can be a midwife in just a year. It's mostly hands on. One of the midwives reckons I have a good chance at being accepted. I just need to do my graduate year, then I can apply. They offer it yearly so I can start in February the year after next.'

'Go for it Em. Don't hold back. I'm sure James would be thrilled to have your company, even though I would miss you dearly.'

'I won't stay up there forever, Grandma. Besides, you still have me for a year yet.'

Emily completed her first year as a Registered Nurse at Royal Melbourne Hospital rotating through emergency, paediatrics and recovery. She enjoyed all the areas and each Nursing Unit Manager, NUMs for short, offered her a permanent position once she finished her graduate year. Deep down, she still wanted midwifery and kindly declined each offer.

Chapter 9
Sydney

Emily was amazed how smoothly the application process went. The educators who interviewed her at Westmead Hospital, were impressed with her outstanding grades and recognised her enthusiasm. As a result, she was accepted and she moved to Sydney in the January. Luckily, James and Kira lived near the train line so commuting to Westmead Hospital was relatively easy. She settled into her new life in Sydney with tenacity, embarking on a new chapter.

It was one of her stints on night duty when she met Dr Andrew Phillips, a Senior Registrar of Obstetrics and Gynaecology. There was an instant connection. He was charismatic, had a deep passion for obstetrics and great taste in music. They would spend as much time together as work allowed, chatting and laughing in the corridors. Dinners were limited though, due to Andrew's demanding schedule and long working hours. More often than not, they would grab a bite to eat in the cafeteria. Andrew was impressed and supportive of her desire to be a doctor and possibly an obstetrician later.

'Do you know, my grandmother suggested I be an obstetrician years ago. She knew back then. She's been my guiding light since. I can't wait for you to meet her and see the incredible woman that she is. I have no doubt she'll adore you, just as I do.'

He kissed her and smiled. 'I look forward to it, Em. I may be lucky to swindle a weekend. My friend, Scotty owes me a swap. Let's make sure we do it soon. Christmas is coming up and I won't be able to get time off. Family is such an important part of who we are, and I want to be part of yours. I've never felt this way about anyone before. You truly are a gem.'

Emily's heart swelled. She was falling in love with Andrew. She opened up to him about her fleeting childhood memories and time apart from her family. Through many tears, Andrew offered an attentive ear and helped Emily to heal. It allowed her connection with her brothers to grow stronger. Nights together became intimate. He was caring, affectionate and loving.

During their long conversations, Emily discovered the estrangement Andrew had with his mother. Since his parent's divorce, when he was only thirteen, he had not been in touch with his mother. Though he was brought up by his father, their relationship was strained. Once his father knew of his chosen profession, he chastised him more. "Why would you want to care for women after what your mother has done to you?" his father would cruelly ask.

Andrew supported Emily's career, solidifying her love for him. In such a short time, they both realised the special bond they shared. She felt like she had known him for years. They flew to Melbourne early December. Emily was so excited when May met them at the airport. 'What do you think, Grandma. Isn't he amazing?'

'Yes darling, he is rather dapper.' May was happy for Em, but within a few days, she sensed a quality in Andrew that she couldn't quite grasp. There were moments when Andrew belittled and disregarded what Emily said, then there were times when he would be kind and show affection. Em was happy and that's what counted, she convinced herself.

It was during Emily's graduation ceremony in January, organized by the obstetric department of the hospital, that Andrew blindsided her. He stepped into the limelight and proposed to her. The room instantly shifted its attention to Andrew. The atmosphere was abuzz with excitement and congratulations. Everyone was hugging Andrew, believing him to be the prize catch. The moment now focused on a wedding, rather than Emily's achievements.

The chance to finally sit for the GAMSAT was scheduled for March. Emily dedicated herself to study hard, often postponing dinners with Andrew. He became frustrated and when they were together, he would show his frustration in the bedroom. Their love making was rushed and lacked the usual intimacy. Added to this, Andrew kept pressuring Emily to plan the wedding, constantly badgering her for a date and a venue. Eventually, he took matters into his own hands and booked the Conservatorium of Music for the reception, picking the Saturday before the scheduled GAMSAT.

'It was meant to be, Em. They had a cancellation and I snapped at it. You can still sit it in September.' Though Emily was disappointed, she was also extremely happy at the thought of being, Mrs Emily

Phillips. The next eight weeks were a whirl wind. They tied the knot in a stunning ceremony overlooking Sydney harbour. Andrew opted for a figure-hugging, navy suit that fitted his muscular body well. Naturally his strong abs could not go unnoticed, and Emily was not the only one who acknowledged it, with many of the women vying for a dance.

As the reception unfolded, James with a hint of humour, turned to Charlie. 'Shouldn't the bride be the centre of attention?'

Charlie agreed with his brother. 'He does seem quite fond of the spotlight, doesn't he? A bit of a show off perhaps.'

Emily thoroughly enjoyed the night. She felt a sense of pride and love toward her husband, regardless of other women swooning over him. It didn't matter to her how the girls acted. What mattered was that she was now married. During the night, the three brothers joined together to do a collective dance. As they had only been practicing for two days, everyone had great delight in noticing when one of them stuffed up. With all the attention away from him, Andrew decided to add his touch on the dancefloor, which made the room erupt with more laughter.

Emily couldn't help but notice her father, Bill, spent more time outside smoking than mingling with guests. When the night ended, the hug from him was cold and dismissive. No kiss. No kind words of affection, nothing. She decided to brush it off. After all, he hadn't been a part of her life for the past twenty years. Andrew had taught her strategies to deal with those emotions, and tonight, she had put them into practice.

Chapter 10
The Switch

The happy couple settled into married life, renting a three-bedroom apartment overlooking Parramatta Park. One night, over dinner, Andrew was eager to share some exciting news. 'Hey, Em. I have been given the opportunity to attend a conference in London. The obstetric department are even paying for us to go. It will support my application for a Fellow position next year. We can stop over in Italy for a couple of weeks on the way home. Can you apply for holidays?' Emily was excited yet her enthusiasm soon wavered when he informed her that the trip was in September.

'But I'm sitting the GAMSAT,' Emily reminded him. 'You know how much this means to me. I only get two chances a year. Please can you go on your own?'

'No, Em. That wouldn't work. Isn't my career more important? There will be nightly events and I need you by my side.'

Andrew was getting angry. He couldn't believe that Emily would sit a stupid test and miss out on three weeks overseas. 'What's wrong with you? Anyone else would jump at the chance of London and Italy. And you just want to stay and study. Don't you want me to succeed? It's obvious that time with me is not a priority to you. I thought you loved me?'

Emily felt a sense of guilt. 'You know I love you, Andrew. Of course I support you.'

'Well then, what!' He poured himself another wine and sculled it. Emily was shocked with his temper. She had never witnessed this behaviour before. 'My parents didn't believe in me,' he continued. 'My mother doesn't care, and my father despises me, yet look where I am now. Everyone tends to abandon me and now even my own wife is.'

Emily was trying to backtrack. 'I'm sorry, Andrew. I believe in you. I suppose I could reapply next year.'

She gave him a kiss on his cheek. 'I'll put in for leave tomorrow.'

Andrew switched. He was now hugging her, a beaming smile on his face. 'Oh, Em, you are so special.' He bent his head, gave her a kiss that lingered for a long while, allowing his hands to roam downwards, cupping her beasts, rubbing her nipples and stroking her thighs. He edged her toward the lounge, his clothing left far behind. Her wrists now pinned, he prized her legs apart, enabling him to enter her, thrusting fiercely. She tried to speak, but he shook his head to stop her. Emily didn't understand, but she knew she had to obey. She felt it was an act of necessity rather than of love. The movement went on in a savage urgent silence, striking her over and over with impact. She was on the edge of pleasure and pain, and then he finished within moments.

Releasing her arms, he got up and walked away; still no words. She rose and stealthily walked to the bathroom.

What was that about?

She found him collapsed on the bed. Climbing under the covers, she woke him. He rolled over and again began kissing her breasts, then stomach, then headed downward till finally he reached the spot of euphoria. She gasped and within seconds, he was inside her, each jolt felt deep into her stomach. Her thighs were bruising with every impact, yet the moment was over as quick as it began. He turned her on her side and curled his body around hers.

She felt sore in every muscle on waking the next morning. Glancing down at her inner thighs, expecting to see bruises, there were no signs, yet they were so tender on the slightest touch. Andrew had risen early to go for a bike ride. He had recently taken up the sport, joining other doctors. Their own small manly club.

She wobbled to the kitchen and noticed Andrew had the coffee brewing, a cup with sugar already prepared. Next to it was a note, a love heart written on it and signed with an "A." Lifting the pot, her wrists felt they would break. She was thankful she had a day off and could rest.

Chapter 11
GAMSAT

Emily continued to work a fulltime rotating roster, involving evenings and night shifts, which Andrew despised. 'Why can't you have more day shifts? I miss you, and I hate being home alone.'

Their trip to London and Italy in the September proved to be divine. They spent hours walking the cobbled streets, visiting churches and museums, and then eating at secluded restaurants, ending their days making love till the early hours. Andrew was passionate, loving and tended to her every need. The holiday was magical. The GAMSAT was far from Emily's thoughts.

The following year, Andrew was offered the position of a Fellow in Obstetrics and with that they were invited to dinners, functions and weekends away with consultants. Emily found the spouses were pretentious, questioning her desire to study medicine. To them, it was a preposterous idea. "Don't you want children?" Andrew questioned the same thing over and over. 'You should be pregnant by now. Maybe something is wrong. I could line up an appointment with Scotty. He is sure to fit you in.'

Emily was adamant that a baby was not going to mess up her plans at being an obstetrician. Little did Andrew know, she had been on the pill since first meeting him. She agreed to see Scot, his associate, but conveniently changed her shift to avoid the encounter. Andrew was so engrossed in work, fitness and hours spent with colleagues, that thankfully babies were continually brushed aside. "Sorry, darling not this month." She wondered how long she could keep up the facade.

Sitting the GAMSAT the following March, proved extremely difficult. The test was extremely intimidating, not only did she keep the day a secret from Andrew, but the test itself was gruelling. The three sections of the exam took up an entire day. Within minutes of reading the first lot of questions, she realised that studying anatomy and physiology were a waste of time. She needed to know more about analytical thinking, problem solving, and about cultural and social issues. The second section was two essays, and she spent too long trying to interpret the prompts that she ran out of time. The final part thankfully, was multiple choice on subjects she was more familiar with. It covered biology, physics and chemistry, with mathematical components deciphering graphs, blood flows and statistics and she finished well within the time allowed.

Hurting her pride a tad, the results were way below the score needed to even apply for an interview at a selected university. Emily's aim was the University of Notre Dame. To even be considered for an acceptance interview, she needed a score above 60. The interview was still not a guarantee for acceptance, so the higher the score, the greater chance.

Before taking subsequent tests, Emily researched past exam questions and dedicated time to practice. With each attempt, she was more prepared until finally on her fourth try, she achieved an impressive score of 82, gaining high percentages in every section. Feeling confident, Emily meticulously collated all the necessary information for her portfolio, aiming to secure an interview at the University of Notre Dame. All she could do now was to hope and wait. She was in a happy mood and decided to cook a special dish for dinner. Andrew had been working long hours, so she wanted to treat him. Unfortunately he was delayed. He arrived home in a cranky mood. Not even seafood paella worked. He complained about inexperienced registrars, equipment not sterilised or available. At one stage he even whinged about Jill and Emma, two very experienced midwives. Emily tried to defend them, yet he put up his hand, indicating he wasn't interested in what she had to say. The subject about her university application wasn't going to help matters, so she chose not to bring it up. To lighten the mood, she brought up his birthday party. He was turning thirty-five in just three weeks.

'Do you want to see who is coming to the party?' Emily passed him the list.

'Why is your grandmother coming?' Looking further down the list he also noticed the rest of the family's names. 'Why the brothers, I didn't have them on the list. And what's all this, why are all these midwives coming?'

'It's also a housewarming, Andrew. Remember we decided on combining the two.'

'I don't remember agreeing with it. It's my birthday after all. Besides, I don't like your friends, they're not good enough for you. I don't understand why you spend time with them when they don't value you, like I do.'

They had moved to a large home in Baulkham Hills, consisting of five bedrooms, three bathrooms and a massive backyard. Emily thought it was too extravagant. "I deserve it, besides, we need lots of room for our kids," he broadcast at the time.

The guest list had escalated to around ninety people. Even though Andrew rejected people on the list, he loved the attention. He met up with caterers and wine connoisseurs. "Nothing but the best for my guests, Em," he stipulated. "No matter the cost. We can afford it on my salary. I'm not going to be seen as a cheapskate."

Chapter 12
Dad

Two weeks out from the party, Emily got a call from Ben.

'Hi Em. Sadly, Dad died this morning. He had a heart attack sometime through the night and I found him on the floor. James has just arrived and we are seeing the funeral director later today. Charlie is in Brisbane but will be here tomorrow. At this stage, the funeral will probably be Friday. I hope you can feel it in your heart to come. It's bad timing with Andrew's party though.'

'Don't worry about that. His party is the least of our worries. Death never happens at the right time anyway. Of course I'll be there. What do you need me to do?'

'Thanks Em, but Kira and Julie have it all sorted. Just being here will mean a lot.' After Ben hung up, Emily rang her NUM to organise the next three days off. Next, she rang Andrew. He was out riding with the usual crowd and planned to head straight to the

Private Hospital for a departmental meeting. She was not surprised to get his voice mail.

'Hi darling, can you call me when you get a chance. Dad died this morning, please call me back?' Surprisingly, Andrew did not call back at all. Her shift started at ten thirty am and his meeting would have been finished around eight thirty am. She kept phoning and leaving messages. By one pm, she rang the Private Hospital only to find out that his list was finished, he'd already left. She rang his rooms, and Jane, his secretary, said he hadn't checked in yet. She assured Emily that she would pass on the message once she laid eyes on him.

Emily never heard from Andrew all day. On arriving home that evening, she found him on the lounge, earphones on and playing the X-Box. She stood in front of the screen hoping for him to acknowledge her. Instead, he shooed her away and continued with the game. She remained where she was, indicating to take the earphones off. In frustration, he threw them onto the lounge.

'What the hell Em, I finally got up to level ten and now I've got to start all over again.'

'Didn't you get my messages? I've tried calling all day. Dad died this morning.' Emily was getting angry and Andrew became defensive.

'I've been busy today, Em. Besides, it's your Dad. Remember, the man who didn't give a shit about you. Why are you upset with me?'

'It's still my Dad. I thought you could have at least rung me back. The funeral is Friday, so I'll head up tomorrow. I don't expect you to come.' She stormed off and went upstairs to pack.

Andrew followed her. 'What, so you're planning on going without even consulting me. How will it look if I don't show up? That's more ammunition for your brothers to despise me.'

'I don't expect you to come. I know your schedule is tight. I'm going up to support Ben mostly. He needs me there.'

Despite wanting to drive up on her own, she was grateful for a driver. She had woken with a bad headache and as the day continued, her body ached. Not a great time to get sick.

The funeral was only a small affair, with most people being local parishioners and mates of Ben's. Andrew had got into a heated argument with Ben and Charlie and she decided it would be best to just leave that afternoon. The flu was taking hold and all she wanted was to be home.

Ben and Charlie needed help to sort out the farm. They were hopeful Emily could come back up and give them a hand. Getting more time off work was a tall order. Andrew couldn't care either way. His party was the next weekend, and he was now pleased that the brothers decided not to come. May, her grandmother also declined. 'Why do you need me there, Em. It won't be my thing. Andrew doesn't want an oldie like me there.'

'I want you there, Grandma,' Emily pleaded.

'Yes, but it's about Andrew's birthday, darling. You'll enjoy it more if you don't have to worry about me.'

The flu had a significant impact on Emily, leaving her bedridden for four whole days. It wasn't until Andrew managed to persuade her that she eventually agreed to start taking antibiotics. By the Friday morning she had turned the corner.

'I wish you had started the antibiotics earlier like I said,' Andrew pointed out to her. 'I have the department heads coming to this party. I want you by my side. Hearing you cough and blowing your nose is not a good look for me. Did you manage to get that red dress I showed you?'

'Yes, I bought the dress. I promise everything will all be fine.'

Andrew was awake early and full of energy the next morning. Emily meandered into the kitchen. 'Tonight will be a fabulous night Em. I'm going on a ride. I'll be back to help sort the wine. Can you help the caterers set up the tables?' He gave her a peck on the cheek and was gone.

Emily drew in a deep breath. It will all be over in eighteen hours, just hang in there.

People started arriving at five pm despite the invite saying six pm. Andrew had pressured her to get ready early. 'Em, I asked a few to come early so I could show them the wine cellar. I don't want everyone knowing about it.'

As the dignitaries arrived, Andrew guided them to the downstairs cellar. He had already set up several bottles of both red and white wine with glasses alongside. One of the waiters opened each bottle on Andrew's command. Emily was also expected to try the wine. Each time Andrew handed her a glass, he glared at her insisting she try each one. Without food, she could feel the effects almost immediately.

Other guests were arriving, so she excused herself. The night was a huge success. Andrew was in his element showing off the house, joining in on singing and dancing. He played the perfect host. Throughout the night, Andrew would top up Emily's glass with bubbles. She had no idea how much she had drunk. By the time everyone left, she was very tipsy. Stumbling up the stairs, she felt a pull, or was it a tug, on her hair and fell backwards. Andrew caught her. 'Wow, someone has had too much to drink.' He guided her to the bedroom and began stripping her.

'This dress was perfect on you. Red always suits you.' He pushed her onto the bed.

Emily couldn't keep her eyes open. She had no control over her body. Andrew didn't care, he dived on top.

'I want you now. I want to be deep inside and leave my seed in you.' He was in his element, as he always was, with an unwavering determination etched on his face.

Emily tried focusing, now aware of what was happening. 'Stop, Andrew, please, you're hurting me.' Beads of sweat formed on his forehead as he persisted on and on. He was not going to stop, harder and harder. Then Emily passed out.

The early morning light shone on her face. Andrew was already up and had opened the blinds. He left a note on the bedside table, it said, thank you for last night darling. You were incredible. It was signed with an A.

Emily couldn't remember anything after the party. She clambered out of bed. Looking at herself, her reflection was far from pretty. Her hair was knotted, eye make-up smudged. Pain was felt in her inner thighs and her vagina was very swollen. What happened last night? Why can't I remember?

She stayed in the shower for a long time, the heat soothing her muscles. Andrew came bounding through the door as she descended the stairs.

'Good morning my little vixen.' He grabbed her and twirled her around. Emily's head felt like it would flop off. 'I feel invigorated. The hills were a breeze today.'

'I need some of that energy. I feel wrecked and nauseous.' Emily poured herself a coffee.

'Maybe it's morning sickness.' He whistled as he headed up to the shower.

Not likely, she thought.

All Emily could do was to keep busy. The waiters had cleared all the glassware, the tables and chairs had been stacked ready for collection, and food had been placed in Styrofoam containers in the fridge. She just needed to remove the decorations, vacuum and wash the floors. By five o'clock, the house was back to normal. She was lying on the lounge resting her eyes when Andrew crept up on her and stroked her hair. She opened her eyes to see a bunch of roses.

'I love you so much, Em. We make an incredible team. You stay there. I'll sort out food.'

A month passed. Andrew was attentive and romantic. Emily noticed a massive change in his moods since the party. He was like the old Andrew, the one she fell in love with. She didn't want the bubble to burst but she knew she was needed at the farm to help the boys. Andrew had resisted talking about the subject. It was now vital, as she planned to leave in the morning. She was not looking forward to the evening ahead. She opened a bottle of wine downing two glasses before Andrew got home.

Chapter 13
True Colours

Waking up in the shed back at the farm, Emily was unsure how long she had been sleeping. The sun was setting over Mount McDonald and she felt a cool night settling in. Ben's ute pulled up near the shed. Hearing all doors closing, she got up from her father's chair.

'What have you found in the boxes, Em. Is there anything worth keeping?' Charlie bent down to check the boxes himself. 'What's the photo?'

Emily showed him the photo and he just stared at it. 'Is this from your birthday party?'

Emily nodded.

'Here, let me see.' Andrew grabbed the photo from Charlie. 'Wow, how old were you then?'

'Four,' Emily replied in a soft, reflective voice.

'Oh, right. That was that day!' Andrew said, with sarcasm, and walked off. 'I'm parched, anyone else ready for a drink?'

'Doesn't have much of a heart,' Charlie whispered to James.

'Come on Em, let's see what's in these other boxes.' Charlie rummaged through a few boxes finding old linen tablecloths, crockery, bedspreads and underneath old newspapers, he found envelopes of various sizes, a rubber band holding them together. On the front of each one, in his father's handwriting was written, "Emily." Afraid of what the contents might reveal, tears started to fall. Charlie put his arm around Em. 'Do you want me to open one?'

She nodded.

Peeling back the lip, a birthday card came into view, Today you are 5. A few words were written inside ending with Love Dad.

She quickly grabbed the pile, opening each envelope. There were cards for each birthday.

'I thought he didn't care, Charlie. Why didn't he just post them?'

'Who knows what Dad thought, once you left with Grandma, he never mentioned you or Mum again. He died a lonely old man.' They both headed back to the house arm in arm.

'There you are, I was about to send a search party out,' Andrew barked, as he handed a glass of red wine to Emily. 'Try this, Em. It's one of the bottles Professor Jones gave me for my birthday. It's delicious.' He completely dismissed Emily's depressive mood.

Late in the day, Andrew and Emily were alone in the kitchen. Andrew wanted to leave, yet Emily felt she wasn't ready. Grabbing her by the shoulders he shook her. 'All this trip has done is make you miserable. You can't snap out of it. Well, I've had enough. I knew it was a bad idea. You don't need this. You don't need them. You never listen.'

Emily shrugged herself free and started to walk away, when suddenly she felt a pull forcing her backward. Slipping on the floor, she landed on her wrist. The pain was instant.

James was standing at the dining room table. 'Hey! What the hell, Andrew.'

Andrew's quick thinking saw the water on the floor. 'Em, are you okay? You slipped.' Looking at her arm, swelling now becoming obvious, he grabbed some ice and a tea-towel and wrapped her wrist. 'Oh dear, I believe you've broken your arm. Best we head on home. I'll call Ed and he can meet us in emergency. In no time, he had packed their things and had Emily resting in the back seat the car, her arm on a pillow. Before anyone could speak, Emily and Andrew were driving down the highway.

'That bastard pulled her hair. I saw him do it. Em didn't slip at all.' James was furious. 'I've a good mind to follow them and punch the living daylights out of him.'

Kira was trying to calm him. 'That won't help Emily. We'll give her a ring tomorrow and see what she believes happened.'

'I wouldn't lie about this, Kira. I know what I saw.' James stormed out, slamming the front door.

Emily had her arm in plaster for six weeks, so she couldn't work. Andrew took a week off to look after her. Painkillers affected her memory. She wasn't sure if she slipped or if Andrew did in fact pull her hair and then she slipped.

Her brother James kept trying to tell her that Andrew did cause her injury. Now she was confused. Did he? The more Andrew told the story, the more he influenced her.

'Who do you believe, my love, James or me? You slipped. It's okay that you don't remember. Probably best to not take any calls from James. He's never liked me.'

The pain finally eased and Emily stopped taking pain relief. Her mind became clearer. Staring out the window one Sunday morning, she watched Andrew mowing the lawn. He stopped to pick up something with his gloves and stomped across the road. Alice, the neighbour, opened the door, only to have Andrew hurl the object in her direction. Startled, she let out a piercing scream prompting Tony, her husband, to retaliate with wild punches, missing Andrew each time. With a smug look on his face, Andrew casually strolled back and resumed mowing the lawn. Tony was yelling after him but Andrew just ignored him.

'What was that all about?' Em asked, when he returned.

'I'm over their dog pooing on our lawn. So I gave them a taste of their own medicine.'

'Oh, Andrew, you didn't?' She turned and started to walk down the driveway when she felt a tug of her hair.

'Don't you dare go over there,' while pointing his finger at her. 'They deserve it.'

Memories flooded back. How many times have I felt this? She was glaring at Andrew. 'It's true. Everything James said was true.' She ran into the house.

Realising his actions, Andrew was backpedalling fast. 'Em, stop. It's not true. I wouldn't hurt you. I love you. Come here, please.' She was not going to listen and ran upstairs locking the bathroom door.

Calling through the door, he was starting to beg. 'Please, Em. Come on. Let me explain. Open the door?'

'No, Andrew. Leave me be.'

After about an hour of constant knocking and soppy pleas, he left. She heard the front door close.

Peering out the window, she saw him ride out on his bike.

She quickly gathered some belongings and drove to James's place. Upon opening the door, James greeted her with a long, tight hug. Through flooding tears, she mustered the strength to share with James the painful memories of Andrew's verbal and physical abuse. In that moment, she recalled the incident at the farm.

'He's a bully Em. A narcissist even, a real manipulator. He has influenced your thoughts since you met him. But he hasn't fooled me. I'll expect a fight, but he'll be crumbling to his knees when I've finished with him. Not to mention Ben and Charlie when they hear about this. Now you're aware of what he is capable of, it offers you a great defence against his tactics.'

Kira settled her into the spare room. 'I was so blind, Kira. All this time, he has misled me. I'm such an idiot.' Emily was distraught. Her mobile started to ring. 'I'm not speaking to him.' Before even checking the screen, she switched it off.

A few hours later, Ben arrived. Both boys decided to confront Andrew. They arrived at Emily's home. A police car was parked in the driveway. Two policemen were opening the car doors. They stopped and approached the boys.

'Hello, I'm Sergeant Peters, and this is Constable Palmer. We are trying to get in touch with Mrs Emily Phillips. No one is answering the door. Do you know where she might be?'

Ben piped up. 'What's he been saying? He's the abuser, not Emily. He's a liar. It's all him.'

Both policemen had puzzled looks on their faces. 'I'm afraid there has been an accident. Mr Phillips, sorry Dr Phillips's bike collided with a car around ten am this morning. He's in a critical condition and we need to locate Mrs Phillips.'

Chapter 14
Karma

Ben and James drove Emily to Westmead Hospital. Andrew was already in ICU on a ventilator. She was approached by one of the doctors. 'Hello, Emily. I'm Craig Cross, the ICU consultant tonight. We have actually met before, at an obstetric dinner a couple of years ago.'

Emily couldn't remember. 'I'm sorry Craig, I don't recall.'

'Never mind that, unfortunately, Andrew has suffered severe head trauma. He crashed into a parked car and then flew over the top of the roof, hitting his head on impact. The swelling has caused significant pressure causing extensive damage. We have performed relevant tests and he shows no brain activity. I'll leave you to spend time with Andrew.'

Emily, James and Ben all stood beside Andrew's bed. He looked peaceful, calm, even innocent. His chest was rhythmically rising and falling. A heartbeat was present on the monitor. Other than what the machines allowed, there was no life. They all hugged each other. A nurse entered the room and discussed the possibility of organ donation with Emily.

'We hadn't actually discussed it. I'm quite certain it's what he would have wanted. I'm more than willing to sign the necessary papers.'

The drive back to James's house was quiet. Emily was dumbfounded. The morning had been a whirlwind of shock, anger and now grief. Her mind was in a turmoil.

Throughout the following week, she drifted through life in a haze, as May, Kira and Julie took charge of all the funeral arrangements. The service for

Andrew was well attended. People Emily had never met came and offered condolences.

Following the wake, she reflected on the entire nightmare and confided in Ben. 'I'm torn between feeling sadness and relief,' she confessed.

'It's okay to feel both, Em. Look toward the future and what you want to do. No barriers, no pressure, just the path you choose.'

Emily was in a daze. She was uncertain whether to go back to work or not. Her energy was still depleted, and a constant feeling of tiredness waved over her. Her friend, and G.P, Jenny Palmer, ran tests to delve into the cause of the increasing fatigue.

A few days later, Emily received a call from Jenny's receptionist. 'Hello Mrs Phillips? Dr Palmer would like to schedule an appointment with you. She has an available slot at four thirty pm today.'

Emily didn't have to wait long before Jenny called her in. Hi Emily, I'm sure the last few weeks have not been easy. I have an answer to your tiredness though. These are your blood test results,' pointing to the paperwork in front of her.

'Not showing anything bad, I hope,' Emily said.

Jenny looked her straight in the eye. 'It depends on how you look at it. Em, you're pregnant.'

Emily was shocked. 'How, because I've been on the pill for years, it's not possible.'

'Let's think back. When did you have the flu? You took antibiotics back then, didn't you. They can interfere with the pill, remember.'

The memory of the week preceding Andrew's birthday party came to mind. She had been on antibiotics. Andrew had insisted on it. Emily couldn't recollect exact moments, but she did remember Andrew claiming they had an intimate night. Did he know she was on the pill?

Lying on the bed at the radiology centre a week later, the sonographer turned the ultrasound screen around. Emily was spellbound. She was looking at the image in front of her. There it was. A baby, a heartbeat, a spine, wow! She wasn't listening to the technician. 'Mrs Phillips, Emily.'

Her mind back on track, Emily tuned back in.

'You are around fourteen weeks. Would you like to know the sex?'

Emily shrugged. 'Mm ... yes ... okay.'

'Congratulations, Mrs Phillips, it's a girl.'

Emily was in a state of delusion. Andrew, her husband, a narcissist, a bully, now dead and she's expecting his child. Should she keep it? Should she have his baby girl?

Checking the letterbox the next morning, Emily had received a letter bearing the emblem of the University of Notre Dame. With a mix of curiosity and reluctance, she gingerly opened it.

Dear Mrs Phillips

It is our utmost pleasure to inform you that your application to attend an interview at the University of Notre Dame, for our medical degree program, has been accepted. Congratulations on this significant achievement.

We highly value your dedication and passion for pursuing medicine. In light of this, we kindly request your presence for a series of interviews with our esteemed medical advisors, on November 10th, 2022, at 9:30am. These interviews will provide you the opportunity to showcase your qualifications, ambitions, and potential as a medical student at our esteemed university. In the coming days, you will receive a detailed email with further instructions on the interview process and what you can expect.

If this date is inconvenient for you, please notify our office as soon as possible so that we can make alternative arrangements.

We look forward to meeting you to discuss your future studies and aspirations at our renowned institution.

Regards,
Professor David Simpson.
MBBS FRACP PhD in Surgical Medicine.

Emily felt she was living a fantasy. Now pregnant, and a chance to finally do medicine. She retrieved the photo frame off the sideboard. Looking at her own self captured in the family photograph, taken twenty-eight years before, she reflected on herself. What did the younger version of Emily know of her future then?

Lost in contemplation, she turned her gaze toward the reflection in the hallway mirror. Well Emily, you have the chance to follow your dream and pursue medicine. What is it that you truly desire? Do you want to be a doctor, a mother, or both?

The Chase
by Desley Polmear

Chapter 1
24th April 2004

Seventy-year-old Charlie Johnson went in search for something on the top shelf of the bookcase which he'd hidden a long time ago. It was time to get rid of the memories. His mood quickly changed and his hands began to shake as he read once again the headlines in bold print on the now yellowing fragile newspaper from way back in 1979.

At approximately 16.45 on Friday the 10th August 1979, in the town of Haywood, NSW, two brothers, in their late thirties, were shot at close range. They were dead before the killers left the building. A search is underway.

Chills ran down Charlie's spine as he searched the smiling faces plastered on the front page of the local newspaper. The photo of the two parents and their teenage children bunched together, made him flinch. He stared long and hard wondering what had happened to the wives and children over the last twenty-five years. He smothered his feelings as there were some things in life he knew he couldn't change. Things long gone he couldn't mend.

Before long, a sharp pain had surfaced in his chest. He bunched over, the severe pain diminishing all thoughts. He tried to reach his mobile phone, but he hit the floor first, the fragile newspaper following in his wake.

Chapter 2

It was just on six pm when fifty-two-year-old Gloria Talon found Charlie slouched on the worn fabric chair, his greying hair tousled.

'You're looking a strange colour, Charlie. What's been happening?'

'I…think I had a funny turn. I had dreadful chest pains and the next thing I knew, I found myself on the floor. I got a bit clammy there for a bit when I came too. I'll be right as rain shortly.' He tried to get up but his energy was depleted.

'Let me get you on the bed then I'll bring you a hot cuppa. You're not looking too good at all. There's no way you're going to the Anzac parade tomorrow if you're looking like this in the morning.'

'Awe, stop fussin'. No bed for me.' He looked at the clock on the wall. 'I'll sit out the back with a beer and wait for the sun to go down. It's well past me drinkin' time.'

'That's half your problem you drink and smoke far too much. You'd be better off having a lie down.' She could tell something wasn't quite right with Charlie. His skin was as grey as a moody sky. Someday, the drink and smokes would kill him, she reckoned. After a couple of attempts, she got him to his feet and he shuffled out the back grabbing a beer from the fridge as he went. She grabbed one too and went out to join him. He started telling her about the old days. She'd heard a lot of it before but she sat and listened, yet once again. For a long time now, Gloria reckoned Ol' Charlie had a touch of dementia.

Charlie stared at the darkening landscape working out the distant mountains. He opened his bottle of beer and took a long swig before he rolled a cigarette. As he relaxed, he started to tell Gloria about his childhood. 'There were times, on me bike that I'd have to double me mate all the way along the potholed track to the forests near the river. At other times I'd head east to the mountains, picking up our customised slingshots from secret hiding spots that were mostly hidden in the hollow trees on the way.' He chuckled before he went on. 'Once we'd entered the cover of forest, we all fanned out with the intention of bagging small birds using carefully selected stones as ammo.' He stopped to take a drag on his cigarette. 'We were only young boys then and all this hunting at such a young age was invigorating. The whole thing was about mateship really, the wonder at the seasonal variations in birds, orchids, and tree cover. Those were the days.'

Gloria knew he was on a roll, it showed in his singsong voice. 'You've had an interesting childhood Charlie and I've heard it all before, but you don't talk much about your family life.'

'Not much ta tell ya really. I didn't have much of a childhood that's why I headed off often with me mates.' He gazed into the distance thinking about the difficult foot journeys they all undertook, and the peace he had being away from his very dysfunctional family life. He chuckled when he thought about those fun days with his good mates.

'What's so funny?'

'I was just thinkin'. Having a weapon in school back then meant being caught with a Slingshot.' They both laughed at that.

'I was always in trouble in school too. I went ta school ta escape me home life. I thought it'd be fun but I was in more trouble than any other kid in the class.'

She looked across at his frail body and had a little empathy. She'd always thought he was unschooled, but crafty too, in many ways. There was a lot that was hidden with Ol' Charlie. At times, she never knew the real person. She suspected he had a secret life with all the bikies and young blokes knocking on his door at all hours. When she asked him one day, she got a shock with his reply.

"You mind your business and I'll mind mine." He said it in a threatening way, so she never spoke of it again.

'I was born in 1934 when times were tough. Me father was in and outa work while me mother looked after the six kids in the home. At times we all went ta bed without food.' He let his mind wander thinking about those days so long ago. His parents drank away what little money they had, and they didn't seem too concerned about whether there was food on the table or not. As soon as he turned fourteen, he went to work on a nearby farm and slept in the run down barn near the milking shed. He never went back home but as his siblings grew, he often saw them in the village. He learnt that all the boys had left home at around fourteen or fifteen years of age too. Both of his parents died in a car accident after a raging night at a bush dance ten minutes away from their home. It happened just after Charlie's twenty second birthday. He gathered the contents of the rented house and he shared them amongst his siblings. He didn't feel the loss of his parents then and he didn't feel the loss today. They were never there for the children.

'Do you ever wonder what happened to a lot of your mates?'

'I know of some that are still livin' in the area. I remember spending quite a lot'a me youth hanging out with an aboriginal kid. It wasn't frowned upon openly, but I knew racism was a cloud hanging pretty close to home. Sleepy Sam was a kid with lots a talent and tons of charisma. I'm sure that at times it was hard for Sam to hold his head up and hold his tongue, but to his credit he's still holding up that head today, keeping his pride. Yes, I had a lot of time for Sleepy Sam. He was, and still is a real champion and a good friend. He and a few of the old mates catch up with me now and again.'

'Did you ever move away from here?'

He looked across at her as he took a long sip. 'Ah, moved away with me mate Greg Pemberton for a while, but that was years ago and not worth thinkin' about or even mentionin'.'

'Well, you're lucky you still have a few mates left after all these years. The only people I call friends are the drinking mates in the pub after work…and you of course.' She poked him in the ribs, and he smiled his cheeky smile.

'Ya know, one day I came across me old photo album me mother had kept from me youth. I'll go fetch it as it'll give ya an idea what I'm talkin' about.' He threw the beer bottle in the rubbish bin and shuffled back into the house not saying another word. Gloria called out for another beer on his way back.

He chuckled as he flipped the page and spotted cheeky young Blackie, another aboriginal he'd befriended. In the photo, he had a black face and broad smile showing healthy white teeth. He pointed to the picture. 'He was showin' the boys how to make a Shanghai. He had picked up the technique from someone at Harry's Bridge behind Coopers Valley. He used to cut the correct shape from the fork of a young Banksia or Cheese tree and then he roasted it over a fire to achieve the correct amount of spring through boiling the sap out. Then he'd carve the rubber-holding grooves and select the correct type of rubber from the car tyre tube. Next, he would wire up the rubber without splitting it using copper wire taken from electricity cable. To make a pouch for the stone, he'd cut the leather tongue from old shoes. See this picture?' He pointed to Blackie. 'To the right of me in the picture, Blackie is hidin' behind a green shield sneaking up on some quails in the foreground.' It brought another smile to Charlie's face. 'Memories,' he said. 'Mind ya, we all learned the value of birds and their beauty, probably more than anyone else because we all knew their nesting cycle and every facet of their behaviour. Towards the end of our adventures, we all came to the realisation that it was just too traumatic to actually take a bird's life.'

'And I repeat. You had a magical childhood with your mates. Escapism from the oldies brought good friendships into your life, friends you still value today.'

He let out a long sigh. 'Ah! It was magical at the time to have the opportunity to know so much about birds and their calls. I'm a lucky fella to have all me memories come back. Those were the days.' He closed the album and stared out at the distant mountains, the long-ago memories filling his head. 'The best thing I did was join the army just after the parents died.'

'Have you got any photos during that time?'

'Nah, not many to speak of, there's probably a few layin' round but I never kept in touch with any of the guys. Except Greg Pemberton, we were mates from day one when we joined the army.'

'You've been friends a long time then. You mentioned earlier that you left the area for a while. Where did you and Greg Pemberton go when you left town all those years ago. And how long were you away?'

He took a puff and waited for the smoke to disappear before he spoke. 'I can't remember…too long ago.' There's no way he's coming into this conversation. What's gone is gone and where he went was no ones' business. Gloria loved to collect information, but he told her little. A flash appeared before his eyes of the two brother's photograph on the front page of the local paper back in 1979. He shuddered.

'It's getting a little cool, I think you'd better come on inside. I'll cook up something for dinner for you before I head to the caravan.' She pointed to the sky as she stood. 'Can't get better than that can you?'

'Never will,' he said, as he watched the fading sunset. He picked up his album and walked inside and placed it on the top shelf of the bookcase. He bent down and gathered up the yellowing fragile newspaper and added it to the top shelf too. Out of sight, out of mind, but tomorrow when he'd be on his own, he'd throw the newspaper in the fireplace, light a match and watch it burn. The shocking headlines printed in black and white had haunted him for the last twenty-five years.

Chapter 3

Anzac Day 25th April 2004

Thirty-eight-year-old Tony Wiggins found it hard to control his shaking legs. Moisture built under his armpits.

He fought hard not to let his feelings show next to his cousin, James Wiggins. He looked across at him, and sure enough, he seemed calm and relaxed. He often wondered about the difference between the two cousins, although they were born in the same year, they were like chalk and cheese, but had formed a great friendship since a young age, similar to what their fathers had done.

They had a good steak and a couple of beers during the evening but right now their interest lay more in watching the floorshow, like the drunks and the pretty young girls hanging off the blokes, unsteady in their high heels.

The Federal Hotel was crowded and noisy. They sat in the back corner amused as the hours' ticked away, the vocabulary altering by the minute. Every pub in Australia would be kicking on till the small hours as they celebrated Anzac day.

His cap lowered, Tony walked up to the bar and ordered two more beers. A scuffle could be heard out on the street and the girls screaming filled his ears. His chest was tight with anxiety as he walked back to join James. He threw the packet of chips on the round table. 'Get into 'em.'

'What the hell's going on out front?' asked James.

'Sounds like a lot of screaming women. There are a couple of old drunks punching into each other out near the road.' Tony's facial muscles tightened. He mixed in different circles in the City of Brisbane and the uncomfortable feeling he had amongst the seaside village locals, didn't fit with him. He had been separated from his wife, Katherine, for about three months. The loneliness was the hardest. He started out in the marriage being faithful because she was a wonderful woman and a great mother and he loved her. After the children came along, she started abandoning him in the bedroom. He'd heard from his mates that it was not uncommon. The children, ten year old Todd and twelve year old Alice, always came first with Katherine and he was sick and tired of her molly-coddling them. Before the separation, he only came home to shower and sleep. He spent more time drinking with his mates than working on his marriage. On looking back now, he realised he took everything in his marriage for granted, blaming Katherine for the majority of their arguments. When the whole idea of a separation was mentioned, it smashed his heart into pieces. He knew the life he wanted with Katherine, and he knew what he had to do to get it. To even consider they get back together, she'd suggested that he attend Alcoholics Anonymous. He agreed, if it meant getting back with the family he loved. Yes, he'd do it one day.

James reached for his mobile phone and put it to his ear. 'Hey Hon, how's the kids?' He turned away whispering.

'They are doing okay. We miss you,' said his wife, Sonia.

'We won't be long here. I'd say I'll see you within the next few days.'

'I hoped you'd be home on Saturday. There's a good deal on a three-day cruise to the Melbourne Cup in November and the cut off day is Saturday.'

'Perhaps I'll make it home in time. I'll do my best anyway. I miss you honey. Love to the kids. I'll talk about the cruise real soon.'

'At least think about it...please.'

'I will hon. See you real soon.' He flipped the lid closed.

'Is everything okay back home?'

'Yes, all good. She wanted to know if I'd be interested in going on a three-day cruise to the Melbourne Cup later this year. Told her I'd talk about it when I get back home. I said I'd be home within a few days. Are you right with that?'

Tony nodded. He wished he would've brought his own car so he could leisurely drive back home to Brisbane. He didn't want to be in any hurry. His manager was taking care of the business. It was different for James he had a wife and two kids to go home to. The noise inside heightened as the locals began to fill the room. With the music turned up, the young girls stood in a circle moving about to the beat.

James looked across and noticed beads forming on Tony's forehead. 'You alright mate?'

'Yea, sure, but it's bloody hot in here.'

'It's because the place is packed. Maybe you need to get some fresh air. Why not go outside for a bit.'

Tony shook his head. 'Nah.'

Chapter 4

At the bar there was a scuffle and raised voices.

'Right'o Ol' Charlie, I think it's time for you to get on home.' The publican, Neville Harrington walked over to him and tried to lead him outside.

'I ain't ready. I've still got another couple on the bar. I'll go when I've downed 'em.' Charlie pointed to the younger guy itching for a fight. 'He reckons he knows what's happened to me Eddie, but he won't let on.' He pulled away from Neville and found his way across the room to the bar and joined his marching mates. 'Me boy Eddie didn't turn up for the Anzac march today and somethins' goin' on.' He turned and pointed to the younger guys gathered in a group. 'Bloody bastards…all of em,' he yelled, volatile voice. He grabbed his beer and downed it in one go. The younger long-haired bloke tried to throw a few air punches his way.

'Leave him be young fella? He's had far too much to drink and he's better off going on home. Get on back to your mates.' A dark-haired young guy grabbed hold of his arm and guided him towards the group. 'C'mon Dino, Leave the old codger, we'll get him later.' They all laughed loud and long, raising their glasses towards Ol' Charlie.

As soon as Ol' Charlie had downed his beers, the publican got Larry O'Reilly to help him out the front and be on his way. 'See him up to his car Larry, and put him in the back seat. We've done it before. Take hold of the keys too.'

'Geez, same old story every Anzac day, he can't hold his flamin' grog,' said Larry.

'He won't remember a bloody thing in the morning. I tried to get him outta here an hour ago, but he wouldn't budge.'

Larry grabbed hold of Charlie's arm and led him up the hill to his vehicle. Charlie fought to go back to the bar but Larry kept telling him he could come back later. He'd say anything to Ol' Charlie to get him in the car and let him sleep it off. He took the car keys from Ol' Charlie's trouser pocket and pushed him in the back seat.

Cousins, James and Tony, downed their drinks and left via the back entrance leaving the dull sounds of the pub behind them. Tony's spine went stiff and hard when he heard footsteps following in the dim car park.

Chapter 5

The sun had peeked through, and reflections had formed on the expansive blue ocean. Patricia Chadstone was in her element on her early morning walk soaking in the yellow, oranges and pinks in the vast sky. Her hat covered her pale skin and her long muddy-coloured hair. She noticed the tiny dew drops glistening on the grass as she put one foot in front of the other. Her husband, Brendon, forbade her bringing her camera to snap photos. "It will slow us down," he'd mentioned often. Within minutes, her heart began to race when she looked across at the flowers from the Anzac day ceremony. She noticed a man's body slumped against the epitaph, as if he was sleeping.

'Keep walking. Don't look back,' said Brendon. He grabbed hold of her arm with force.

'He could be hurt Bren, and besides, it could be someone we know. We need to help him.'

'We don't want to get involved.' He dug his fingernails into her arm and pulled her along. Brendon was over six foot tall, solid build, tanned wrinkled skin. He had an accountancy business, and some say he'd crack the mirror if he smiled.

His nails dug into her skin and she struggled to get her arm free and when she did, he pulled it back.

'Keep moving, I said.'

Patricia ignored the tone of his voice. 'No Bren, we have to investigate. It's not right.' She made a scene and broke free running towards the body lying at the base of the cenotaph. A shiver ran down her spine. His head had slumped back and the early morning light gave a sparkle to his medals that were pinned to his bloodied suit jacket. His eyes were open, unblinking, unseeing, staring towards heaven. His stained crooked teeth were more noticeable as he lay in the silence. She turned away from his blood covered egg-shaped face. The life force had been drained from him and she suspected his heart had stopped beating long ago. She covered her eyes with her hands. Her lips twitched and her body went limp. The scream began deep in her belly roaring through her lungs bringing people running. They ran from the camp site huddling amongst each other, whispers circulating as they eyed the local as if he were sleeping.

Brendon crouched down beside his wife and pulled her into him. 'For God's sake, stop making a scene,' he said, taut voice. He looked down at the corpse and knew he wouldn't miss that lying cheating rogue for a minute. His face hardened as he turned away and led his wife to a bench seat.

'Patricia, try to control yourself. You're making a spectacle.'

People shook their heads in disbelief. Screams and sobbing filled the air in the tiny seaside village. 'Ol' Charlie, poor Ol' Charlie,' they echoed. The local policeman, Sergeant Bill Norris, pushed his way through the line of onlookers. He bent down, waited to feel a pulse: nothing. The stench hit his nostrils. He checked the pockets. Charlie's wallet was untouched; it held money, licence, a credit card and a couple of receipts. The licence proved that the body belonged to seventy-year-old Charlie Johnson. Not that Bill Norris needed proof. His face was recognised all over the seaside village of Rocky Shores.

'Away from the body please,' Norris called out. 'Move back.'

The curious crowd reluctantly followed instructions. Cries were heard amongst the children as parents dragged them away.

'Stay well away, move right back. Who found the body?' Norris called out.

Neville Potts pointed to the bench seat. 'They were the first ones here.' Norris looked across and saw that Brendon Chadstone had his arm around Patricia's slumped shoulders. He strode across to the seat.

'Did you come across the body first?'

'Yes. Trish noticed the body before I did.'

'It's a real shame. He'll be missed,' Norris said to the two of them, meaning it. 'I'll need to talk to you both. Just hang around. I'm going to call for backup from Coopers Valley. Are you holding up okay Trish?'

'In a bit of shock as you can imagine,' Brendon answered.

'Look after her mate. Just stay put and I'll get back to you soon.'

Trish couldn't help but think about Ol' Crayfish Charlie. She knew he was a larrikin around town, but hell, everyone knew him, and yes, he would be missed. On an overcast morning the previous day, she'd watched him struggle as he marched in the eleven am service. Not even twenty-four hours later, he was dead. She couldn't get the vision of his face out of her mind. She pushed her head into Brendon's chest. He rested his chin on her muddy coloured head, his eyes darting amongst the gathering crowd.

Chapter 6

Neville Harrington left his pub and rushed across the road to speak with Sergeant Bill Norris. He was 5'7' tall with a huge tummy, and by the time he arrived he was out of breath. He took off his light jacket and handed it to Bill indicating with his hand to cover the body.

'He'd had far too much to drink. I had to stop a fight last night between him and some young bloke. I ended up telling him to get on home.' He pulled up his trousers over his stomach and adjusted his shirt for comfort.

'What time was that?'

'Around 8.30. He didn't want to go as he was in the fighting and drinking mood. Larry saw him off the premises and walked him up the hill to his car. I told him to put him inside the car and take hold of the keys. He told me Ol' Charlie was ready for sleep when he slammed the back door shut.'

'Who was the young bloke?'

'Never seen him before but he was with Chad Hawkins and his mates. Mind you, I saw him rush after two blokes who'd been sitting up the back all night drinking beers.'

'Do you know if they were locals?'

'I've never seen them before.'

'Righto. I'll have a chat with Chad. Around the same age as Chad, was he?'

'Maybe close to mid-twenties or a bit older perhaps.'

Sergeant Bill Norris ran his hand through his thick blonde hair taking it all in. An uncomfortable silence fell between them as they both studied the corpse. Norris threw the light jacket over the top half of ol' Charlie. He looked across at the ruddy face of the publican, Neville, also known as Nifty Nev. 'Stay here for a while, I'll be back shortly. Also, would you tell Brendon and Patricia to wait in your pub for now? Patricia seems quite distressed.'

When Norris walked back to his residence, his wife Carla was standing out front. 'Look behind you at the hues in the sky Bill. I've taken a couple of photos earlier. It's so majestic.' He and Carla made a habit of watching the sun rise each morning with their first cuppa of the day as they sat in the front room facing east, but today, well, Ol' Charlie carking it was his main focus. 'I'm just about to dish up your hot breakfast,' Carla called out as he rushed through to the office.

'No time for that right now,' he called back. He walked into the office and called an Ambulance as well as backup from the Coopers Valley police. He called out to Carla and told her about Charlie being found dead at the epitaph. He didn't have time to go into detail right now. 'You have your breakfast and sit tight. I have a lot to do and I don't know when I'll be home.' Norris was known to be an enthusiastic cop. He chased things up and got answers and got the job done. He went to bed satisfied.

He ran down the steps two at a time and rushed down the road and across the grass to the epitaph. He cleared away all the stragglers who were waiting for answers. They sounded like a flock of squawking birds. He began to cordon off the area, and Nifty Nev insisted on helping.

Chapter 7

Detective Inspector Barry Peterson, Sergeant Robert Morton and two young constables arrived from Coopers Valley Police station. Peterson handled the introductions before getting on with it. He pulled the publican aside. He'd need to find out about the goings on the evening before, the night of the Anzac celebrations. More trouble than anything on Anzac day, even in Coopers Valley. His men had quite a few call outs from booze related incidences overnight. One day of the year when the ex- soldiers can get together with their mates to celebrate and have a drink for the ones who never came home.

'Excuse me Nev. Do you mind if we use an area at the pub to conduct the interviews?'

'Sure Bill, I'll get my wife, Jan, to set something up. I've got the Chadstone's sipping on a cuppa over there now.' A feeling of importance took over as he sprinted across the road to the pub.

'What do you know?' someone shrieked out. The detective fobbed them off with a wave of his hand. The two young constables tried to move the crowd on but they took two steps back then shuffled forward wanting answers.

Sergeant Bob Morton had been woken up early on his day off and having to work today left him with little patience. He mentally ordered them back from the taped area but that wasn't working. He'd made plans to go fishing and that was in the back of his mind right now. He and his mate Stretch had the spot picked out and the beer cold waiting in the Esky. He didn't expect to get away from here in a hurry. 'Some of you folk must be deaf and dumb. Can't you understand English? Move along, I said.'

Chapter 8

Sergeant Bill Norris had been stationed at the seaside village for six years and he looked around at the grim-faced onlookers. He turned to Sergeant Bob Morton. 'They're all locals and everyone knows everyone here. They care what goes on, and Ol' Charlie was a legend. Being in the state he was in last night, he obviously hit his head. The whole thing was an accident.'

Bob Morton pulled his trousers up over his oversized belly and stepped closer to the corpse. He wanted this over with so he could keep his fishing appointment. He pulled the cover back. 'I agree.'

Detective Peterson turned towards them. 'Inside with the others Bob, interview anyone who can speak. Someone may have seen or heard something.' Bob Morton grabbed his notepad from his inside pocket and took off. He realised then and there that his day off didn't consist of fishing with his mate Stretch. Earlier, Sergeant Norris had directed the onlookers towards the pub. He figured someone in the crowd may know something. The quicker they solved Ol' Charlie's death, the better.

Detective Petersen turned to face Bill Norris. 'Nev told me Charlie had quite a bit to drink last night. He seemed eager to get into a fight around 8 o'clock, and that's when he and a couple of workers asked him to leave.'

'That's right. Nev told me all about it. Knowing old Charlie and the state he was in, I'd say he didn't know where he was and fell over and hit his head, an accidental death.' He shook his head, with thoughts of Charlie lying out there in the cold night.

Petersen shifted his large body slightly and fixed Norris in his gaze. 'Like I've said many a time, you just can't assume anyone you find dead has hit his head. You must realise we have to have a full investigation.'

'Maybe you're right.' Norris nodded. 'I have a different point of view to you. I don't see it your way because it happens all the time, especially on Anzac day. Too much to drink and they don't know what they're doing or where they are. It happens every year, you know that yourself.'

'The other thing I heard was that one of the workers put him in his car and took the keys.'

'You heard right, but as for Larry putting Charlie

in his car, I haven't checked whether he took the car keys or did he just throw Ol' Charlie in the back seat and leave him with his keys.'

Detective Petersen nodded his head. 'I'll be checking all that with this guy, Larry.' He pointed to the corpse. 'Has he got family?'

'Yes, he's got a son Eddie and a daughter in law, Louise. Don't know a thing about any woman in his life. Besides Eddie and Louise, the whole town was his family.'

'Let's go over to the office and we'll get forensics out here, and a police photographer. You can get in touch with the newspaper. No doubt they'll be hungry for a story.' He turned to Constable Canning and called out to him. 'Keep an eye here. The ambulance is on its way and we've got a few calls to make. The corpse stays right here until forensics have done their job. Just keep everyone at a distance.' He put his notebook in his inside pocket and hurried with Norris across the grassy area and onto the road to the police station. They accepted a coffee from Carla and drank it while they made the calls.

Bill Norris stared out into the street. 'Poor old Charlie... the village will miss the old bugger. He carried information better than any phone company or newspaper. He knew where the fish were biting and everyone's business as well.'

'We see trouble every day in Coopers Valley. We deal with it, get over it and move on. Quite likely the young bloke pursued Charlie and kept the fight going. We'll know more after the interviewing's done and we'll also see what forensics come up with. We'll get to the bottom of it. We'd better get on over to the pub and do some work.' He put the coffee cup down and headed for the door, but not before calling out to thank Carla Norris for the cuppa.

Bill Norris didn't like the detective's theory. He knows how to handle things in Rocky Shores and he knows the locals. It's not the first corpse he's dealt with in the area. It's pretty simple really. Ol' Charlie had too much to drink and collapsed, hitting his head on the marble and bled to death. No point in the Coopers Valley mob trying to make a big case out of it. He was protective of his people in the seaside village as he'd been for the last six years.

Chapter 9

The reporters got to talk to Detective Inspector Barry Petersen and a few others who were lingering in the street. Then they moved inside to Neville's pub. The noise from the locals rose and fell around them.

The policewoman, Cassie, who worked in evidence, and the policeman, Phillip, the photographer, took prints at the scene and looked for signs of what could have happened and who was there. The two officers would later piece together a story from the pictures. When Cassie was training, the chief in charge told the group that everyone lied and not to believe a thing they said. You have to find out the truth is what he rammed down their throats. Standing there, she had a feeling that it was not just going to be an open and shut case. Something devious went on here last night. Phillip snapped at all the coloured tattoos which were situated in different areas on Charlie's body. He took close-ups of the bloodied face, the clothing and a thick gold ring on Charlie's right hand. The fingers were swollen and knotted with age.

Phillip felt something lodge in his chest before swallowing hard and quick. A tear trickled and landed on his Nikon. Ol' Charlie looked a similar age to his beloved grandfather. What a waste of a life if he died from consuming too much alcohol. Cassie and Phillip re-covered the corpse before walking away. Cassie overheard Sergeant Norris say that Ol' Charlie had probably hit his head and bled to death. She reckoned that the local cop wanted to close up the case quickly but Detective Petersen had different ideas. "Check everything then write up the report," he'd told her earlier, gruff voice.

Detective Petersen left the pub and went back to the Epitaph. He lifted the cover and walked slowly around Ol' Charlie Johnson's corpse. He beckoned Sergeant Morton to join him.

'Someone was in a rage.' He grabbed his handkerchief from his pocket and wiped his brow. Peterson's shirt was ripe with sweat.

'Not just a crack on the head from a fall then.'

'No. This is no accident this is a murder.'

Chapter 10

Forensics officer, Jill Brennan, got busy collecting fingerprints, footprints, and soil tests. Everything would be sent off to the toxicologist and they'd have to wait for the results. A search warrant was issued and later, they would search the house of Charlie Johnson.

The Chase

'I'll go back to the morgue with the corpse. You all ready to get on with it?' Detective Peterson called out for all to hear.

'Bloody born ready,' said Sergeant Norris under his breath.

One of Ol' Charlie's mates, Stew, told Bill Norris that Charlie had a good win playing two-up at the Anzac day celebrations the previous day, and by the end of the night he wanted to get into a fight, but could barely stand. He remembered the publican asking him to head off home. He told Norris that he'd tried to talk some sense into Charlie too, but the drink had taken hold.

'Yes, unfortunately seen it all before. Bloody drink is the ruination. What time did you leave the pub?'

'Ah, around about nine o'clock, could've been a bit after.'

'Did you see Charlie after he left?'

'No. I went in the other direction.'

'Driving?'

'Well, er…yes.'

'That'll be all. If I need you again for anything, I know where to find you.' Bill Norris walked away knowing full well half the town drove home with a belly full.

Forensics and the photographer had finished their job and as far as the locals knew, Ol' Charlie had hit his head in a drunken state; a simple accident.

The corpse was placed on a stretcher in the back of the ambulance with a white sheet loosely covering the seventy-year-old. Ol' Charlie would be transported in the ambulance to Coopers Valley morgue.

Bill Norris stood by watching and reflecting as thunder rolled across the sky. To his dismay it was only yesterday, on a rain-drenched day, that Ol' Charlie marched along with the locals in the eleven o'clock service in the sleepy seaside village. Now, not even twenty four hours later, his body was transported off to the morgue. Ol' Charlie was dead. It was hard to believe he was actually gone, as he was known in the village by all. Norris wondered what they will find? Did he fall or was it foul play?

Chapter 11

It was just after sunrise the day after Anzac day, 26th April, when seventy-six-year-old Meg Hobbs leapt out of bed at the first sound of the Kookaburras. Tying her apron, she stoked the fire in the combustion stove and added more wood to get the oven hot for the scones. She busied herself making the mixture and placed the doughy mixture in the oven.

Carrying the tray which held the small teapot and rose patterned china cup, she set it on the small table under the awning at the front of the house facing east. A lizard scarpered and slithered into the tall grass. Sipping on her black tea she sat listening to the birds as they began planning their day. She watched the mist as it rose from the mountain tops in the distance, and the dew glistening on the rose bushes. Yes, this is what brought peace to Meg each morning, this small window of time. She used to tell her children it was the best time of the day but they always brushed their mother's words away, like her suggestion was of no value at all. She was born in the seaside village of Pretty Beach, and she reckoned the only time she'd leave the area would be in a wooden box.

It took her a few goes to lift her heavy frame from the chair as her joints were filled with arthritis. The hot scones had been baked, now rolled up in a tea towel. She undid her apron, grabbed her purse and headed to the old Toyota sedan. She left Fred sleeping, like he always did after a heavy night. Yesterday was the biggest day of the year. Fred and some of his mates marched at the eleven am Anzac service and continued on until their bellies were full. The old truck had made a racquet around ten pm the evening before as it sped recklessly on the gravel path towards the shed. The sound of the door slamming in the still night would wake the household and the dead. She heard the microwave going and Fred mumbling to himself.

The cows would have to wait to be milked this morning. God only knew what time Fred would rise. He was born on the outskirts of Pretty beach, about one hour north of Rocky Shores, and Meg's parents had moved here well before she was born. When Fred's parents passed away he was left the property and the running of the cattle. All their married life they'd never wished to travel overseas as Pretty beach was their holiday place every day of the year. They'd often picnic on the headlands after swimming in the ocean on summer afternoons. They had a vegetable garden, loads of fruit trees, fresh milk, cream and homemade butter. "Why buy butter when I can make it," she'd said to the children often.

There was not another car in sight as Meg drove along the narrow road into town. Spunk, their German shepherd, hung his head out of the window, his tongue flapping in the wind. She parked outside the newsagency like she did every day to purchase the daily paper. She knew Derrick Hanson, the newsagent owner, was only open until ten am today as it was a public holiday.

It was just after six am when Meg Hobbs got out of the car with Spunk and shuffled towards the front door. Not another soul was to be seen. She'd seen big changes in the town in all these years. She knew everyone and if she didn't, she made it a point to find out. The wonderful smell of bread from the bakery hit her nostrils.

Spunks bark was deafening. 'Behave yourself. You'll wake the bloody neighbourhood.' His eyes were fixed on the spare block of land covered in overgrowth and spindly spikes of flaxen. Her eyes followed his gaze. It wasn't the spatters of blood on the brick wall that captured her gaze it was the site in the tall grass in the gap between the two shops. What she saw set her heart pumping. Her screaming filled the empty street. She stumbled to the gutter, buckled over and vomited time and time again until a stream of liquid trickled from her mouth. She wiped the dregs with a handkerchief she kept in her bra cup, and then tried to find support against the brick wall.

William Sheldon ran from his cottage. 'It's important to remember to bring an umbrella Meg. Even though it's early, the sun is still strong.' He grabbed hold of her as she slid down the wall. 'What is it Meg you're as white as a ghost. Is something wrong love?' Her waxen face turned towards the gap. William held her tight while taking in the sight before him.

'Daphne, here quick,' he yelled to his wife. Within seconds she appeared at the doorway. 'Stay with Meg while I go in and make a call?'

Daphne sat beside Meg on the ground. 'There, there. What brought this on darlin'? Are you not well?' Meg's eyes were as big as marbles under the owlish glasses. Her fast breathing and her trembling body worried Daphne. She wiped aside the tendrils of grey hair that clung to Meg's face while Spunk nuzzled into his keeper.

The Newsagent owner, Derrick Hanson, popped his head out the door. Before he uttered a word, William Sheldon appeared and cocked his head towards the tall grass. Derrick took one look in the dew-covered grass before his knees buckled. He crept closer to Greg Pemberton's lifeless body. His skin colour told him that Greg was long dead.

'Poor bugger. Geez must've been a bloody heart attack.' When he looked closer, nestled into Greg was his faithful dog, Bear.

'Take Meg into the house Daphne. Settle 'er down with a cuppa.' Meg's knees wobbled as Daphne attempted to support her.

William Sheldon had a grin on his face as he watched the two local policemen running down the street as though a killer was chasing them with a knife. By the time they arrived, they stood, catching their breaths. Within no time, locals were milling around, voices low.

'Okay, move on everyone,' said Detective Malley Porter. 'Better call an ambulance,' he said to Constable Reginald Davis. Davis looked at the man facing him, a frown creasing his forehead before he headed away from the crowd. In his mind the body in the tall grass was long dead.

'Looks like Greg may have had a heart attack,' said William Sheldon.

'I have a feeling it's more than that. His face and the top half of his body are covered in blood.'

William had another look. 'Maybe you're right.'

'You'd better call Coopers Valley Station and Clearview as well. We need to get a good team out here.' He knew Clearview station was well over an hour away, but they had top cops there, and the more the better. They'd get to the bottom of this.

'Right, step aside everyone,' yelled Porter. He leant into the man's body pulling the grass aside to get a better look.

'Christ,' he yelled. 'Hey Reg, let the ambos know there's a slight pulse.'

'Want me to run and tell the constable,' a pimply faced boy said. He could see him fifty metres away on his phone.

'Yes. Run....' The young boy hovered, stomach vile, but he ran like a bolt of lightning.

The cops fired questions at William Sheldon and Derrick Hanson. 'Who was the first to spot the body?'

'From what I can tell, Meg Hobbs saw the body first,' said William. 'She's a bit shaken right now. Daphne is looking after her in the cottage.'

Derrick's thoughts went back to the previous evening at the only pub in Pretty beach. It was a busy day being Anzac day, and Greg was also celebrating his sixty eighth birthday with his mates. Earlier that day there was the dawn service, and then the eleven am service followed. He remembered that Greg Pemberton had a good win at two-up in the afternoon. After Greg filled his belly with grog, Derrick tried to coax him to go on home around eight pm.

"Won't be long me ol' mate? Just got a few more to down and I'll be on me way," he'd said. "I've gotta celebrate me birthdy." Greg had lined up three beers in front of him at the bar. Like always, with a belly full of grog, the coaxing didn't work. A surge of irritation hit Derrick as he thought about that last conversation with his mate, Greg. If only he would have waited to see him home safely. When he went to wipe his brow, the top half of his body was drenched in sweat.

Chapter 12

The police tape was still hanging in strips around the cenotaph in Rocky Shores after twenty-eight hours. The questioning at the pub had finished and to the locals, it seemed an open and shut case. The cops got the same story about Ol' Charlie's movements on Anzac day. How he'd had a good win playing two-up and by the end of the night, consumed with grog, he was ready to get into a fight, but he could barely stand.

Nifty Nev, the publican, asked him to head off home somewhere between eight thirty and nine pm on the evening of Anzac day. Everyone had their own version of events, but close enough. Detective Peterson had heard that Charlie had a few enemies over his life time but nothing to be too concerned about at this stage. The biggest concern now for Peterson was to solve this case. He reckoned it was some sort of a frenzied assault. He'll be on the lookout for the young guy who wanted to fight Ol' Charlie the night before. From the interviews, he learnt that it was the same guy who followed the two blokes out the back entrance.

It'd be a start.

Chapter 13

As Sergeant Norris and Sergeant Morton approached the front porch, Norris noticed the empty wooden chair rocking slowly in the wind.

Norris knocked on the front door. Louise Johnson held Grayson in her arms and went to see who it was. A cold dread took hold, knowing what the two cops were about to say was not going to be to her liking. Her husband, Eddie, was always in some sort of trouble and he hadn't come home last night.

'Hello Louise. Is Eddie home?' asked Bill Norris.

'Eddie's not home yet.' Time stood still and all she heard were the birds singing in the distance. 'Is something wrong with Eddie?'

'Can we come inside,' asked Norris. She stared at them with an unfocused gaze. Unsteady, she waved them through the screen door and trailed in their wake. She brushed aside the paperwork from the kitchen table.

She was beside herself when they told her about Eddie's father, Ol' Charlie, and how he'd most likely hit his head and bled to death. Louise was holding her young baby, Grayson, when her knees buckled beneath her. Sergeant Norris pulled a chair close and rushed to help her sit down. Grayson began to whimper so she grabbed the check tea towel to cover herself while her baby snuggled into her breast, his little lips to her nipple. She blinked back tears as she thought about Charlie lying all alone in the dark night on that slab of marble.

Norris stared at the discoloured beige curtains as they flapped in the morning breeze while waiting for the news to sink in. He liked Louise. She used to serve him with a huge smile at the bakery before she left to give birth.

The Chase

Since the baby was born and she had lost her father to cancer only four months ago, Ol' Charlie had made a habit of phoning her each morning like her father had done. She wasn't concerned today, as she knew he would've had a big day like every other male on Anzac day in Australia.

Young Louise had been bought up in the bush and went fishing with her father from an early age. Back then, the area was surrounded by heath lands and forests teeming with birdlife and every spare moment she had, involved surfing. Her and her brother, Hugh, always got a lift to Rocky Shores with his friends or anyone that was going that way. She went and watched the boys play soccer on winter weekends, charging up on Coca-Cola at the halfway shop in Coopers Valley before kick-off.

If Sunday was flat and her ol' man hadn't lined the two of them up with some forced labour, they'd be up and away on their pushbikes down to the creek where Shorty would be snoring on his mattress in a converted Blackie house on the edge of a swamp, with the mosquitoes humming outside, and Mud Gudgeons swimming past a couple of metres away. It was magical learning about the bird life and she learnt from them too. All those memories came back in an instant as she was sitting here opposite Sergeant Norris and the cop from Coopers Valley who she hadn't met before. How could she take another loss so soon after losing her own father? He was the one who taught her all about the bush.

'I'd better skedaddle on back to the office. We were keen to let Eddie know, but you can pass on the sad news and when he is ready to know more, he can see me at the station.' He took a look at Louise and noticed the skin on her face had changed colour, a sickly colour.

'Will you be okay here on your own Louise?'

'Yes,' she whispered.

'Is there anyone I can call for you?'

'I'll be okay.'

The two officers stood, pushed the kitchen chairs back where they belonged, and walked towards the screen door. 'We'll be in touch, but in the meantime if there is anything we can do, don't hesitate to give us a call.' She waited until they were out of sight before she slumped into the armchair and cried like the baby that she held in her arms.

On this day, the 26th April, Louise Johnson didn't need any more stress. The bloody cops had brought her the news that Eddie's father had been found dead in the centre of the village, and it made her nervous. Where was Eddie?

Chapter 14

In Rocky Shores, Sergeant Bill Norris drove to Misty Mountain, NSW. In full police uniform he headed out to see Gloria Talon. She lived on Ol' Charlie's property.

As soon as Gloria saw the local cop at the front door, Charlie came to mind. She knew he hadn't come home the night before, as his car wasn't in the carport.

'May I come in?' Her greying hair was tied in a bun, and she wore faded jodhpurs and a flannelette check shirt. Without hesitation she ushered him into the kitchen. Her demeanour was as cold as charity, and her down-turned mouth seemed a permanent fixture. Norris had met her when he first moved to Rocky Shores and he knew from day one that she was a strange one. She was one of the boys.

Gloria sensed that Norris was about to tell her something she didn't want to hear. Her intuition told her that he was here about Charlie.

He took a deep breath. 'It's Charlie. We found him lifeless beside the epitaph early this morning.'

She flashed her green eyes at him, as if what she just heard wasn't real, but by the sullen look on Bill's face, he wasn't joking. He ran to support her as her legs gave way and she slid down the kitchen wall next to the combustion stove.

'Here, here, Gloria, let me help you. Come and sit down?' He led her to the wooden chair by the kitchen table and she sank into it. She held her head in her hands as she tried to catch her next breath. She wiped her eyes with the sleeve of her shirt. 'I warned him time and time again about drinking too much... the silly old sod.'

'Well, it was the Anzac day celebrations and you know each year it turns out the same. The old boys get together and after a while they're not sure how much they've consumed. Remember, there were a few years he woke up down by the beach, another by the creek. It's a wonder he survived then.' Norris walked over and filled the kettle and put it on the stove to boil. 'To be honest, if you must know, I think he fell, hit his head then perhaps bled to death. The Forensics team are hard at work in the surrounding area where he was found. Of course, the cause of death will be reported to the media as soon as the coroner does his job. I'm only surmising of course.'

He watched her clasping and unclasping her hands. He knew she wasn't well liked in the village by the women, but the blokes reckoned she was one of them. They said she had balls. Every afternoon at the close of business, Gloria strode across to the pub and joined the men at the bar for a beer. After catching up with the gossip, she headed off home to her caravan on Ol' Charlie's property on Misty Mountain. She'd never married nor did she have the inclination she'd told the boys in the pub. Her needs could be met any time after office hours with no commitments to anyone. She could take her pick and come back for seconds.

She paid Charlie a small amount of rent for the piece of dirt where her caravan sat and she helped out with odd jobs as well. When called for, he received a little extra on the side. They'd made the deal from day one. If she wanted to keep her animals and caravan on the property, she could put a little effort in for him as well.

Back in 1979, he kicked his wife, Meredith, out of the house. Well, that's what he told everyone in the village. The truth was that he beat her once too often, and she ran off and started a new life without her son, Eddie.

Gloria's green eyes were small, and her long face reminded Bill Norris of the horses wandering in the back paddock. He guessed she was comfortable in her riding gear at home, but working in the post office, she wore a white blouse and a navy pencil skirt with a blazer to match. She looked the part.

Gloria was an open book. Everyone in the village knew her story of how she finished her education in Sydney years ago, securing a job managing a horse stud in Bedstead, in western NSW. That was until her parents became ill nine years ago. Her father had a stroke and shortly after, he passed away. Her mother ended up a nervous wreck and found it difficult to work in the post office anymore. Gloria took over the job under duress in Rocky Shores, but it left a bitter taste in her mouth. She was in a job she hated. She wasn't shy of letting everyone know. On weekends, she worked on Charlie's property. At this time in her life, she told her customers, her animals were her life.

Chapter 15

Thirty-nine-year-old Justin Pemberton, a bulky figure, stood blubbering like a baby. He couldn't remember the last time he cried like this. Whoever murdered his father, Greg Pemberton, would pay, he was certain of that. He glanced back at the corpse on the slab in the morgue and his spine went cold. His father had been battered around the head several times. The police said it was a violent attack. He knew he wouldn't rest until the culprit was dealt with.

Sitting in the wicker chair on the porch, Justin's mother, seventy-year-old Mandy, had a lot of time to contemplate. She wanted to leave Greg many a time but commitment was something that was instilled in her by her mother. She repeated it like a mantra. "The man works all day long and provides for the family. It is your duty to have the house tidy, the kids quiet and a home cooked meal on the table." So divorce never seemed an option for Mandy. Way back in her mother's day, society frowned on couples separating or getting divorced, especially a woman with children. In the back of her mind, she always thought of the children, so she stayed. And in her mind, by staying together, there was an accomplishment, something valuable and intangible. They'd been through a lot together. Like most marriages they had survived hardships including lots of financial stress, due to the terrible droughts. And over time, in spite of all this, she realised that something solid had formed. And the grass is not always greener on the other side. That is why she stayed married.

She wondered about her dead husband, Greg. Had he really loved her? They'd closed each other out over the years, conversations stilted, lack of intimacy. And the two of them often passed each other in the house without a word spoken. She supposed a boring wife could force a degree of distance in the marriage. They were like peas in a pod. Greg was the social type, and she, the stay-at-home wife and mother, who avoided conflict at all costs. She remembered her mother's words. "It is your duty to stay in a marriage." Could she dare have a future now, alone?

Sitting in her soft leather couch, she closed her eyes. In her dream, she swam in the deep ocean, and the huge waves broke over her, sending her whole body out of control, finding it hard to resurface. She struggled time and time again. She jerked awake. The reality of the dream was exactly how she felt right now with the grief and loss of her husband.

She made a cup of tea and sat outside under the leafy Jacaranda tree. She loved the view of the trees and the mountains in the distance. The Australian ghostly white eucalyptus trees stood tall along each side of the gravel road which led from the old farm house to the bitumen road. The house had been in the Pemberton family for generations. Tough grass clumps hugged the fence posts which glistened with dew from the early morning. A melodic warble filled the air. The house with the wraparound veranda was tucked away between two Jacaranda trees, its tin roof rusting. Greg, her late husband, was the sixth down the line to make it his home, and Justin, their son, was the seventh. Memories came back of him as a young boy with his sister, Madge, traipsing down the gravel track to collect the mail on the days they were home from boarding school. That seemed so long ago. They were good old days then, bringing up the young children while she kept herself busy with sewing, cooking and pottery. They were company while Greg was out all day working on the farm. He came in for lunch and dinner and went to bed early. That was life on the farm she reckoned, and just accepted it.

Chapter 16

On Friday, at the church, the pictures on the screen that her forty-year-old daughter, Madge, had put together of her father, were just a blur to Mandy. Pictures of a baby Greg in his mother's arms, a toddler, a young boy in his school uniform, a photo on their wedding day, and so on. The pictures showed a happy couple. She dabbed her cheeks with her lace handkerchief as she clung to her daughter's arm. She wondered when they'd changed, when they stopped communicating lovingly. Well, he's gone now and looking at the photos of happier times, brought a small smile.

When they all started to sing, "Abide with me," Madge whispered in her mother's ear. 'Mum, Dad was born on Anzac day and he died on Anzac day. Don't you think that's a little creepy?'

After the funeral and the wake, Mandy went home to an empty house. She wandered through the large rooms aimlessly. Today was the first time in all these years that she would be responsible for the rest of her life.

Chapter 17

A tear escaped and glided down her cheek. It left a trail of salt in its wake. Her little one kept sucking, oblivious to all that was going on in her mother's life. Something bad had happened to Eddie, she knew it. She didn't know what he was mixed up in but whatever it was, it didn't sound good, and the other thing, he had detached himself from her of late. When she'd asked him where he'd been till all hours, he just shrugged his shoulders and walked away. The distance between them concerned her.

She hadn't showered for two days or washed her greasy hair. All she could do was to take care of her baby. Grayson was her main concern.

The following morning, she dressed in a wheat-coloured trench coat, bulging at the waist, put a hat on her head and walked out the door. She had to get into town and open her ears to any whispers. It'd be the talk of the town that Eddie Johnson hadn't been home for days and his father's funeral was coming up in the next few days. How would she tackle a new life without Charlie and Eddie?

Chapter 18

'The autopsy results are in,' said the medical examiner, Jack Hennessy. 'It's impossible to determine the actual cause of death of Charlie Johnson. He was obviously inebriated and whatever happened, I reckon he'd hardly be able to fight back. From what I gather from the injuries, he definitely hit his head, but someone else could have done that, because his head was hit with force more than once.

Someone has bashed his head into the marble over and over again.'

'Poor old bugger. Not a nice way to go,' said Norris, as he stared into space. 'He'll be the talk of the town for some time. I wonder if he had any enemies that we don't know about. It might be worth my while to visit Charlie's son, Eddie, and his wife, Louise.'

'Eventually, a suspected killer will show his face,' said Sergeant Morton. 'They like to gloat.'

'Has either of you got anything substantial to go on, like pieces of information from the folk you interviewed?' asked Norris.

'We're doing a follow up on the young bloke who was ready to have a punch up at the pub that night. They call him Darkie. His real name is Dino Black, and he has no fixed address.'

'Has he been up on any charges before that you know of?'

'He's been checked out and he's been before the courts many a time on theft, and bashings, and has a violent temper to go with it. Someone we interviewed saw in the early hours, a black or dark blue 4WD leaving the parking area not far from the epitaph. One driver and one passenger and the registration plate; illegible.'

'I'd like a chat with that someone.' Norris had a good relationship with the village folk and he reckoned he might be able to get to the bottom of this his own way.

'The report reads, "Frenzied assault" on Ol' Charlie Johnson,' said Detective Petersen.

'In all this time and that's all you've come up with?' said Bill Norris. 'We've got no answers and no leads as such, except this young bloke and maybe this someone who saw the 4WD.' He threw his hands in the air and stormed off. 'Be in touch with me when you have something to go on,' he yelled back. The high-profile cops have come up with nothing. He'd do some investigating himself. He knows where to go for information. He's got a good relationship with the village folk.

Chapter 19

Bill Norris called the Coopers Valley station and the local fire and rescue. Someone had rung in and reported a burnt-out vehicle down by the swamp on the outskirts of Rocky Shores. Within thirty minutes, three cars met at the crossing of murdering creek road and swamp creek road. Detective Inspector Barry Peterson and two young constables joined Bill Norris, and all trudged by foot to the remains of the burnt-out vehicle.

'Geez, what a bloody job they've made of it,' said Peterson, as he blew out his cheeks. They began to walk around the vehicle, inspecting the remains. 'Certainly hasn't been done recently. I'd say it's been sitting here for a few days. Just stay back from the remains, I don't want any evidence destroyed. I'll step away and make some calls. Just walk side-by-side and look through the dense vegetation away from the burnt-out car for evidence that may have been left behind.'

Chapter 20

Louise Johnson sat cross-legged on the floor and wrote in her journal about how she was feeling over the last two days. She found it hard to focus, but writing in her journal had become a daily ritual since she was about thirteen years of age. She learnt about it when she watched the Oprah show.

After, she began to iron Eddie's good shirt ready for his father's funeral. A news flash popped up on the TV. A picture of a burnt-out car with police and fire trucks everywhere was plastered on the screen. When she heard the reporter mention Rocky Shores, she put the iron down and turned up the volume and sat on the couch, listening. Her hand went to her chest as the cameraman focused on a policeman who was telling a room full of reporters what he knew so far. 'I'll now pass you over to Crime Investigator, Lance Graham who has the latest update,' the policeman said.

Lance Graham stepped toward the microphone. 'I have organised a major investigation. Firstly, my officers need to find out if anyone was in the car at the time and if the burn was suspicious. Investigators are gathering information at the scene as I speak, and after, when they see fit, the vehicle will be taken away for forensic examination.' Someone handed him a note. He took his time reading it. 'I've just been advised that a crime scene has now been established. The investigators have found skeleton remains in the vehicle and assistance has been sought from the homicide squad. I am also calling for any assistance from the public. Someone may have information which can assist our enquiries. Come forward if you saw something suspicious in the area or perhaps strange behaviour, different vehicles, anything.'

'Have you any idea how long the vehicle has been there?' someone asked.

'That will be determined later.'

'How easy is it to trace the owner of the vehicle?'

'A trained investigator knows where to look and what to look for inside a vehicle. Weather and time can destroy some of the evidence, but it is still possible to identify certain things.'

'How long will it take to determine the human remains?'

A post-mortem examination will have to be done, so at this moment, the identity of the deceased person is not known.'

'Please God, don't let that burnt out car be Eddie's,' Louise said out aloud. She looked down at her baby and he tried a smile. She took him in her arms and held him close to her chest. When she looked back at the screen again, the limbs of the trees, surrounding the burnt vehicle, looked like ropes of liquorish.

Louise rocked her baby. 'What should I do Grayson? I haven't told anyone that your Daddy hasn't been home for two days.' Her mind had been on Charlie's funeral and wondering where Eddie was for the last two days. There were other times when he hadn't come on home but he'd always phoned her and let her know that he'd had far too much to drink to drive. She got that, it was sensible. That was before she'd given birth to Grayson when he had no family responsibilities. Right now, the main reason that she was worried, he hadn't called her.

A young policeman walked over to Lance with a piece of paper. He inspected it before he spoke. 'The skeletal remains found in the burnt-out car have just been confirmed to be human.'

'Any idea if the human remains could be a local?'

'It's too early to answer that.' He glanced around the room. People were wanting answers, he knew that. Rocky Shores was a small village, and they all knew each other from what Bill Norris had informed him. He was speaking from head office, in Sydney, NSW, so he wasn't familiar with the area. 'It's quite possible that the human remains could be a stranger to the area, but we have experts who can determine who the skeleton remains belong to. Male or female, they will find out in time. Once we know something, I will make an announcement when the news comes to hand.'

Louse's thoughts were racing. Could she be jumping to conclusions? Maybe it's not Eddie's remains. Perhaps he is safe somewhere. It could be a female in that burnt out car. She realised it was pointless worrying when she didn't know the facts. That'd happen in due time. She took her little one and lay down on her double bed and when she woke it was four o'clock. She had no idea how long the phone had been ringing. She rushed to pick up the phone.

'Hello Louise, it's Bill Norris.'

'Yes,' she said, quivering voice.

'Have they got a date for Charlie's funeral yet?'

'Yes. It's on Friday at eleven am at the Catholic church.'

'Thanks. I'll be out that way shortly. Will you be home?'

She took a while to answer. 'Yes.'

'I'll call in and see you then.'

She brushed her hair and put a skirt and blouse on to make herself look tidy before he arrived. Why on earth did he want to come and see her? Did he know something about Eddie? Maybe he was in trouble. As she closed her eyes, she had a bad feeling. It started in her tummy and rose to her chest. Her breathing quickened and she went all clammy, then everything went black, and she went down. Falling, falling…

Chapter 21

Tony and James Wiggins were about an hour out from Brisbane. They'd told work and family about their three-day fishing trip. James wanted everyone to know that since Tony was separated from his wife, he needed to get away. He wasn't coping. They took swags, food supplies and a slab of beer.

Tony started to express his feelings, but James put a stop to it. 'It's over,' he said abruptly. 'We discussed it on the way down. We planned on this over months. I don't want to hear another word about it. So now forget all about it and move on. Our fathers can now rest in peace.'

Since Tony had separated from his wife, he'd been sullen, and moody. James had spoken with him at length many a time, but he knew there was only so much he could do and say to help. Turning to drink to drown his sorrows wouldn't help one bit.

He slowed down as he neared Tony's rented house. 'The fishing trip did you good if anyone asks,' he said. 'Rather than unload now, I'll keep the fishing gear at my place for now and return your stuff in a few days. Okay with that?'

Tony grunted before grabbing his swag, walking away without even a goodbye.

James drove north. He'd be home in thirty minutes. Tomorrow, he'd put on his uniform and head into the police station in King Street where he led a team of twelve professional cops in the drug squad. He had thoughts running around in his head, but over time, they'd disappear but he wasn't too sure about his cousin, Tony. Could he trust him to keep his mouth shut?

Chapter 22

Louise stood by the window which looked out onto the dirt track leading to the bitumen road. Her breath fogged the window then disappeared, then fogged up again while she waited. Her mind was full of so many thoughts as she twisted her hands back and forth. Earlier, she'd found herself on the floor and remembered the horrible feeling she'd had before everything went black. She noticed the cloud of dust, so she ran back to check on Grayson. He stirred when she opened the door, but he went back to sleep.

She stood in the doorway as Bill Norris made his way up the stairs.

'Hello Louise. How's the little one?'

'Good thank you. He's sleeping.' Her breathing quickened. What in hell did he want?

'May I come on in?'

She led him through to the kitchen table. He took his hat off and placed it on the bench. He waited for her to sit.

'When did you last see Eddie?'

She looked down at her wedding ring before looking up at Norris. 'About two days ago. He was supposed to march with Charlie but I was told he didn't turn up. He got dressed to go and he told me not to wait up for him.' She gave a smile. 'It's always been the same with him and his father on Anzac day. They both used to come home at all hours as drunk as skunks.'

He stalled. 'There was a fire down at the swamp…'

'I saw it on the news, it was a burnt-out car,' she said, flat voice.

He leant into the table locking eyes with her. He didn't want to just blurt it out, but he figured there was no other way. 'I received word a little while ago that the VIN number which was etched onto the metal tag was located. Also, the remains of Army medals were found in the ashes. We believe the medals belonged to Eddie's father, Charlie. The skeleton remains were located and tests were done, and we believe the remains to be that of your Eddie. I'm sorry Louise to bring you this news.'

Panic blurred her vision and her body froze. It took a while for her to focus.

'Louise, are you okay?' Her eyes were glazed over, her skin pale.

She took some time to speak. 'He always wears some of his father's medals. I pinned them on for him on Anzac morning.' Tears filled her eyes and rolled down her cheeks. Bill raced around and pulled a chair close. He placed his hand over hers and sat and waited for her to settle.

'Why don't you fetch a few things for you and Grayson, and come to our house for a while?'

'No. I want to wait here. You could be mistaken. It may not be Eddie in that car. The remains could be someone else, even a woman or a kid. I'd rather be here when he comes home.' Her body trembled as she shook her head back and forth. 'No, I'm staying here.'

He stayed quiet for a bit. 'Well, how about you come with me so that Carla can look after you for a while. Then we can all find out the latest news on the TV together.'

Her vocal cords refused to co- operate. Her breathing was heavy and laboured. Her body slumped forward. She rested her head in her hands on the table. Her scream filled the tiny room.

As she sat there hunched over, he patted her back like a mother does to her baby, when it has wind.

She stood and shuffled off to the bedroom without saying another word. He checked the kitchen, turned off the power points and locked the back door. He felt for the poor girl and what lay ahead, as she was only twenty, and she had no idea the life Eddie lived behind her back. He mixed with the wrong crowd and had done most of his life, and it was well known in the village about father and son.

When Norris had first moved to Rocky Shores, the previous cop, Sergeant Paul Brooks, had filled him in on the father and son's activities.

Since the two have lost their lives within hours of each other, Bill Norris reckoned house checks would be under way. When Ol' Charlie was found at the cenotaph, Norris was sure he'd hit his head and died an accidental death. Knowing now, about what has happened to Eddie and his father, the deaths were definitely suspicious, no doubt about that.

Chapter 23

As Tony Wiggins slumped in the chair in his rented house, he gave deep thought about the fifth commandment. 'Thou shalt not kill.' Murderers are evil dark Souls. A surge of anger took over. He knew too well that secrets are a heavy burden to carry. He also knew that he couldn't live with what he'd done. His skin was as grey as a dull day when he passed by the hall mirror. Katherine had served the divorce papers and it threw him for a sixer. The thought of not being married to her broke his heart into a million pieces. And talking to her didn't get him anywhere. He'd lost out on being around his children. They needed a full-time father. Although he went to bed each night, he's not sure whether he had slept at all. He lay awake, hour after hour. He'd gone off his food and taken to the drink instead. He found it hard to focus on anything, except the next step. It seemed to be foremost in his mind. Who would care? He had lost his wife, his children and he couldn't see a future without them. He repeated over and over again. 'Murderers are evil dark Souls.' His only focus was...how, when and where.....

Chapter 24

Charlie and Eddie's funeral were held on the same day. It was Louise's decision. How could she go through the pain twice? She'd found a long black dress amongst her mother's things and matched it with a shawl to drape over her shoulders. The church was overflowing out into the grassed area. People came up to her, but a lot of the faces were unfamiliar. She'd been in the seaside village most of her life but when she tried to focus on different ones, she was left in the dark. She couldn't even hold a conversation, but they seemed to understand and moved on. She wanted to get out of there, but the village had arranged a wake at the local club.

Bill Norris came and stood beside her. 'Carla is heading off home, would you like to spend some time with her instead of heading off to the club Louise?'

Louise stalled for a moment. 'Yes please,' she whispered.

'C'mon, I'll take you to her car. You wait beside it and I'll go get her.' Louise followed like a puppy. She was grateful that Bill thought of her in her grief. The last thing she wanted to do was be amongst a rowdy crowd at the local club. She'd never gone to the club with Eddie and his mates. She stayed home and found peace in reading her latest book.

'I'll be right back.' Bill Norris rushed off in the direction of the crowd who were gathered on the grassed area around the church in small groups.

Grayson began to stir. She lifted him from his pram and held him tight. He had no idea what this day was all about. He'd lost his father and his grandfather a week ago and now they'd be buried side by side in the local cemetery.

She saw Carla rushing towards her. 'Come with me love. We'll go away and find a little bit of peace and quiet.'

'Thank you,' she said in a small voice.

Chapter 25

Carla's sister, Giana, sheltered Louise and her baby over the next week. Giana's property was thirty kilometres west of the seaside village. Louise had collected her two dogs along with a small suitcase for her and her baby.

Eddie and Charlie's homes had been cordoned off by the police. Bag after bag, box after box was carted from both premises and placed into a waiting van. A stash of money and cocaine had been found under the floorboards at Charlie Johnson's house and small amounts of money had been found in Eddie's work shed along with drug paraphernalia, like bongs, pipes, tin foil and needles and small spoons.

Louise wondered how he could have hidden this other life from her all this time; Charlie too. She had a fondness for Charlie and he seemed to care about her too. The news of the father and son's illegal drug dealership shattered her and the news was the talk in the village and surrounding areas.

Giana kept Louise busy away from the news on the TV, but she found ways of gathering snippets from her best friend, Tania Montgomery, who worked at the bakery in the village. She needed to know, especially news of the hunt for the killers. Two murders happened in the village, father and son on Anzac Day and the police were looking for the killer or killers. They believed that the murders were related to drugs. They were also investigating the murder on Anzac day of Greg Pemberton. He lived one hour north of Rocky Shores at Pretty beach and was a good mate of Charlie Johnson. He was found in a bad way, but with a slow pulse. When the ambulance arrived, they carted him off to the hospital, but he was pronounced dead on arrival.

Chapter 26

Investigations were carried out regarding the yellowing fragile newspaper which was found on the top of the bookcase at Charlie Johnson's house. Was there a connection somehow to Charlie and the two murdered brothers? Did he know them personally or perhaps a family member? Why did he keep this paper for twenty-five years?

In December, 2004, the DNA results came in from the stored blood samples back in 1979. The results turned out to be the find of the century.

There was a clear DNA match with Charlie Johnson and Gregory Pemberton and that of the two murdered brothers.

Twenty-five years ago, two masked men stormed into the newsagency in the tiny country town of Haywood, in western NSW, demanding the money from the safe. The brothers, Alfred and Mark Wiggins, fought the robbers with kitchen knives, slashing the two in the ribs and neck before they were forced to open the safe.

After stuffing their bags with the weekly takings, the two brothers were shot dead before the killers escaped via the back door and into the secluded laneway where the stolen car was parked. That much they knew at the time but where the killers went from there was something the police couldn't ever pinpoint. The stolen car was found by the local creek, one kilometre out of town, which is where they surmised they'd left their own vehicle and walked by the river into the town to do the job.

They vanished into thin air. Searches were done for the killers, but the leads led to nowhere. The case was opened many a time when information was put forward by the public. The killers were sighted here, there and everywhere, but when the supposed suspects were interviewed, there was nothing to hold them responsible. All names were kept on file all these years and often a new cop thought he'd follow it through, but nothing became of the murderers.

Except one cop who never closed the case. It was his lifetime goal to catch the killers. In February 2004, he did a deal when interviewing a sixty-four-year-old long-time drug dealer, by the name of Fred Bales, also known as sticky fingers. Fred wasn't about to talk, but when questioned day after day by Sergeant James Wiggins, he finally gave in. Secrets were revealed about the highly profitable drug business going on in Rocky Shores and Pretty Beach. Fred's job while working for Greg and Charlie for the last twenty-one years was to deliver along the NSW coastline by boat with his mate, Jim Lockyer.

Fred revealed a lot. By opening up and ratting on his friends to Sergeant Wiggins, he avoided a long jail term. Maybe he could change his habits.

Fred Bales walked away as free as a bird and was told to shut his mouth, or he'd be next on the list.

Chapter 27

Two young boys found a body near the mangroves at Grants beach, twenty kilometres north of the City of Brisbane. At first, the boys thought he was a homeless person, but when they called out to him, there was no answer. They went closer and realised the man in the swag, was dead.

The police found a phone number and a message addressed to James Wiggins on a small piece of paper in his top pocket.

"I'm sorry cousin, I couldn't live with it." And underneath, in small handwriting was James's phone number.

Chapter 28

Days after Greg Pemberton's funeral, the police came and questioned Mandy. Did he have any enemies, owe anyone money etc. She had to think back about his life and places he'd been, people he'd known even in his youth. They said they wanted to piece things together, because maybe he had enemies recently, or in the past. She wanted to help find the killers of her husband of forty two years.

'I remember a time when his mate, Charlie Johnson, wanted to take off for a week to a country town in 1979, after his wife ran off. He wanted to go and find her and talk some sense into her. He asked Greg to come along for the ride.'

How could Mandy forget the dates, because while he was away, she gave birth to a daughter, but the baby was stillborn. It was gut-wrenching at the time.

'I'll never forget the time and date. It was at two thirty one am on Sunday the twelfth of August, 1979. The worst part for me was not being able to contact Greg after I lost the baby. The two of them were supposed to be gone for a week but it was three weeks before they came home.'

'I'm sorry about your loss,' said Constable Tim Hinds.

'After Greg consoled me, he went off and purchased a brand-new car for me. I argued about it at the time because we had financial problems, but he told me not to worry about the money as I deserved it after what I'd been through, losing my baby and all.'

She had no idea why any of this information would help the police, but they thanked her and left with their notes.

A search was done two days later of the house and shed at the Pemberton property. Fingerprints were taken and a van left the premises, full of boxes.

Chapter 29

Two weeks after Greg's funeral, Mandy blacked out when the coroner's report was handed down. Someone had deliberately bludgeoned her husband to death around ten pm on Anzac day as he walked to his car from the pub. His wallet was untouched and so were his car keys. Whoever did this, wanted him dead. She still can't get the thoughts out of her head. Why would someone murder an innocent hardworking man?

Weeks later, she drove to the highest point in Pretty Beach to watch the sun go down over the skyline and have time for herself. It was a majestic sight and she planned on getting used to it. She came alive just watching other people. When Greg was alive, he insisted that his lunch be on the table when he came in from his chores. Her son, Justin, took over the farm and he was happy to get his own lunch. She found more time now to take the car and have an outing; time for herself.

She sat on the bench seat overlooking the sandy beach and the deep indigo ocean. There was one lonely fisherman standing in the shallows, the water lapping around his ankles. She filled her glass with the white wine and watched the colours fade into darkness. What she had just witnessed would be someone else's sunrise. She found it relaxing and wondered why she had never found time before. Without warning, she could hear her mother's words. "The man works all day long and provides for the family. It is your duty to have the house tidy, the kids quiet and a home cooked meal on the table." She guessed she never found the time to come and sit on the bench seat and watch the sun set, as her days were full, even after the children had left home. Greg expected her to be home at all times. He demanded a cooked breakfast early, lunch, and then a cooked dinner, three vegetables and meat. She thought that was a normal farm life.

She had to admit, she was lonely in the rambling house. Greg never let her talk about what she wanted to talk about, like her emotions, her wants, but she listened to him moaning and groaning and hearing all about the cattle and the crops. She guessed, deep down, if she were honest, she missed any sort of communication. Her son, Justin, talked a different language, and her daughter, Madge, lived five hours drive away with her husband and two children.

Chapter 30

A special team was formed to fully investigate the burnt-out car and the reason behind Eddie's death. It wasn't hard to find Dino Black and his druggie mates sorting out the takings under the bridge in Coppers Crossing. They had make-shift accommodation made from materials and fixed it around a wooden structure by one of the pylons.

The five young men were cuff-linked and dragged off to the police station. Two thousand eight hundred dollars had been seized in the raid and bags of cocaine worth over three thousand dollars, perhaps ready for delivery. The men would spend the night in custody and would be dealt with the following day. No bail was granted.

Police had come up with more information about Greg Pemberton and his murder. It turned out that he was the main drug supplier bringing it in by ship from offshore. Ol' Charlie had his men do the pick-ups and deliveries. It turned out to be a lucrative business between the two long-time army friends.

***

It took just on two years for the jury to find Dino Black a guilty man charging him with murder, the possession of cocaine and a supply of drug money. He revealed to his lawyer that he met up with Eddie Johnson before the eleven am march on Anzac day. It was ascertained that he had murdered Eddie Johnson over an argument about owed money. He bludgeoned him to death with a steel bar before driving him two kilometres from Rocky Shores to the swamp. He then threw Eddie's dead body in the car and set it alight.

Since all three murders happened on the same day, 25th April 2004, it was automatically assumed that Dino Black had something to do with it. No charges were laid against him regarding Charlie Johnson and Gregory Pemberton's death as no evidence was found. The police surmised, with Dino's connection with the three men, he surely had a lot to do with their deaths.

'Would the defendant please stand.'

Twenty-eight-year-old, Dino Black, stood facing the judge in his borrowed dark suit, his hair all slicked back, like he did in his youth when he was dating. He didn't want to think of how many years she'd give him. He pleaded guilty which may take some years off, he reckoned. He tried to block out any thoughts of prison. His right eye began twitching as the anxiety built.

'Have you got anything to say Mr Black before sentencing?'

'No, your honour.'

Judge Cameron Peterson, when summing up, addressed the courtroom.

'What a deplorable act Dino Black has committed. To take a life so violently all because Eddie Johnson owed him money seemed like another day at the office for the defendant. Dino Black has had a history of violence, theft and drug use since the age of fifteen. The court hasn't seen any improvement in his behaviour since his last stint in prison, at the age of twenty-two.'

Murmurs could be heard amongst the courtroom.

'For the murder of Eddie Johnson, I sentence you to fifteen years in prison, no parole. For the charge of drug dealing, I sentence you to eight years in prison, no parole.'

Dino dropped his head. His lawyer, Randell Hart, tried to speak to him but Dino brushed him away in anger. Two guards led him away.

***

Back home in Brisbane, James Wiggins was eating a poached egg on toast when he heard the news of Dino Blacks sentence. He's more than pleased with the outcome. Rats like him don't deserve to be kept alive.

It was different for him and his cousin, Tony Wiggins. It was an eye for an eye.

Chapter 31

In 2006, Grayson's second birthday was celebrated with Tania and Carla in Louise's tiny cottage which she'd purchased after selling the large property her and Eddie had owned. She purchased her little cottage in the seaside village of Rocky Shores, a place close to the ocean.

The Chase

She had made the decision to not sugar coat the facts about her husband's other life. She would make no excuses for the life he led, and how he deceived her. She worked three days a week back at the bakery putting Grayson into day care. Before she collected him each afternoon, she walked in the sand and let the waves roll over her tiny feet. The ocean air helped to clear her mind from the terrible thoughts from her past. The man who married her and told her often how much he loved her was nothing but a liar.

Day after day, as life moved on, she found joy in the little things, like making new friends and watching her son grow. That was enough. She was enough.

Deception
by Nola Turnbull
Chapter 1
2021

The portrait of twenty-one-year-old Mary Watson hung above the fireplace gathering dust. Geoff Montgomery-Brown glanced at it occasionally, but guilt took over. Mary's eyes followed him accusingly everywhere he went in the room. It was as if Mary knew his secret. Along the wall hung portraits of the Watson family going back as far as 1897. A photo of the property, 'Tall Trees' hung above. Mary's portrait hung proudly beside her parents, Jim and Rose. He'd often thought of taking it down but the Watson family came to mind and he was concerned it may be a jinx. It was a family tradition all these years, so how could he break that? Jim and Rose Watson inadvertently left him the property in unusual circumstances. Nothing he was proud of.

2020

Geoff appeared to be madly in love with Mary Watson, although he didn't show as much interest in her as he did her father's grazing property. He definitely had a fondness for the family's fortune. The

Watson family was well known for their fortune. 'Old money,' Geoff's mother, Jennifer, said.

'Any money is fine with me, I couldn't care less how old and mouldy it is,' Geoff snapped. He liked to dress well. He had a collection of expensive watches, brand-name shoes, and had cultivated more than a fetish for driving fast cars. And he was a popular handsome bachelor around town. He was known to be lazy and made no attempt to hide the fact. 'I realise that there are lots of jobs which need to be done to keep the world running smoothly, Mother,' he said off handily, while drawing on a cigarette. 'As I readily observe, they all seem to be getting done without any of my involvement. My life is pretty full and interesting.' He picked up his car keys before checking the time for the first race to start. 'No point being late, I need to be there early to get the best bookie price. See you later, Mother.'

Mary's parents, Jim and Rose, had never warmed to him. He was a 'know all' and he accepted their generosity too readily, and he displayed an air of entitlement. They had worked hard to run their property and a lot harder to hang onto it at times. Over the years, they withstood many setbacks, including droughts, floods and bushfires. Blackleg, a bovine disease, was hard to manage in their early years on the property. It usually affected the prime beasts, those that looked like they were the pick of the herd, fat, healthy and full of zest. They had been on the land a couple of years when Jim recalled going out to muster one morning, only to find fifty head of prime beef cattle all dead or dying. There was nothing that could be done to save them. What a setback that had been. They had been relying on these cattle to sell well at the sale yards. Prices had been good. They needed the prices to stay high to pay the bills, and for once get a little bit ahead. Now, seeing these cattle dying or already dead, they were well and truly behind the eight-ball again.

Rose had worked in hospitality before she married Jim. After setbacks, like the cattle dying, she made the phone call to the local café which was fifty-six kilometres away. She was able to secure three days' work a week to keep their heads above water, but Jim hated to see that happen. Mary was just a toddler at that time. Jim loved taking care of her, but it certainly did impede his work program.

Rose settled in to her new job and would leave home at six am. Jim would get Mary dressed and fed, and pack lunches for them both. He secured her old bassinet to the trailer he dragged behind the tractor, and head out to the back paddocks to fix fences or plough huge paddocks in readiness for pasture planting. Mary was such a lovely child. She fitted in with whatever was required of her. She slept in a makeshift bed on the trailer and often played in a huge tree stump that had been burned out, leaving only the surrounds of the base of the tree about two feet wide. The inside was charred and she always got filthy dirty, ate charcoal and scratched patterns in the red soil that formed the base of her naturally formed playpen.

Jim would be gone for some time, maybe half an hour while ploughing a drill on both the outward stretch to the back fence and return. He would whistle as he came close to the stump playpen and Mary would giggle with excitement while trying to climb up to get a good look as he approached.

They were certainly tough times. Their wealth didn't fall from trees, no, it was the result of hard slog, self-denial and living within their means, and more often than not, very meagre means indeed.

Jim and Rose appreciated their good fortune when the seasons leant in their favour, and the property was swathed in lush green fodder, and their cattle grew fat and profitable. He'd grown up in similar circumstances seeing his parents start all over again after the droughts and rain. Jim and Rose would often sit in the cool of the afternoon breeze after a hard day's work, enjoying a stiff scotch and recall some of the calamities they had endured on their journey. The setbacks only seemed to make their success sweeter.

As Mary grew into her teens and beyond, she was a real head turner with long dark hair, and despite the harsh environment she grew up in, her skin was soft and blemish free. She was a natural beauty.

After she finished college, she arrived home with Geoff Montgomery-Brown in tow. They made a striking couple. She was so in love and hung on to his every word. He had studied agriculture, though he hadn't done very well in the theory, and his practical had never been tested. He was quite open about that, but he had the family convinced that he knew all there was to know about running a successful cattle property. And he was only too willing to step up and take over the reins, letting Jim and Rose step away and take a rest. Perhaps a couple of overseas trips, organized bus trips and a cruise would do them the world of good, he reckoned.

Mary had introduced Geoff to a few of the adjoining neighbours. Rose noticed some were raising an eyebrow at Geoff's comments on how to farm in the outback. She noticed that he was left standing alone as people moved on to talk to others. Most ol' farmers didn't take to braggers.

'Jim, I do want Mary to be happy. She really does have her heart set on this fellow, but I am having grave reservations. What do you think about the match?'

'Well love, she is a young lady. I don't much care for him, but then I guess it's only important that Mary cares for him and him for her. I must admit, she appears to be more invested in this relationship than he does.'

'Mary and I were talking about where they would live after they marry. She asked me if we would mind if they moved into the little bungalow. It's been vacant for years since Mum and Dad died. I guess it was Geoff's suggestion, but I didn't ask. What do you think Jim?'

'I will have to give that a bit of thought love. This fellow seems to be planning a lot of changes, very few of them that I agree with. He has little to no understanding of running a property. He is quoting textbook stuff, and I don't have to remind you of how seldom that runs true.'

Deception

One day, Jim and Geoff rode out the back paddock checking fences, and encountered the neighbour, Bob, doing the same. They stopped for a chat and Jim introduced Geoff. He leant forward to shake Bobs hand while remaining seated in his saddle. For the well initiated, this wasn't a difficult manoeuvre, but Geoff didn't take a good seat in the saddle, and while trying to look suave and casual, he inadvertently pulled on the left rein, dropping the right one, causing his horse to take a quick sideways step, almost unseating him.

He gathered his composure, cursed, and gave his mount a kick in the ribs, then pulled on the reins until the horse's head was held high. His horse shook his head from side to side trying to free himself while stepping backwards, crouching down, and was almost sitting on his back legs. Geoff released the tension on the reins. His mount bounded forward and took off at a fast gallop, just managing to squeeze between Jim and the barbed wire fence. A barb caught Geoff's mole skin pants and ripped a massive tear from the knee to the bottom, right through the hem and all. Geoff's feet came out of the stirrups, his arms flapping about. He looked like a juvenile pelican on its first take off; not a pretty sight. Bob and Jim watched the duo disappear in a cloud of dust, the hooves sending up divots of soil, grass and twigs. He'd completely lost control of his mount, which was hell bent on clearing anything in its path. The horse cleared a fallen log, but Geoff didn't quite make it, he fell heavy and in an awkward position.

Jim took off to inspect the damage and offer whatever assistance he might need. The sound of Bobs laughter faded as he moved closer to the catastrophe. Jim hoped that he could wipe the smile off his face before he got to within eyesight of Geoff, who by now was on his feet and looking like he had done a couple of rounds with a heavy-weight champion. The leg of his pants was torn and flapping. His shirt sleeve was ripped from the shoulder, most of the buttons gone. What a mess he looked, but oh so comical.

'Why haven't you taught that horse some manners? I have never ridden such an arrogant, uneducated beast in all my life. I'll be teaching it some lessons in the next day or so, or it will get a bullet. It isn't worth feeding, and to think that you would allow me to ride it without as much as a warning of its intolerable traits,' Geoff yelled.

'Hang on a minute young fellow, that horse is

well-bred and well mannered, probably more than I can say for you at the moment. Are you hurt? Well, apart from your ego that is.'

'I could have broken every bone in my body, and all I could hear as it took off was that dopey neighbour laughing. Does he not have any brains at all?' Geoff by now was white with rage. Jim whistled and the horse came trotting back to him, though giving Geoff a wide berth. It was showing the whites of its eyes and snorting, also pounding the ground with its left hoof to register its disposition. Mary was almost hysterical when she saw Geoff on arrival back at the homestead.

'Oh, darling, what happened? Are you alright?' Geoff was covered in dust and dirt, pieces of dead grass hanging from his jacket, not to mention his mole skins. There was no saving them, and he'd paid such a high price for them at the Country Road outlet. 'Our wedding is only weeks away and look at you your face is scratched and grazed. You have a gash just above your eyebrow. Oh dear, what a mess, no more horse riding for you until after the wedding. We don't want our wedding photos to include broken arms or legs, do we?'

'Well, I must say,' Geoff replied. 'I will be taking that steed for an educational ride tomorrow and give him a lesson or two in manners.'

While Jim sat at the kitchen table, he'd overheard the entire conversation and was teetering between rage and laughter, while trying to bring Rose up to date with what had taken place. Rose had a wonderful sense of humour and could visualize the events as the story was unfolding. Listening to Jim's account of the episode, and the bits she could overhear as it wafted from the back veranda where Mary was affectionately administering some delicate first aid, started Rose laughing.

Geoff wasn't a brave patient it seems. Jim and Rose were trying to stifle their laughter as he yelled and moaned each time Mary dabbed at an injury. 'Not so bloody heavy handed. You certainly don't know how to be gentle do you?' He admonished her more than a few times, each time with a bit more authority creeping into his tone. Mary was apologizing over and over. Jim and Rose hated to hear the way she was being spoken too and worse than that, how she was grovelling to this arrogant piece of work.

They all retired early. Jim and Rose lay awake talking for some time about how things were shaping up. Not what they had ever envisaged for their sweet Mary. Rose decided to take her to town the next morning for a bit of shopping, and to have a quiet word about her thoughts on the future. Jim would stay home, if for no other reason but to keep Geoff off the horses. If there was anyone needing lessons in manners, it wasn't any of the horses on the property. Jim hoped for an opportunity to bring it up with Geoff while the girls were away.

Geoff slept late and everyone had eaten breakfast and the dishes were done. The place was tidy, and mother and daughter had left before he rose to greet the day. Earlier, Mary had tip-toed into the bedroom to say goodbye before leaving. It didn't appear to please him too much. Jim and Rose heard him grumble about being woken in the middle of the night. Really, it was eight thirty am, and the sun had been up for hours. Mary was apologizing over and over, before tip toeing out, closing his bedroom door ever so quietly behind her. Her father noticed her long face as she kissed him goodbye and headed towards the car where Rose was waiting.

Chapter 2

The trip to town was less than sixty kilometres. It would probably take about an hour as the dirt road needed grading, the corrugations were bone rattling, and dodging the potholes could add another five kilometres to the trip.

Mary sat quiet for a while, fiddling with her purse.

Rose glanced across and was sure that she had seen Mary blinking back tears. 'Is there anything in particular that you'd like to look for in the shops when we get to town?' Rose asked.

'Not really. I could use some new makeup and hair products, but I'm not much in the mood to shop really. I know I'm not good company for you either. I'm sorry,'

'There is no need to apologize to me darling. I am having a day out with my daughter that is so special for me. I don't like to see you glum. Is there anything that you would like to talk about?'

'Well, I know you and Dad don't like Geoff very much, and I understand. He hasn't been engaging or really given the two of you any reason to think that he is a good choice for a husband for me. I just wish you could see him when we are together, as he is so charming and attentive. I guess he has picked up on the vibes that you and Dad are not blown over by his charm. And that only makes him feel worse, and then he doesn't display his real self, his nice side. Do you think that you might talk to Dad please? Perhaps be a little friendlier towards him, for my sake. Please Mum, I love him.'

'Well of course darling. We only want your happiness. If you feel that we are causing him to be arrogant and moody, then we will see what we can do to lift our game. That is not behaviour that either of us has ever been known for, as you well know. I'll talk to Dad when we get home. Now let's cheer up and get ready to have a nice day out together.'

Chapter 3

The two of them had a wonderful day out. "A bad start, a good finish" her grandmother used to say, well, that was true today. They had gone into the café for lunch and met up quite accidently with some of Mary's old boarding school friends. It was like old home week. Everyone talking and laughing, just the tonic that Mary needed today.

All of a sudden, everyone fell quiet. Mary looked around to see what had happened, and that is when she saw June Evans flounce through the door and head for the big table, the one set centre stage and usually used for large group gatherings.

June looked exquisite, long blonde hair, with the largest sky-blue eyes. She and Mary had been friends since the age of six. Their friendship continued until the first year in high school. That's when Mary met Joe. They had a sweet little romance going on and June felt neglected. That's when she became nasty in her loneliness. Mary was too wrapped up with her love for Joe to notice June's sadness. In no time, June became resentful and spiteful.

One day at recess, June turned on Mary. 'You think that Joe really likes you, well by the end of the week he will be my boyfriend. There is more to being a girlfriend than holding hands and looking coy, you know.'

Mary was taken aback, and speechless. But surely Joe wouldn't be so gullible. She knew he really liked her and she was sure that he would remain true to their relationship. Sadly, though, that was not to be. Joe and June were as she predicted, a couple by the end of the week, perhaps even sooner. Mary had noticed June in those coming days, making a play for Joe and she saw the effect it had on him. He was smitten and made no attempt to hide it. Mary was sad that both her friendships had fallen apart.

The following week, June had lost interest and moved on from Joe. 'He was too easy to attract, and win,' she said to Pam Sanders, Mary's friend. It left

Joe heartbroken, but Mary couldn't find it in her heart and go to console him. She knew exactly how he felt, because he'd caused her to feel the same way.

***

Six months after dumping Joe, June sat alone and sad at the big table in the Café. She took her powder compact from her purse and dabbed the puff on her nose, freshened her lipstick and flicked her glistening blonde hair back over her shoulders. She beckoned to a couple of her friends to come and join her. Betty and Julie rushed over and grabbed a seat. In no time, they began talking and laughing. June's mood had certainly changed in an instant. Then, to everyone's surprise, Mary walked over and pulled out a chair.

'Do you mind if I join you all?'

'Be my guest. It appears that I am going to be your guest shortly, so yes, please sit down.'

Mary couldn't hide her surprise and confusion at this statement. 'Oh! What do you mean about being my guest, I don't understand?'

'Well, you have invited James Cooke, and friend, to attend your wedding haven't you? It just so happens that James is my latest conquest and until something better comes along, we are a couple. He has asked me to come to your wedding with him as his friend,' she said, giving a somewhat disdainful glance at Mary.

James Cooke was the son of Jim and Rose Watson's closest friends, Bert and Nancy. James was named after Jim. They had all secretly hoped that Mary and James would wind up together, but that wasn't to be.

'When I heard your wedding was on the cards, I just had to make sure that I got to go to it. I suspected I wouldn't get an invite, so James was my ticket to attend. He is rather boring, but one can put up with anything for a short time to get what one wants. You know the old saying darling, 'the end justifies the means,' or something like that. I'm going to your wedding; I wouldn't miss it for quids.'

Mary swallowed and sucked in an involuntary gasp. 'Oh, that's wonderful June, I am so pleased. I did want to invite you of course, but you understand what it's like, it's so hard to keep to the numbers. It gets out of hand very quickly.'

After Rose had done her shopping, she came and joined her daughter. Once the pleasantries were out of the way, Rose suggested that they should be heading for home.

Deception

Mary said goodbye to her friends. She remarked to her mother what a lovely surprise the day had been. It was so good to catch up with everyone, except con artist, June, of course. She wouldn't get her off her mind in a hurry. She left the café and headed to the car, parked nearby.

Chapter 4

The drive home was similar to the ride to town earlier in the day. Mary was obviously broadsided by the fact that June would be attending her wedding. She knew that June would make a play for Geoff, like she did with Joe. The girl has no shame and would do so for no other reason than to make Mary jealous. It was a game to June. Also, crossing Mary's mind was how Geoff would react to the attention from such a stunningly good-looking admirer. This might be an awkward situation, she thought. She already knew that he was not in the good books with her parents.

'Never mind too much about what June had to say darling, everyone knows what she's like. Let's face it, she will only be there for a few hours then you and Geoff will be starting your new life, and you will probably never see her again. Don't let her get the better of you. In this world, there are all sorts, some we gel with, and some we don't.'

What surprised Mary and Rose was that in recent conversations with Bert and Nancy, there had been no mention of James's new girlfriend. Perhaps they hadn't been made aware yet. James would have heard about the tension between June and Mary, and the reason behind it. He couldn't be blamed for being attracted to June, as she was stunning, however her looks beguiled her true nature.

Chapter 5

Jim and Rose invited Bert, Nancy, Mary and Geoff for cocktails and dinner, a week before the wedding. Mary had to make excuses for not attending as Geoff was not interested in meeting any of the old fogies who had been around for years.

'Oh Mum, Geoff has organized a private dinner for the two of us. He had booked into Danilo's ages ago. It is a beautiful Italian restaurant and apparently expensive, but people say it's worth it. Definitely first class, and Geoff told me to dress up. He said he wants to show me off to the locals.'

'Really,' said Rose.

'I'd better rush and get ready before the guests begin to arrive.'

Geoff feigned surprise as Mary entered the lounge room. He went and kissed her on the forehead. He held her at arm's length and eyed her from top to toe gasping at how beautiful she looked. She swivelled around, showing off her emerald green gown. She wore the diamond pendant he'd purchased for her on their engagement. Mary glowed.

Rose searched Geoff's face for a sign that Mary was his love. The two lovebirds said good night and managed to leave before the guests arrived. It made Jim and Rose happy to see a display of affection from Geoff; a display they hadn't seen before.

It was a warm summer evening as they drove into Hamilton. The ride in Geoff's long wheelbase Merc was a lot smoother than Mary's mother's old vehicle. Geoff made a few negative comments about having to take his Merc on such a rough and dusty road. As he got closer to the restaurant, on a bitumen road, he was in a romantic mood. He reached for Mary's hand, glanced at her and patted her on the knee. Before long, his hand started to roam. She pushed it away. 'Please,' she said. 'There's a time and place.'

'How about having a bit of fun? What's say we find a spot by the water and make love on the sand?'

'Are you out of your mind?'

'You're so frigid.'

'I'm not frigid.'

'You're as cold as a fish. Most girls would be taking their clothes off by now.'

'You're disgusting. This trip so far is not turning out how I expected. How about you take me home?'

Chapter 6

Jim and Rose served the cocktails on the back veranda overlooking the property. Bert and Nancy had arrived not long after Mary and Geoff drove down the road. They said that they'd passed them along the way.

Rose mentioned the trip to town and the happy but unexpected catch up with some of Marys' friends at the café. 'Oh, and we met up with James's new girlfriend, June. Have you met her yet?' Nancy appeared a little taken aback.

'I haven't been formally introduced as yet, but I do know of her of course. She was once fairly close to Mary when they were younger, wasn't she?'

'It's funny how kids grow apart from their friendships once they grow up,' said Rose.

'James maybe is a bit smitten, though in no hurry to bring her home to meet us.'

"All in good time," he'd said, when I asked if he was seeing anyone. 'I thought we might have had a chance to meet her on his birthday. We wanted to have a bit of a gathering with friends. We wanted to invite you and Jim, Mary and Geoff along with a few of our neighbours, but he declined. He said he didn't want any fuss as it was just another day to him. Bert bought him a nice car, not new, but new to him.' Bert looked at Jim and laughed.

'I always wanted a convertible myself Jim, but never had enough of the folding stuff. I would have been over the moon if I had been given one. James was very nonchalant about it, he is happy with it I think, but he didn't jump up and down with excitement. I noticed he tore off into town to show his mates and an unnamed girl. We don't hear too much about her, I think he is being cagey about something. Time will tell.'

'Best not to get too involved until you get to know the person, I suppose,' Rose said. She nodded to Jim as she refilled the glasses.

Jim looked a little worried. 'I know what you mean, Rose and I are feeling a little fazed about our soon to be son-in-law, as he seems a bit too self-centred for our liking. He likes the good things in life. He recently bought another set of golf clubs he tells me, but not too interested in cracking a sweat to use them.'

Jim went on to tell Bert about the calamity when the horse threw him out at the back boundary. They all enjoyed a good laugh at his expense.

They were relaxed and enjoyed one another's company. They'd known each another for so long. Both their parents had been friends and even went back further in the family. They had watched their children grow up together and went through similar good and bad times on the land. It was always a welcome experience to catch up, have a comfortable conversation and know that they each had one another's back. Nothing was usually off limits. However, Nancy was reluctant this time to mention anything about their son James's new romance.

Dinner was easy, salad was made and ready, while Jim cooked the steaks on the BBQ. They had killed a beast a week ago and had it hanging to age. The steaks looked wonderful, and they would be a real treat to share with good friends.

Chapter 7

As Geoff parked his car outside the restaurant, a red convertible with its top down went dashing by. A shock of gold hair swirled around in the breeze and he could hear the couple laughing. Marys' heart sank. She recognized James driving the car and just knew that the cloud of gold hair that was blowing in the breeze belonged to troublemaker, June Osbourne.

Oh please, don't let them come into the restaurant. I don't know what I have done to make June treat me so bad. Let us have a wonderful night please, please. Her silent prayer was answered. The car kept going by.

They had a wonderful evening. Geoff had asked for a table way down the back of the restaurant. They were seated in a little alcove, away from the crowd. The table looked so pretty and romantic with the candles and fresh flowers. Mary could see whoever came in through the front door in one of the ornate mirrors. Earlier, she had asked God to please send June and James on their way, and her prayers were answered. They ate lobster that Geoff had pre ordered the week before.

'It was flown in from Western Australia,' the waiter, Paul said, when he set it on the table. As he went to pour the wine for tasting, Geoff waved his hand indicating to go ahead and pour.

'I have an expensive taste. This one hundred and thirty five dollar bottle of red is my go-to wine, and I've never had a bad one yet.' He raised his glass to the waiter. 'Thanks for ordering it in. We may need an extra to take with us,' he said, giving Mary a wink.'

'I doubt it,' she said, with a laugh.

'Listen to me, my soon to be bride. I have booked a room at the motel next door. We'll be staying the night, so it might be an idea to call your parents and let them know you won't be coming home. You know they'd worry.'

It was after ten pm when Mary made the call explaining they'd had too much to drink and would be staying in town the night. She wondered what her parents would think, as they had old fashioned ideas.

'I just hope none of our friends see them coming or going from the motel,' Rose muttered to herself, as she put the phone back in its cradle before joining the others. They'd all enjoyed the steaks Jim had cooked.

He was a pedantic cook. Every steak was timed so it was done exactly to everyone's liking. It was getting late and Jim kept topping the glasses. Bert protested feebly, as he put his hand over the rim of the glass.

'We have a spare bed so why not enjoy the evening and the wine and stay the night. If you need to be home early tomorrow, we can set an alarm. You can just get up and go when you need to. You can help yourselves to a cup of tea and some toast if you get up before seven thirty. Sunday is the only day I stay in bed until eight o'clock, but I would make an exception if you stay,' Jim said, laughing.

Rose was taken aback. 'Oh, Jim, you know what it's like if you're asked to stay overnight and you're not prepared. We should have thought of that when we invited you,' she said to Nancy.

'That's fine, thank you Rose. We'll take up the offer. Bert has had a busy day with some heavy fencing work that needed to be finished. It is nice to see him relax and enjoying himself. I'd be a bit concerned with him getting tired behind the wheel and driving home. As you know, I have never learnt to drive. I never thought I would have the need, although it might have been handy from time to time, but we have managed.'

Deception

Bert settled back in his chair and pushed his glass toward Jim. 'There, Jim, it looks like we are going to be staying, so I won't hold back. I'm ready for a top up. It is a delicious wine and really doing its job on me. Thanks mate.'

Rose knew that the news of Mary and Geoff staying overnight in the motel was not going to be a secret for long. Nancy and Bert would notice their car missing in the morning as they were leaving. She pondered the idea of telling them now and getting it over with. She wasn't sure of her husband's reaction though. Would he take the news calmly, or seethe and fall into a rage and spoil the evening? Perhaps telling him now wouldn't be the best time, as she wouldn't want Bert and Nancy to witness a temper tantrum. Good God, the two were engaged to be married, wasn't that supposed to be the time to get to really know one another, Rose thought. No forget it, she decided, these days things were not as they were when she and Jim were courting. Mary and Geoff are both over twenty-one years of age, it really isn't anyone else's business.

At the motel, Geoff set the key in the door. It was the usual layout, one double bed and a single. The room looked clean and tidy but it certainly showed its age.

'Good God,' Geoff yelled. 'Doesn't anyone outside the city limits ever update things? I apologize to you darling, I wanted better for you.'

'Not to worry Geoff, it is just somewhere to sleep and the beds are fine. Do you mind if I take the double bed? I can be a restless sleeper after a few drinks.'

To her surprise, Geoff didn't mind, he didn't even suggest that they share the bed or engage in a sexy romp while they had the opportunity. She didn't want it like this. She wanted to wait for their wedding night.

'Not at all darling, I hope your parents aren't too concerned about us staying in a motel together before the wedding. The truth is, I have had far too much to drink tonight to offer my best performance and I don't want to scare you off before the wedding.' He drew her in and hugged her. 'I love you Mary Watson, soon to be Mary Montgomery-Brown.' He nestled his head into her neck, then found her lips and kissed her. 'Good night, my darling Mary.' He pulled away and held her at arm's length. 'Gosh, I meant to tip the young wine waiter, Paul. I feel bad. He wasn't around when I paid the bill. I'll just duck back into the restaurant and see if I can catch him while you prepare for bed. I won't be long.'

Naturally, Mary hadn't bought any night clothes with her, so she decided to strip off her dress and bra and sleep in her panties and petticoat. She was tucked up in bed and had dozed off to sleep in no time. She heard Geoff as he entered the room. She opened her eyes but was too tired to speak. She turned over and went back to sleep. When Mary woke in the morning, the aroma of coffee wafted through the small room.

'You slept well my girl. You merely stirred when I returned after catching up with Paul. He is a top young fellow. I am going to ask your mother if it will be okay to invite him to our wedding. He has made quite an impression tonight. I think we could become good friends as he plays golf too.'

Mary shrugged her shoulders and went to the bathroom and made good use of the toiletries left for the comfort of travellers. 'I never make use of the toiletries at motels,' she called from the bathroom. 'However, I'm pleased for the use of them today.'

Geoff had showered and dressed before making the coffee. 'I'll pop next door and see if we can get breakfast delivered to our room. Wish me luck,' he said.

Deception

Mary glanced through the window and noticed the waiter, Paul, from the night before. She watched as Geoff strode towards him, his right hand extended before throwing his arm around him. He pulled him in with a very endearing hug.

Strange, thought Mary, she had never seen him demonstrate so much affection to anyone before, let alone a stranger. They were both smiling and having a chuckle about something. Geoff gestured towards the direction of their room. Probably sorting breakfast, she thought, with little concern. He walked with Paul as they both went into the restaurant. Mary had never seen Geoff in such good humour. He had appeared to have found a new friend. He's obviously found someone with similar interests, and she was happy for him. Mary tried to fix her hair and make-up with the meagre few items she had in her handbag.

***

Geoff arrived back in the room and placed two little parcels on the small table.

'Bacon and egg rolls, dear girl. They don't serve breakfast until eight thirty and I thought we would be on our way well before then. Dear Paul offered to make these up so we can head on home.'

'How kind,' she said, as she pulled the chair in to sit.

'I'm going to come over on Friday after lunch and have a hit of golf with Paul. You don't have anything planned, do you?'

'No, nothing I can think of. Although Mother might have plans, she hasn't told me about yet. I'm pleased that you have made a new friend.'

After eating their breakfast, Geoff went off to fuel the car. When he returned, Mary was ready to leave.

'I'll just pop in and tell Paul that the breakfast was divine.'

Marys' eyebrows went up involuntarily. Divine, she thought, it was just a bloody bacon and egg roll. It was nice, but not rocket science. As she gathered the wrappers to put in the bin, she noticed a little heart drawn on Geoff's wrapper. Strange, perhaps there was a different sauce on his, but a heart? Really!

She gave one last check of the room to make sure she'd left nothing behind. Not likely, as they were wearing everything they bought with them. She chuckled to herself.

As they headed for home, Geoff was full of chatter, cheerful. She'd never seen him in such a happy mood.

'You had better not be so chirpy when we arrive home, or Mum and Dad will never believe me when I say nothing happened between us in the motel room. I doubt that they will be very happy about us spending the night together. She didn't say much when I phoned her, but they had Bert and Nancy there for dinner. I'd say a bit awkward.'

'They have nothing to worry about on that account my dear. I would never take advantage. I respect you, and I hope that they trust me.'

'It didn't start off that way in the car.'

'I was only messing around, teasing you.' He gave a wink.

Jim and Rose agreed that Bert and Nancy hadn't noticed the absence of Geoff's car under the enormous carport, which housed cars, Utes and the occasional tractor.

Geoff and Mary arrived home and raved about the beautiful lobster dinner they had enjoyed the evening before.

'Geoff has made a new friend named Paul. He works as a waiter at Danilo's in the evenings and cooks the breakfasts as well each morning. They are going to play golf on Friday afternoon.'

Rose looked at Mary. She was trying to work out what, if anything had gone on at the motel. As soon as Mary had the opportunity to talk to her mother in private, she would tell her what went on the night before.

'Nothing went on. Geoff was a perfect gentleman. He left the room for me to get settled into bed then he woke me the next morning with a fresh cup of coffee to enjoy while he went and bought breakfast and fuelled the car. Then we drove home. He was in a great mood and happy to have found a new friend. He was really impressed with the food and service at Danilo's. Perhaps his demeanour might change now that he has found the local town is not so primitive.'

Chapter 8

The wedding plans were going well. Mary and Rose were 'no fuss' people, they just got on with the job and didn't let any hiccups ruffle their feathers. Mary had popped into town to gather some artificial flowers to put on the back fence just behind where the ceremony would be taking place. That's where she bumped into June again. Seeing her sent her blood cold. Mary always felt inadequate, stupid really, and no idea why.

Deception

'Hi Mary, I just saw your fiancé going into the golf clubhouse. I managed to catch up with him to say hello before he took off to play around, ah, that is, to play a round of golf.' I might have to do a bit of work to get him to do the other sort of play around, but I'm sure I could get him interested; I've got plenty of time.'

Mary was at a loss as to how to handle this type of conversation. If she confronted June, she would carry on about people not having a sense of humour anymore, which would just make Mary feel worse. She felt annoyed and angry. It was pretty obvious that June delighted in Mary's reaction.

'Not to worry dear Mary, I'm sure that he is totally in love and besotted with you and he would resist all my advances. Surely you'd agree. You're not concerned are you Mary, if I turn on my wily, womanly charms?'

'Not at all June because our relationship is built on love trust and honesty, but you wouldn't know about that.' Mary stopped herself short of telling June to look up the meaning of the words on Google.

Geoff arrived home a bit late for dinner looking flustered. He rushed off to the bathroom not stopping to discuss his golf game, or his new friend, Paul.

Mary looked across to her mother and shrugged her shoulders in response to Rose's raised eyebrows.

When she heard him come from the shower, she called out to him. 'Dinner in about ten minutes, I'll set it on the table.'

'Okay darling, I'm on my way,' Geoff called back. Five minutes later, he walked into the dining room and took his seat. 'June bailed me up as I was going into the club house before the game this afternoon. She was puffed and out of breath after running to catch up with me. I barely recognized her. I think I have only met her once briefly. She is friendly, but she seems to like oversharing information about herself and her family. Is she always like that?'

Mary wasn't surprised. 'Really!' is all she said.

'She tells me that their property is more than six times the size of ours, is drought proof because of the number of bores and dams on it and runs ten times the head of cattle that we do. Is all that true?' Jim looked up from his meal waiting for her to answer.

'Yes, theirs is a sizable property, not sure about six times as big, but it is significantly larger. That does seem a strange thing to be telling someone, particularly someone that she barely knows. They would run ten times the number of cattle that we do however, the quality of their stock is nowhere near the standard that we produce and maintain. We always attract a higher price per carcass than they do, but we are not in competition with them. We do our own thing. The way we manage our property is our business, and the way they run their property, is their business. That was a strange conversation indeed, don't you think Geoff?'

'I thought very odd. Anyway, Paul and I had a great game. I really enjoy his company and we have decided to make it a regular thing each Friday afternoon from now on, and if possible, and time permits, we will fit in another afternoon during the weekend.' He leant in and whispered. 'Oh, and I have asked Paul if he will be my best man. I know we'd decided not to have bridesmaids and a best man, but I was sure that you wouldn't mind. After all, there will be more of your friends and family here than any of my lot. You don't mind, do you?'

She lowered her tone. 'That's nice that you've asked him to be your best man, and I don't mind, but I hope I don't have to put your photo on the fridge so that I remember what you look like. I'm not ready to be shoved aside for one of your golf buddies.'

'I'm heading out now,' Jim called out.

'Okay Dad, we'll catch up later.'

Geoff stood, gave her a hug and kissed her on the forehead. 'Living and working out here together all the time, you will probably be glad to see the back of me before too long. I just hope that your friend June doesn't make a habit of hijacking me every time I'm at the club. It was a bit embarrassing really. When I was trying to get away from her, she yelled out to me. "Why don't you come out for a visit one day? But come alone, it will be more fun that way." She may be a good looking bird, but to me, she seems a bit pushy and full of herself.'

Mary lifted the plates and took them to the sink. Her breathing quickened. Geoff would be blind not to notice that June was perhaps doing a line for him. She wondered why he even mentioned it. Was it to hurt her feelings? Confidence, self-doubt and loathing crept back in, all at once. June was always out to go after whatever boyfriend she had. Well, things will change once she is married. She'll make sure Geoff puts her in her place. Besides, now that June is going out with James, she must have her eye on the valuable property his parents own, which will be passed onto him once his parents pass away.

Chapter 9

The day of the wedding arrived. It seemed a little chilly to start out, but the sun soon shone through and promised to be just as Mary had imagined it to be.

Geoff had stayed away on the day, so as not to see his bride before the wedding.

Geoff Montgomery-Brown didn't sit well with his soon to be father-in-law, Jim Watson, but he just couldn't put his finger on why. Jim and Rose decided to move into the bungalow while the newlyweds took off on their honeymoon. It made sense to swap homes. Jim and Rose didn't want for much and the smaller accommodation suited them. Besides, they intended on taking overseas holidays and enjoy life. Jim had been taking lots of photographs in the days and weeks leading up to the wedding. He intended putting together an album for the happy couple as a surprise, like before, and after. Unbeknown to Mary, he had taken a snap of her while she sat on the back veranda just on sunset, as she looked out over the pastures. It was a glorious shot. She looked relaxed and wistful, and the light was perfect. He reckoned he couldn't have done any better if he had asked her to pose for him. He took the photograph to the artist, eighty-four-year-old, Harry Clark. Harry had done most of the portraits which hung on the wall in the lounge room. While there, Jim chose a gilt frame. On the return from their two-week honeymoon, Harry promised it would be hanging above the fireplace in the main lounge room for Mary to see. Jim couldn't wait to see Mary's face when she saw it.

***

As the guests started to arrive, the caterers swung into action. They were locals and knew most of the guests, so it was a bit like old home week with lots of chatter and laughter. Pauline Bellows, the Celebrant, arrived. She always looked amazing but was mindful to not outshine the bride or the bridal party. She had a great knack of putting everyone at ease.

A friend was organizing the car parking on the property. One of the last cars to arrive was a red convertible. James and June arrived with lots of noise and fanfare. June had reached over and pressed the horn, blasting it way too long to be funny. She stepped from the convertible wearing a white strapless gown with a pale blue satin sash, silver high heels. Her skirt hugged her slim body a bit too firmly to be elegant. 'Hello everyone,' she yelled to the onlookers, as she swung her hips and strutted in her high heels. She was the centre of attention, just like she wanted.

Mary was almost ready to make her entrance when she heard the commotion. She looked out and saw June's performance. She would've made a good living being an actress, Mary thought.

Poor James looked embarrassed, as did his parents. Mary's father, Jim, was quick to show them to their seats. He hoped that she would take the hint and tone her enthusiasm down a tad.

Paul, now standing by Geoff's side waiting for the bride to appear, gave Geoff a nudge.

'Geez, where'd you spring her from? She has no shame, no class, and she could be real trouble throughout the night.'

Geoff turned around to get a look at what was going on. He laid his eyes on June, and she him. June Osbourne certainly knew how to make an entrance.

What a stunner she looked in that dress, the blonde hair and the beautiful tanned skin and wearing a permanent smile. Like a bolt of lightning, there was a connection. Sure, she lacked class, not a patch on Mary when it came to social graces, but maybe at some stage he might consider her offer to come over some time, alone. He might see another side to her. He felt his face reddening, moisture building on his forehead.

'Watch it mate, remember this is yours and Mary's wedding day, not hers.'

The music started. Rose walked in front of Mary looking glamorous in a pale blue chiffon gown. Mary came down the stairs leading off the back veranda, holding onto her father's arm. Jim was beaming with pride. He could tell that Mary was really struggling to keep her composure.

'You look beautiful love. Hold your head up, I have you.'

As Mary walked past June's chair, June stuck her foot out, then quickly pulled it back, giggling like a ten-year-old. People stared her way. James squirmed while watching her dreadful behaviour. He would never have thought that this was what she had planned all along. Since they were dating, he had feelings for June and had actually thought that he was one lucky guy. How wrong he was, and what a fool he'd been.

Chapter 10

Pauline delivered a lovely service, but she was quite aware that when the happy couple stood facing each another to make their vows, she saw Geoff steal a long look at June, the town's troublemaker.

It is too late Miss June Osborne, he is mine now. Mary steeled a look at June as they made the walk through the crowd, this time on the arm of her husband, Geoff Montgomery-Brown.

James's parents, Bert and Nancy joined June and James at the table. Nancy was unable to hide her displeasure with the performance and June sensed it, but it didn't faze her one little bit.

'It's okay Nancy, don't worry, I'm not planning on becoming your daughter-in-law. I just like to have a good time and let my inhibitions run wild, like, Rod Stewart's song, 'Do ya think I'm sexy?' She nudged Bert in the ribs. 'You let your inhibitions run away occasionally don't you Bertie? I'll bet you do, come on Nancy, spill the beans?'

Nancy made a beeline for Rose and Jim, June following. 'I am so sorry for this outburst. We would never have allowed her to attend the wedding if we had known what she was like. James is too embarrassed to speak. We are leaving and taking this awful creature with us.'

'Oh, no you're not. I'm not going anywhere just yet. I want some champagne and cake before I go anywhere. I have to toast the happy couple, remember.'

A short distance away, Geoff gave Mary a hug. 'I'm going to sort this mess out.' He headed over to where June and James stood, surrounded by some of the guests, she getting all the attention. Geoff took June aside. 'I think you've done enough showing off. I think maybe this party is far too dull for you.'

'Maybe you're right.' She leant in close. 'I have a proposition for you. I want to see you when you come back from your honeymoon. I want to show you how a fellow like you should be appreciated. If you like my deal, I'll go quietly now. Can we shake on it?' She extended her hand the other went for his groin. Geoff brushed her hand away and walked swiftly back to his wife.

James was furious with June's behaviour. He headed for the car and June had to quicken her step to catch up. Aware that everyone would be watching, she swung her hips, waving her arms in the air as she sang Rod Stewart's song, 'Do ya think I'm sexy?'

Deception

Nancy was in tears, Bert was furious and James couldn't wait to get this tarty piece of trash back to her home. He wondered how he would ever face anyone again, especially Mary, she was such a sweet and gentle person. Mary oozed class and style and he was devastated that his guest had ruined her wedding. He knew that he would never be able to make it up to her. He drove way too fast and skidded to a stop outside her homestead, without a word. He reached over and opened her door, and gave her a shove to help her on her way out.

'Don't worry diddums it was going to be a dull party anyway. Thank your lucky stars that I was there to lighten things. Thank you for the invite. I'm sure you can't wait to phone me when you have organized another ripping date.' She stepped out of the vehicle and laughed all the way to the front door. 'I'll be available until something better comes along,' she yelled back. 'See ya!'

James put his foot on the accelerator once she had closed the front door, and sped down the road, his anger building. He had no idea how he would face anyone after tonight. He wanted to go and apologize to Mary, but he just couldn't bring himself to do it tonight. She had probably left on her honeymoon by now anyway. Presumably most of the guests would have taken an early leave. Embarrassment would have put a dampener on the festivities for sure, he reckoned. He drove home more than a little despondent, with thoughts of packing up and leaving town foremost on his mind. He noticed his parents' car in the driveway. He knew they didn't deserve this sort of behaviour, and he guessed he would be blamed, but how was he to know that June Osborne had been hell bent on ruining the wedding. He wondered what on earth made her tick. He's sure not about to hang around to find out.

Chapter 11

Today was the day to hang Mary's portrait. She was the next heir in line to have her portrait hung in the big house. Her eyes seemed to follow Jim around the room as he admired it from several positions. Harry, the artist, had done a great job, so life like. He was sure Mary would be happy about it when she returned. He wondered how Geoff would feel about it, as he had commented that he was looking forward to having his portrait hanging there once the wedding was over. Jim had tried to explain the family tradition, but Geoff didn't seem to be interested in following that. Geoff had mentioned that there is always room to introduce new traditions. "You know Jim, out with the old, in with the new, or a new broom sweeps clean, all that stuff. We'll work it out, don't worry," he'd said one day. Jim knew he had to act fast and get the portrait hung while he had the chance.

Mary had questioned Geoff at great length about his actions and June's response just before she left the wedding. Geoff passed it off lightly. 'I just told her she looked more beautiful when she behaved herself and that he felt that she should leave the wedding quietly. She agreed and took my advice.' He thought for a minute. 'I also mentioned that her parents would hear of this embarrassing behaviour and would be more than a little upset. They were invited to the wedding of course as you know, but her father was recovering from a hernia operation, and they couldn't make it. Even if they were there, I reckon that she would have performed regardless of who was there to witness it. There's something wrong with that woman.'

They rented a little cottage for their honeymoon in a little beachside place called, Urunga, NSW, south of Coffs Harbour. Two weeks to spend time together. The weather was great but the atmosphere between them was at times a little frosty. Mary conceded that Geoff wasn't responsible really, as she had included the friend on James's invitation. He had nothing to do with that, though there was that eye locking glance that had to have been noticed by more than just Pauline, the celebrant. Geoff admitted that he held the gaze a bit too long, but claimed that the sun was hitting her necklace and throwing little rainbow patterns across James shirt and it had distracted him, nothing more.

Geoff was not an eager lover, preferring to keep up to date with the latest football games and cricket. He often took time to indulge himself back at the farm, watching TV through the day. Her father certainly didn't approve or condone watching TV through the day. She was aware that she was making excuses for him more and more these days and it bothered her. Making excuses for him to her parents was one thing, but she felt she was being untruthful to herself. She didn't believe the lies she was telling herself. And she didn't like the fact of her not confronting him about her mistrust in him. Something deep within her, told her that she'd made a big mistake. He held back making love to her, preferring to find something important to watch on

TV instead. She wanted him in the bedroom, but he held back. She'd made a dreadful heartbreaking mistake. She'd have to find a way to fix it. Maybe things will get better when they are both back on the farm in the family home. She hoped, but silently doubted.

The time in Urunga dragged on. They ate lunch in the local café a few times. She would reach for Geoff's hand as they meandered along the beach in the afternoon, but she noticed that he soon needed to scratch behind his ear, pick up shells etc, so the hand-holding would end. They'd only made love a couple of times and he was awkward and clumsy. Mary gave him a false impression. "You are so good," she'd said each time. More lies. *To thine own self be true.* The words echoed in her head. Yes, she really should live by that. It may not be easy, but she deserved better, and obviously it was going to be up to her to seek the changes in their love life.

Chapter 12

Mary and Geoff arrived home to find her parents, Jim and Rose, fully ensconced in the bungalow. A welcome home sign was pinned to the family home. Such a thoughtful thing to do she'd said to Geoff. He just shrugged his shoulders. He dropped the bags at the front door.

'I'm off to catch up with Paul and see if we can fit in a round of golf this afternoon. Don't bother waiting up for me as I might grab a bite to eat at the club.'

Mary was flabbergasted. Is this how it's going to be? 'What's the hurry?'

'Look, I have a few things that I want to discuss with Paul. It's just an idea or two that came up while we strolled along the beach. I thought it was amazing how a bit of relaxation and sunshine can get the thoughts flowing. Some ideas out of left field just kept popping into my mind, mostly business ideas. I reckon that they could all end up making a killing if they come to fruition.'

He headed off, and once again, Mary felt abandoned. She let out a heavy sigh as she picked up the last of the luggage and carried it through the house and into the bedroom.

Jim and Rose stood on the front porch of the bungalow. 'Geoff is off already, he seems in a bit of a rush,' Rose said to Jim.

'He might have to get something at the shops.'

Rose knew otherwise. Something was not right already. 'I hope they haven't had a tiff, not this soon into their married life.' Jim took hold of Rose's hand. 'It should still be all roses and buttercups. I wonder if he's not well and is heading off to the doctors.' Rose shook her head. 'Let's go and check with Mary and find out about their holiday,' said Jim.

'I think I'll go alone and talk to Mary. Give me fifteen minutes and then come on up. I'll put the kettle on.'

Mary wasn't in the kitchen. Rose walked in through the lounge room, still no sign of her there either. She called out as she entered the hallway leading to the bedrooms. She could hear Mary sniffling. 'Are you okay darling?' she called out. Mary stepped into the hallway and she fell into Roses arms.

'What have I done Mum, what have I done? I feel so miserable and I'm not sure that Geoff is happy either.'

'What's the matter love?'

'We have polite conversations, no arguments, no expression of emotion and very little intimacy. I've asked Geoff if he is happy. He seemed shocked that I would ask such a question.'

Deception

"Of course I'm happy," he'd snapped. "Why wouldn't I be? I have married the most eligible young lady in the district. You are attractive, well-mannered and if I may say so, you have a beautiful figure." Mary cried as she repeated his words. Rose put her arms around her daughter. 'Come and sit and we'll have a cuppa.'

A cuppa fixes everything. 'I must say Mum, I am more than a little miffed that he chose to race off into town as soon as we arrived home. He wanted to talk to Paul about some business idea that came to him as we were walking along the beach on our honeymoon. I thought that he might like to stay and get settled in here, our first night at home. He said not to wait up as he might have dinner at the club.'

Rose put the kettle on and got the teacups out onto the table. She called out to Jim to bring some milk. Mary went to wash her face and freshen up before her father walked through the door.

'Hi darling, how was your honeymoon? We listened to the news, seems like you had good weather most of the time.' Mary looked less like a newly married bride than anyone Jim and ever seen. She burst into tears and fell sobbing into his arms. 'There,

there, what's all this about?' He lifted her head and searched her eyes.

'I think I have made a big mistake Dad, a terrible mistake. Geoff says he is happy and delighted to be able to plan a wonderful life together for us, but I doubt that he truly means it, or loves me. I thought that he was just being a gentleman before we were married as he never put any pressure on me. He always said that he respected me too much and was happy to wait until we were married to be intimate. I don't believe him. He isn't very loving towards me, and as soon as we arrived home, off he went to discuss some business plan with his new buddy, Paul. I would have thought that the proper thing to do was to discuss any future plans with me now that I'm his wife. I really don't know what to do. I will see what happens when he comes home, but I think I have a difficult decision to make, and probably soon.'

After eleven pm that evening, the family were more than a little concerned about the whereabouts of Geoff. Jim called the club, but Geoff hadn't been there today, they'd said. He then phoned the local hospital as he could have been involved in an accident. No one had been into emergency, and no reports of any accidents around the area. Where the hell was Mary's husband?

Mary began to wonder if June had anything to do with his disappearance.

Chapter 13

June was driving home after spending a long night with a new love interest. She spotted Geoff's car parked at the back of the local motel. A scheming smile curled her lips. Surely the new groom was not sleeping alone in a motel room so soon after the nuptials. She turned into the car park and noticed his car was outside room number sixteen. This was an opportunity she couldn't miss. She tried the door, and it opened. For once she was speechless. There was such a flurry of activity, but she couldn't make out who was who. She thought for a moment that she had interrupted strangers and began to back away. She made a rapid retreat, until Geoff's voice boomed out. 'What the bloody hell. What are you doing here? Get out, and don't come back.'

June couldn't believe her luck. Geoffrey Montgomery-Brown was going to be hers. Probably on a shared basis, but hey, she had enough admirers to keep her busy while Geoffrey made himself scarce a few nights a week. She hated dull and boring. She loved how her mind went into overdrive, always in a split second, and always looking for an advantage in her favour. Today, this was pure gold. She could not have arranged it any better if she tried.

'This is not what you think it is June,' Geoff protested. 'Well, it is a pretty good imitation to what I think it is, buttercup. I reckon it would pass for the real thing don't you? Let me see, how do you think your new bride would see this, huh?' Oh, I know, you lost your wedding ring and Paul was helping you look for it. You both thought that it might have gotten lost in your pants, so you took them off to search, along with your shirt too, tricky little things those wedding rings.'

Paul had grabbed his clothes and dived into the bathroom. Geoff sat on the edge of the bed covering himself with his hands and attempting to retrieve his clothes from the floor where he threw them.

'I can't say I'm not surprised, well maybe just a little bit. It is an ill-wind that blows no good, as they say. This could really be an answer to my prayers when I come to think about it. You see, I have worried that marriage would always be dull and boring, like not my cup of tea. It's such a long-term commitment and faithfulness was never going to be my strong point. Now buttercup, I can plan a future, oh, I remember you have that pesky little wife, what's her name, Mary, that's it. I wonder how she will take this news. I guess you would rather her not know. Your secret will be safe with me.'

Paul made a sheepish entrance from the bathroom. He headed for the door, leaving Geoff to explain. If he chose to of course, but maybe he wouldn't even try.

'Remember buttercup, they don't call me blabbermouth for nothing.' Geoff struggled to his feet, struggling to get into his pants. 'So you are thinking of blackmail in some form or another I take it? It will always be your word against mine you know, and after your performance at my wedding who do you think people will believe, surely not you?' He slammed the door and headed for his car.

June opened the passenger door and jumped in alongside him. 'I think I will come with you for a drive. I haven't seen Mary for a while so it will be nice to catch up. You haven't seen her for a while either come to think of it, we can all have breakfast together. How nice would that be.'

Geoff was tempted to drag her kicking and screaming from the vehicle, but he knew what she would do. He thought it might be better if he let Mary think the worst and assume that he and June had an indiscretion, and in time, she might get past that, probably the better of two evils he thought.

Chapter 14

It was almost two am before Jim and Rose finally encouraged Mary to go to bed. They'd offered to sleep the night in the spare room if she wanted them to, but she declined.

'No, Geoff will be home soon surely, and I think I would like to have privacy on his return.' Rose made a cup of sweet tea for Mary and saw her to her room.

When Jim and Rose got back to the bungalow, he poured a mug of tea for Rose and a stiff whisky for himself. They sat on the veranda in the rocking chairs to chat before going inside. Rose was softly weeping, she had managed to hold herself together for Mary's sake, but her emotions spilled over as she wondered what could have happened to Geoff. They both agreed that there was something that didn't sit right with Geoff, as he always appeared to be hiding something. He never talked about his years growing

Deception

up, old girlfriends or even close family. They finished their drinks and made it off to bed for what they assumed would be a fitful night with maybe not much sleep with one ear cocked to hear Geoff's car when he finally came home.

It was after four thirty am when sheer exhaustion took over and they dozed off. Jim woke as soon as the sun streamed through the sheer curtains. He bounded out of bed and looked through the window to check if Geoff's car was back in the carport, but no. He left Rose sleeping and went to join a distressed Mary who sat sobbing on the veranda. Strange, he thought, that is the very spot where he had taken the picture of her, which was now framed and hanging in the lounge room. She was so happy then and looking forward to a bright and happy future. Perhaps he and Rose should have made their feelings known about Geoff earlier, before the marriage. He wondered if it might've changed things. Perhaps not, he concluded, Mary was deeply in love, and nothing would have gotten in the way of her love for him.

Mary told her father that she had called the motel restaurant as she knew it would be open for breakfast. Paul had answered her distressed phone call. "No, Geoff had not eaten there last night, but they'd had a

367

conversation earlier in the evening. I don't know where he might be now, although I had seen him with that crazy woman who was at the wedding. I saw them pull out of the motel carpark earlier this morning. I guessed that they may have been heading for home."

Mary was inconsolable as she clung to her father. She was lost for words, struggling to speak at all. She knew who the crazy woman was. June would always find a way to grab any man, but today it happened to be her husband, Geoff.

Rose had woken up and joined them. She too, was not able to make any sense of the situation. She wondered how Mary would get over this.

Mary pulled herself together and asked Jim to take her to town to see their solicitor later. There was never going to be an excuse to satisfy her and save their marriage. It was over and needed to be annulled. Mary felt hysterical and humiliated. She was sure that she could not face Geoff again. Why would he want to see June? There could be absolutely no explanation for his behaviour and there could be no reasonable explanation for him and June to be vacating a motel room early in the morning. Paul would have no reason to lie about it, he wouldn't say it, if it wasn't true.

Chapter 15

Mary had called Bruce Stranger, her solicitor, as soon as his office was open. He detected her distress and made time to see her as soon as she could get into town.

She gathered their marriage certificate, birth certificates, her newly written will, and any other documents she thought might be required and took the front seat alongside her father, leaving Rose in the back seat. The trip to town took some time as there were lots of roadworks going on. It was a dirt road in need of constant grading and repairs to take out the treacherous corrugations. It was ever so easy for the uninitiated to lose control of a vehicle on these roads especially travelling at speed on corners was so dangerous. Mary had to have many a chat to Geoff who was inexperienced on country roads and far too confident. It was just another demonstration of his stubbornness and over confidence.

They all sat strangely quiet on the long drive. So many questions had been asked, and all possible answers had been offered. Nothing made any sense. The sooner this was all over the better for everyone seemed to be the general consensus. Rose had dozed off resting her head on the cushion that had been in every car they'd ever owned since Mary was born. The fluffy cushion was yellow when new. Two years old Mary wanted it because she said it was the colour of the sun. Over the years, it had been washed and recovered many times.

As they travelled along, Jim made small talk about the state of the countryside, how it managed to recover after severe droughts, bushfires and horrendous floods. He had lived in the area all his life and had experienced it all. Mary tried to be polite and listen, but she had heard it all before and now she had more important things to think about. Her mind was scattered with many thoughts and mixed emotions. They saw a cloud of dust a couple of kilometres ahead of them coming in their direction. One of the benefits of a dirt road was that oncoming traffic was always evident in fine weather, the vehicles always stirring up a cloud of dust.

'Geez, this one is travelling a little too fast, I reckon,' Jim said. He slowed down and clung to his side of the road. It was a straight stretch of road and he pulled right over and slowed to a crawl. As the car neared them, the driver slowed down and the occupants were clearly visible. It was unmistakably Geoff, and sitting beside him was blonde-haired June

Osborne. Her head thrown back, her arm outstretched in the air, laughing. Clearly seen, she deliberately pulled at the steering wheel and directed the car towards Jim's car. The back swung out and the bulbar hit Jim's car on the driver's side and sent it rolling several times, before it went through the fence and down an embankment.

Geoff tried to control the car. He did a three sixty and though threatening to roll, righted itself and he continued on for half a kilometre before he could control the vehicle.

Chapter 16

Geoff was shaken, he knew exactly who he had collided with, and he had seen the look on Mary's face once she recognized him and June. It was an image he knew he would take to his grave. He struggled to turn the car around and go back to the scene, his legs shaking uncontrollably.

He drove back to where Jim's car had fallen down the embankment. Geoff was desperate to help. A couple of property owners who lived nearby had heard the crash and came running to offer assistance. One of the wives returned home to phone for the police and ambulance. The mood was sullen, everyone stood around in shock. The first farmer to arrive had made it down to Jim's car and his expression said it all. Mary and her mother were dead, and Jim was barely alive and seemed to be failing. He needed medical assistance, and fast. The farmers did what they could to stem the flow of blood from a huge gash in his thigh and keep him calm, but he didn't look good.

Tony Harris junior, who owned the property where Jim and his family lay, turned to Geoff. 'What the bloody hell were you thinking? This is a straight stretch, and it's wider than any other section between here and town.' Then he recognized June, the show off at the wedding. 'Get the fuck out of here?' he screamed. 'Go and sit in the car and take him with you. The police will be here shortly, and I hope they lock you both up and throw away the bloody key.'

Two police cars arrived from the closest town. They began to take charge of the situation. One of the officers pronounced Mary and Rose dead. Jim, although alive, was sinking fast and was sent off to the hospital in the ambulance.

On the bumpy ride in the ambulance, Jim was wracked with pain. He wasn't concerned with his body pain it was the pain of losing his wonderful wife and beautiful daughter. Tears formed and the female paramedic held his heavy veined hand tight.

June had a deep cut to her knee and was taken to the hospital to have it checked, and to monitor her for shock. The nurses were polite and professional, but they didn't deliver any of the tea and sympathy that other patients might experience. There was a lot of talk around town already about June Osborne. The police had been to interview her, but she said she was not ready.

'Be at the station at ten am tomorrow then,' Constable Long said.

Geoff escaped injury and passed the usual driving competency test, but the police were grilling him unmercifully. Geoff questioned why his car had been towed away.

'Your car was involved in a major traffic crash, so it will need an inspection. It could be that your brakes failed,' said the constable. 'It will be looked over carefully.'

Geoff was buckling a bit under the strain. He said he was not sure what exactly had happened, perhaps he swerved to miss a rabbit or a dog. That much he couldn't remember. They gave him the benefit of the doubt, but they had no intention of letting him off that easy. After many hours going over and over the events, the police let him go, but ordered him to report to the police station the next morning at ten am to go over his statement. One of the locals dropped Geoff off at the motel and the only room available was room sixteen. Later in the day, June was discharged from hospital and caught a taxi into town. She saw the police car pulling out of the motel car park and on a punt she knocked on the door of room sixteen. She knocked tentatively, could she be lucky two nights in a row, she thought, as she waited for a reply.

'I'm coming, hang on.'

His expression on seeing her was not what she expected. His shoulders were drooped, red eyes. 'Get out!' he yelled.

'I've come to console and comfort you. I can't imagine how you must be feeling.' She pushed her way in to the room and sat on the bed. 'Come here?' she said.

'I said, get out.'

'Please Geoff. Let's stick together. I need to know what you told the police as I have to front up to the station and give my statement tomorrow.'

'It'd be a great idea if you told the police the truth.'

Deception

'What was your truth?'

'I said, get out.'

She went to him and searched his face. 'I can tell the whole town all about your little sleeping partner on the first night you came home from your honeymoon with your new wife. That's before you slept with me, of course.'

He sat on the chair and put his head in his hands and cried like a baby.

'We both have secrets, don't we?'

'You have killed my wife and my mother-in-law by turning the steering wheel.'

'No, you are dreaming. It was you who turned the wheel. You wanted to kill them, you said.'

His face reddened, his temper rose. He stood and grabbed hold of her, shaking her violently. 'You bitch. Who do you think the cops will believe?'

'Stop it. Let me go. Are you crazy?' Right then, June had a mixture of emotions. She had to think clearly about this. She wondered what he had revealed to the police. Maybe she could try another tactic. She fell silent. 'I have another angle.'

'Thinking up more lies are you?'

'How about we nut this out so that we both walk away without any blemishes on our character? In both cases, your relationship with Paul and my turning the wheel, it would be one word against the other, but we both know how mud sticks, and like it or not, I want to live out my time on my family's farm, how about you?'

Chapter 17

When they both reported to police at ten am the next day, they were sent to separate rooms. They asked Geoff why Mary would have had the marriage certificate, her new will and birth certificates in the car. Geoff had no idea and appeared to be as confused as the police.

June revealed she had no idea what happened the day before as she was still in shock over the deaths of Mary and Rose. 'The whole town will be,' she said to the cop as she teared up.

Bruce, the solicitor had contacted police about the phone call he had received from Mary. He told the police that Mary had made a call about some important business that she had wanted to get sorted out as soon as possible. He naturally assumed that she had wanted to add her share portfolio to her will, leaving everything to Geoff. It had been an oversight when she had her will updated just before her wedding. That bit of news seemed to make sense and satisfied the police.

The following day, news had broken that Jim too, had died at six am that morning. The news was too much for the towns folk to bear. It was a small farming community and news like this had people talking about the Watson family and how they didn't deserve this shocking accident.

Chapter 18

Months later, and the court case over, the death of Rose and Jim Watson, and Mary Montgomery-Brown, no charges were laid. It seemed that it was purely a most unfortunate accident. The town went into mourning; no one could believe this could have happened. The Watson families had been managing the property for generations, and well liked, well respected, and loved. They were hard workers and were always willing to help anyone in need. To think that the three of the recent Watson family died within days of each other, was unimaginable. The towns' folk stood in huddles, comforting and supporting one another after the court case.

There were rumours and conjecture about what had happened, but no one knew the truth, except June and Geoff. They were tied to a handshake agreement that neither wanted to break and face the consequences.

Geoff decided to stay on at the farm and remain in the big house. He employed a manager to keep it running as it did before.

June went about her life in much the same fashion as before. There were those who thought her strange, and in some ways she was, others thought she was a cheap little tramp which is more the truth. She ran a good farm and looked after her parents until they passed away just six and ten months after the accident. They died peacefully at home as they had always planned.

Geoff continued a relationship with Paul. Often people in town had whispered about their relationship, but they had explained that the two loved a good game of golf. He had mellowed a great deal since the accident, finally realizing that he enjoyed a quieter life, not so competitive or wanting to impress anyone any more. Marriage was not anything he thought about often, except if ever the subject was talked about, he would marry Paul in a heartbeat.

Chapter 19

Two years later, the wedding was just as Geoff had planned. Attending, were a couple of neighbours who had known about his relationship with Paul over the last eighteen months. Paul's family arrived, two brothers and one sister. Paul had organized caterers for the sit-down reception out on the veranda. All in all, there were fifteen close friends and family.

After the honeymoon, the married couple decided on adopting a child. 'I want to have someone to leave the Watson property to,' said Geoff.

The following short stories were selected for
inclusion by the authors

A Much-Needed Day Out
by Carolyn Williams

"Sunny with slight possibility of light shower this evening, temperature twenty-five degrees," the weatherman had said this morning. The weather forecast for the day lifted Jane Carter and Meg Austen's spirits. After a week of torrential rain and destructive winds, that had decimated the plants of their holiday cottage, they were desperate to get out for the day.

'We must take advantage of the sunshine today. I can't cope with another day of trying to entertain bored, whining kids and teenagers, indoors. There are only so many board games you can play, and getting agreement on a movie that everyone will watch is akin to getting politicians to agree on climate change,' Meg said, as she handed Jane freshly brewed coffee.

'Totally agree, the sooner the better,' Jane responded, as she took the mug and peered through the kitchen window at the rain sodden garden. It looked as if a mini cyclone had gone through it. Jane was not a keen gardener but even by her lowly standards the garden looked dreadful. 'I don't envy the owners having to fix that up. It will take a lot of hard work.' She shrugged her shoulders and grimaced at her friend.

Jane and Meg, good friends since their university days had six children between them, with an age range of four to fifteen years. It was no mean feat keeping them all happy in a confined space. The cottage which had been advertised as cosy and quaint was not exactly as they had imagined it would be. Tiny and basically equipped would have been a better description. Thank goodness Meg had brought her coffee machine and extra essentials, like the bottle opener, extra condiments, and some decent pillows for the beds. Meg was always so organized. Jane was lucky to get all three of her children and the luggage into her car without mishap. She was pathologically late no matter how hard she tried to be on time. As it was, in rushing to get away from home she hadn't really packed enough clothing for the younger kids. Thanks to the atrocious weather, since their arrival a week ago, the tiny lounge room now resembled an industrial laundry rather than a quiet room to relax in.

An hour later with a picnic basket packed, and Jane's youngest child's missing sandal found they set off for a day at the beach. The lane that led to the beach was narrow and they walked single file, like marching foot soldiers, to avoid being taken out by speeding tourists who paid little heed to the oversized Slow Down signs.

'Don't get too far ahead,' Meg shouted, to the older children who were striding out, eager to reach the beach.

'Okay,' they shouted back but showed no sign of slowing down.

Jane gently nudged her youngest son Freddie in the small of his back as she tried to hurry him along. He was only just four and the walk was proving more difficult than Jane had anticipated. *It certainly didn't seem this far when we drove it earlier in the week,* she thought.

'Hell, Meg, that lane is steeper than it looks,' Jane said, as she and Freddie reached the crest of the hill and looked down towards the ocean. Her face was red and blotchy and she could already feel perspiration trickling down her back. Today was turning out to be a real hot one. 'I feel like a pack donkey carrying all this stuff.'

Meg was also red in the face and puffing ever so slightly. She was, after all, carrying an enormous picnic basket and a hold-all that could accommodate at least a week's worth of supermarket shopping. Meg laughed as Jane rested the folding chairs and picnic blanket on the ground.

'It pays to go to the gym,' Meg teased.

'I don't get time for the gym.' Jane groaned as she hoisted the folding chairs back over her shoulder and wedged the picnic blanket back under her other arm.

'Are we there yet Mummy?' Freddie asked, as he sat down on the ground removing his shoes.

'It's not far now sweetheart. Put your shoes back on please. You can take them off when we get to the beach.'

'No thank you,' he replied, as he handed his shoes to Jane to carry. She was in no position to argue so she shoved the shoes under her arm with the picnic blanket and clasped Freddie's hand, as they continued the grueling descent to the beach. The descent was made more treacherous by the ankle breaking pot holes that had been created by the recent torrential rain. After what seemed like an age, they reached the soft white sand of the beach. Meg reached out to take the little folding chairs and picnic blanket from her friend.

'Here sit down, you look ready to collapse,' she said, with a smile of sympathy. Jane flopped down and removed her new sandals, which had produced sizable blisters on her heels.

'Oh goodness they look sore.' Meg reached into her over-sized hold-all and removed a first aid kit. She proceeded to apply a dab of white cream and a couple of band aids to the now burst blisters. Within seconds Jane felt the soothing effect of the cream.

'What is that cream?' She tried to read the name and information on the tube. 'I can't even pronounce it.' Without her reading glasses it was as impossible as reading under murky water.

'It is written in Italian. We picked it up a few years ago when we were there on holiday. Tim fell off a push bike and took the skin off both knees. A local pharmacist sold me this cream. It worked well for Tim's knees so it should work for your heels. It is out of date by a few months, but it should be fine.'

'Ever capable Meg, you really are an apprentice Jack of all Trades,' Jane joked.

'I have to be, to keep up with this lot,' she replied, as she waved in the direction of the children. It's never a dull moment. Pass me that picnic basket over and I will get us a cold drink.' The tide was just a distant strip on the horizon, but three of the children were already happy exploring the nearby rock pools, looking for crabs.

'Come on Freddie, get your bucket and spade. We will go and help the others look for crabs, while your Mum has a little rest, until her feet feel better.' Jane's heels were already feeling much better, after Meg's ministrations, but she relished the idea of a little time to herself.

'Thank- you, I'll just have a little rest and then I'll join you.' She watched as Freddie happily wandered off hand in hand with her best friend. *She is such a great friend,* Jane thought, as she watched them walk away to join the others. Freddie's blue plastic bucket swung from side to side as he skipped along beside Meg.

Emily, Jane's fifteen-year-old daughter was deep in conversation with Susie, Meg's fourteen-year-old daughter. They lay back on a blue check picnic blanket, which was placed a suitable distance away from their mothers. Apparently, it was not cool to be seen with your parents. A wave of nostalgia washed over Jane. Emily was no-longer her little girl, but a stroppy teenager rapidly approaching independence. At Meg's insistence they had covered themselves in sunscreen lotion. Their bikini clad young bodies were poised to catch as many rays as possible in the available sunshine. *They are not too different to me at that age. The only difference being I smothered my body in coconut oil and my pink spotted bikini was made with more fabric,* Jane thought, as she covered her eyes with her new sun glasses. *I must keep an eye on them.* She looked across the beach towards a group of teenage boys playing volleyball, using a makeshift net made from green plastic garden wire. The girls had not escaped their notice and vice versa. Jane lay back, resting her head on the children's discarded clothing and watched the white clouds scudding across the bright blue sky. The warmth of the sun on her face was glorious and as the throbbing from her blistered heels almost disappeared, she felt her body relax.

I wonder if Jon and Phil are enjoying their golfing holiday? She hadn't really thought about Jon, her husband, this week and she doubted that Meg had had enough time to think of Phil either. The children had taken all their mothers' attention. Juggling the needs of all six children in the tiny holiday cottage was a challenge that neither mother had anticipated. It wasn't the first time they had rented a holiday cottage together, but this year the size of the accommodation and the vile weather had conspired against them. *Note to self, checkout the reviews next time.*

A Much-Needed Day Out

I really hope this lovely weather lasts, Jane thought, just before her eyes closed and she was lost in sleep.

When a Town Works Together
by Janette Cooke

'Why did you loan your bike to that little hooligan? You don't even know if he will bring it back.' Kristy was so exasperated with her young son, Danny, she could hardly contain her feelings.

When Danny walked through the front door after school last week, he couldn't wait to tell his Mum of the good deed he did.

'Kody told me that his Mum had to go into hospital last night. He said she had walked into the bedroom door in the dark and broke her nose. It wouldn't stop bleeding and the ambulance took her to hospital to see if there was any other damage.'

As he gave Kristy this information in a very matter of fact, but quavering voice, it was difficult for her not to overthink the situation. Each new snippet of information Danny revealed to his Mum only brought more misgivings for the welfare of Sarah MacLaughlin, Kody's Mum.

'But Mum, Kody wanted to see his Mum and asked if he could use my bike 'cos the bus doesn't go anywhere near the hospital. I thought you would be proud of me, not angry.'

Kristy was shaken by the confusion and unhappiness so very visible on Danny's freckled face.

'Sweetheart, I am sorry for my outburst. I should have asked the reason you offered your bike before I flew off the handle. I am proud of you, and your father will be too, when you tell him. Please forgive me, darling.'

It had been whispered among some of the women in Kristy's gym class, that Sarah probably had an abusive husband. However, not one of these same women was prepared to seek out the truth. No one volunteered to even make a tentative approach to Sarah, to find out if she needed their help in any way. She had heard excuses, such as, "I don't want to be seen as a sticky beak or an interfering bitch, and "It may cause more problems if her husband hears about a visit by one of us," was another.

Each of these expressions of doubt and caution around any intervention, appeared on the surface, to be a valid reason to do nothing. It was only when a few of the women, including Kristy, thought about it a little more, that they admitted it was just using the same old excuse of avoidance that had been used forever. No one admitted having a willingness to seek out Sarah to discover if they could help in any way.

Later that night, Kristy spoke to her husband, David. She told him of a plan she had, regarding how she would broach the subject of possible domestic violence, with Sarah. Kristy and David had been married for almost seventeen years and had always discussed their day's activities before saying goodnight. This routine gave them a peace rather than silly little worries. It allowed each of them to bring their strengths into play. Kristy was a little more bombastic and her *let's do it now* attitude, would sometimes cause her to act before giving enough thought to any possible consequence. David was Kristy's sounding block and had consistently offered a more considered way of approaching any subject. This had worked well in their busy lives. Being a thinking man, it took a little while before he offered his thoughts regarding what they could do. 'Appearances may not have any connection with domestic violence, and there could easily be a very valid reason for the current situation. It would only alienate the family even more if we all go off half-cocked. The subject of domestic violence is so prevalent these days, we think of that first, without looking deeper.'

Feeling quietly reprimanded by this gentle advice, Kristy decided she would just try to be a friend to Sarah, rather than the neighbourhood do-gooder.

Two days later, Kristy finished cooking her family favourite lasagne and a batch of chocolate biscuits, and was ready to put her plan into action. She was going to use the information Danny had told her about Sarah's fall, when Kody had returned the bike. That was a relief in itself. Kristy had wondered if the bike was gone forever, or if it would be returned in good shape. She was coming to terms with the old adage of not judging a book by the cover. Nor should anyone assume anything about others just by their appearance, spread by nameless gossips.

The time showed eleven am on her Smartwatch, as Kristy gave a tentative knock on the McLaughlin's front door. There was a short time lapse before the door opened to reveal a slight, pale-faced woman, holding on to a walking stick. Kristy tried to hide her shock with Sarah's appearance and frailty.

'Oh Sarah, I am so sorry to interrupt your day, but I thought you may need some company.'

'Kristy, sorry for my appearance. I haven't been well lately, and the first things to go are self-care and then the housework. We all know it will wait for us, and I hate to say it, but I think it may be waiting for a bit longer at the moment.'

'Please don't apologise for anything. Kody told Danny you hadn't been well. I didn't come as a judgemental stickybeak. I'm here as a friend. Something I should have done sooner. If you don't mind, I could come in and help you for a bit. I have brought you a lasagne, which I hope your family will like. I also baked a batch of brownies this morning. We can sit down and have one of them with a cuppa, if you like.'

'Thank you, Kristy. Come on in, please.'

'You just sit down while I search your cupboards for the tea etc. Or would you prefer coffee?'

'Coffee would be great. One sugar and a little milk, please.'

Sarah seemed relieved that someone, anyone, would take over and give her a break from her struggle to keep the household functioning.

'Kody told Danny that you had suffered a fall and had been in hospital. How are you now?' Kristy hoped that her question would solicit some information that would lead to knowing a little more about the current situation in the home.

'It probably seems strange to have to stay the

night, or even go to hospital for a bloodied nose, but there is a reason. I would feel better if I told you about it.' Kristy was surprised that Sarah seemed to want to talk.

'I am all ears.' Kristy listened as Sarah began to talk. There seemed to be a bond forming between them as they sat there sharing their coffee and biscuits.

'It is hard to start, but I need you to know I have seen the sideways glances and heard whispers as I walk around the IGA in town.'

This revelation caused a burning sensation on Kristy's cheeks. She knew it hadn't been her doing these things, but she definitely was aware of who the culprits would have been.

'There have been many times I have wanted to turn around and tell them the truth, but then I would lose my courage. You see, if I didn't speak the truth, I could deny it to myself. I guess you could say, I had "The ostrich head in the sand" syndrome.'

Kristy was becoming seriously concerned for Sarah. What would the truth be? What secret was Sarah hiding? Would she be compassionate when Sarah revealed the real reason for her current appearance, her withdrawal from the CWA and Church groups and the gym classes, too?

'For the last three months I have been going from doctor to specialist to pathologists and radiologists, in what has become a nightmare and a never-ending cost and worry for Ron and me. It was only after I fell over and had a night in hospital that all the pieces finally came together in the one answer. I have a brain tumour. At this stage, no one can be 100% sure if it is benign or not.'

This information came out like a dam bursting. Sarah's face seemed to brighten, as though voicing the devastating news lessened the expectancy of a tragic outcome.

'Good Heavens, you poor thing. I don't know what to say. You must be so worried. What is the next move for you? Surely they will operate as soon as possible?'

Sarah wiped her nose with the back of her hand, before reaching for a tissue from the kitchen bench, after realising she had blurted out her news to Kristy.

There was hesitation before she spoke. 'The operation is next Thursday. Ron and I plan to tell Kody tonight. I will be in hospital for two to three weeks for the op and rehab afterwards. I've been told that I'll need to learn to walk properly again, as the pressure on the brain has caused serious vertigo. That is why I stumble like the town drunk, and why I run into walls and doors. I have to admit this house has given me some fairly good *shiner*s.'

'I assume the operation and rehab will take place in the Melrose Base Hospital. Sadly, we don't have great facilities at our little country hospital.'

'Yes. Ron is thinking that he and Kody will stay with his sister in town, but we worry about Kody missing school.'

At last Kristy felt she could offer some practical help to Sarah. 'Well, I can't help with your health, but I can definitely help eliminate your worry about Kody. Kody can move in with us until you are home again, on your feet and on the way to a great recovery.'

'I can't believe my luck today. The last few weeks have been terrifying, and in just a couple of hours you have brought solutions to many of my worries. Someone to care for Kody, someone to confide in, and the beginning of a great friendship, I hope.'

Relief was visible on Sarah's face when she spoke.

Witnessing Sarah's relief was so heart-warming, Kristy was not surprised to feel a tear leak from her own eyes.

'You can be assured of our friendship from now on. Kody will enjoy being with Danny. With them being under the same roof, they can chat about things that worry them anytime they want. It will be good for both of them. Or they can just play on the X-Box.'

These circumstances fitted right in with the very strong belief that Kristy had about her strengths. She was confident in her ability to recognise and then organise help, and assistance for people. This confidence started with her first job in a large office and continued now that she was living in a small town. There was often someone needing help, but not knowing who to approach. Kristy was considered the *go-to* person in town for the first step to a solution.

'Sarah, as you know, this town does have a good heart, but it slips sometimes. We should be able to organise a roster for deliveries of plenty of good home-cooked meals from the ladies in the CWA. We all know how proud they are of their cooking abilities. We can rope the men into mowing your lawn and any general yard-work for a couple of months. That would allow Ron to devote his time to you, instead of worrying about upkeep around the home.'

'That would be welcome and wonderful, Kristy.'

After more chatting, hugs and tears from both women, Kristy left Sarah's kitchen, telling her she needed to get started on putting her plans in action.

Later that afternoon, Kristy jokingly thought to herself. My finger is suffering RSI from dialling our CWA members. Thank God it was easy to arrange a roster and menu for the coming week. She had also organised for the roster to swing into full production when the family returned after the operation and rehab. When the ladies were delivering the meals, they would ask Sarah if she needed any laundry or housework done now, or when she returned from Melrose.

Everyone said they would hold on to the belief that only a benign tumour was going to be the result. No one wanted to accept bad news concerning one of their own in town especially a young wife and mother with so much ahead of her. Positivity was the way to go.

A few wives also volunteered their husbands as yards-men. They intended to organise a roster so everyone didn't turn up on the same day.

Down at the RSL, the manager offered the profits from the Friday night raffles for the next month. That could help with accommodation, incidentals and food costs for Ron, while he was in Melrose and not able to work.

When Kristy laid her head on the pillow that night, tired but happy, she felt pride in her little town.

As she drifted off to sleep, Kristy's last thought was, well God, the town is on board to help this family. The final result is now up to you.'

The Unexpected
by Desley Polmear

Kate Livingstone noticed a slight smile showing wrinkles in the corner of Kenneth's eyes as they walked past the café, filling their nostrils with the aroma of coffee. He stopped by the fountain in the City Square to watch the two musicians, then turned and took hold of Kate's hands.

'This is our song. Do you remember darling? We danced around and around the floor until you led me back to the table, exhausted.' He smiled his silly smile patting her hand, over and over.

'How could I forget my love?' She reached up and kissed his cheek.

Before the music finished, he rushed into the nearby bookstore, his breathing quickening.

'Boat magazines,' he said. 'I want pictures of boats.'

The young girl led him to the section, pointing to the row of books. His finger ran along until he found what he wanted. He grabbed several and hid them in his hessian bag. Kate led him back to the girl and paid for his purchases. Kate smiled, thinking about all the changes in the two of them since the first night they met. She was only seventy four years of age, but her body sagged with fatigue by two pm each day.

The doctor had said, "Remember Kate, you are in your mid-seventies. It's to be expected with all you have to do each day. Your life has turned upside down, far different to what you expected." As he patted her arm, he said, "Do as I say my dear."

"Thank you. I will," she'd said. That was some time ago.

Sitting at a table by the window in the bookshop, sipping coffee, the light, a warm buttery shade, shone on Kenneth's face. His eyes were closed. Kate squeezed his hand, leant into him and listened to the distant music too, coming from the square. They both had a love of music, and that love brought them together at the Italian club one Friday evening. Kate went along because her son played the drums in the band. Ever since that night the couple had shared many things and travelled far.

The date would forever be fixed in Kate's mind. It happened to be her mother's birthday. *God rest her Soul.* The doctor sat her down and told her that the days ahead may not be easy for her. Kenneth had early stages of dementia, and how later down the track, she would be reliant on extra help as taking care of him would become difficult. The news crushed her that day sixteen months ago, but she'd learnt a lot about the illness since then. She'd formed close friendships with other carers, and they had been her lifeline many a time after collapsing from exhaustion.

She began to notice things, really notice things more now. How he went down to the garden shed, his coffee left untouched. She found unopened mail in the rubbish bin in the study. He began to wander off without telling her. He smelt his food before eating it. 'Lovely my darling,' he'd say, before his first mouthful.

'Who are you?' he asked her one morning while she picked roses from her garden. Tears forming, Kate knew it was time for full-time care.

A Day in a Lifetime

by Julie Deegan

Mary Cole was lost in a daydream, not daring to share her fantasy aloud. She was sitting in her writing group, trying hard to focus, yet lost in thoughts of love and remembering the promise her boyfriend Tom Mathews made the night before. Mary and Tom had sat on a bench in the park, bathed in the glow of a full moon. Mary imagined a rosy future with Tom, but was it to be just an illusion? She dearly wanted her fantasy to come true.

'Can you read your story aloud please?' the writing teacher asked.

Coming back to the reality of her class, Mary related her daydream – story, while changing names to protect the innocent. Mary's writing group friends were left to ponder the possible outcome of Tom and Mary's lives. Would they get together as life partners and would Mary get her rosy future?

Two years go by before Tom proposed to Mary under the glow of a full moon. He held her hands in his as Mary replied, 'Oh, yes please.'

They married in their local church and honeymooned on Daydream Island, before moving close to the city to start their married life together.

A Day in a Lifetime

Living with her love Tom, goes so well. They rented an apartment close to the train station so they could both commute into the city for work. They worked in offices close to each other and met up in their lunch hour. Walking through the Botanical Gardens every day, munching on their sandwiches and chatting easily with each other, gave them so much pleasure. Sometimes Mary couldn't wait for five pm so she could run down to the station and see Tom again. They were both excellent cooks so they took turns making tasty meals to share. Tom made a mean spaghetti bolognaise and Mary cooked a delicious chicken roast.

Their holidays were a joy to plan.

'Shall we cruise to New Zealand?' Tom suggested.

'How about we fly to Japan?' Mary said. Whatever they decided their holidays together were adventurous and fun.

Two near blissful years went by and their thoughts turned to starting a family, but no new marriage was without a few challenges. Was married life always as rosy as Mary hoped it would be? Sharing their lives in a small rented apartment was a squeeze and tensions rose as they negotiated the details of life together.

'Please use the appropriate cutting board for your food prep. Is it so hard to close the toilet seat?'

They loved each other, however the strain of negotiating the small details of life, allowed resentments to build. Mary thought to herself, I love Tom but the tension between us is getting me down. I love sharing a bed with Tom, but sharing other aspects of our life is getting too difficult. Had the thought of starting a family given Mary cold feet? After only two years of marriage, Mary and Tom decided to take separate holidays, as a chance to think about their lives. Tom was shocked by Mary's suggestion but goes along with it because he sees no other option. He was upset, the rejection hurt.

Mary drove up the coast and rented an apartment close to the beach. Here she walked the beach, swam, and enjoyed her favourite brand of coffee each day. The time away gave Mary a chance to evaluate her own life and her marriage to Tom. Mary gave herself a good talking to. Surely, I can be flexible and make allowances for our differences. Don't sweat the small stuff, she thought, as she walked along the water's edge. As Mary drove home to the city, she resolved to keep her silence with the tiny details of her life with Tom that riled her so. With a skip in her step, Mary returned to their city apartment ready to apologise and have a gentle talk with Tom.

Tom had been away down the south coast, also pondering his life with Mary. On the two-hour drive down to the south coast his mood was sombre. He was blindsided by Mary's decision that they take stock of their marriage and their future. He drove into the carpark of the Mollymook Golf Club at eleven am. His twin brother David played golf at the club every Sunday morning. He had agreed to meet Tom after a distressed phone call from him, earlier in the week. David was in the bar waiting when Tom arrived.

'Take a seat while I get us both a drink,' he said, as he gave his brother a hug. He was shocked at Tom's dishevelled appearance. His face was pale and he looked like he had lost weight. Tom had always been the smarter dresser of the two brothers but he looked like he had slept in his clothes for a week and grey stubble covered his usual clean-shaven face.

'Sorry to interrupt your golf match but I had to talk to someone. I think Mary wants out of our marriage,' he blurted out.

'Surely not, you have always been the ideal couple. Not that long ago you were hoping to start a family.

What's happened? Has Mary found someone else, or have you been having an affair?'

'Of course, I haven't been having an affair and to my knowledge neither has Mary. This whole thing has come out of the blue. I had no idea her feelings towards me had changed. She has always had a romanticised view of marriage so maybe the reality hasn't lived up to her expectations. If she can't cope with the little minor differences we have now, how is she ever going to cope with motherhood and parenting. I thought I knew her so well but reflecting on the last two years since we married, I realise I don't. I'm not sure I can risk having children with her now. I have agonised over this all week. I am driving back home later today, and I am no closer to a solution.' Drops of beer splashed onto the table as he banged his glass down.

'I am so sorry. This is so unexpected; I don't know what to say. My only advice would be not to make any hasty decisions until you have had time to think this through, and while you are so upset.' Tom had previously made hasty decisions that he later regretted. All work related, but he was prone to run from problems rather than tackle them head on sometimes.

'I have thought of nothing else for the past week.' He checked his watch. It was midday and the club would be closing soon. I need to get going before the afternoon traffic starts to build.' David noticed the tension in Tom's face and knew their conversation was over. Tom picked up his jacket and gave his brother a hug before heading to the carpark. As David watched him drive away, he wondered what scene would play out when he got home to Mary.

It was late afternoon when Tom and Mary met up again in their apartment, each with different thoughts in their head. Mary had rehearsed what she wanted to say but before she had a chance to speak, Tom put a hand up to silence her.

'I think you were right to question our marriage, although I thought we were both happy. Having thought of nothing else for a week, I think we should part and go our separate ways. Love is not always enough.' He turned and walked away. The room started to spin and Mary sank to her knees. How had all her dreams come to this? This was not the ending she wanted.

Bubbles
by Monica Hales

Jenny Knight was brimming with excitement as her father's horse, Bubbles, prepared for his maiden race at the Port Cup on the weekend. Jenny had been there watching Bubbles grow from a foal and giving him his name. In contrast, Jimmy, Jenny's father, seemed noticeably nervous and apprehensive about the race. He held the belief that Bubbles was not ready.

'We should scratch him,' Jimmy announced to Bill, the trainer, down at the track. They were observing the final training session before giving Bubbles a well-deserved rest day. Bill had worked with and disciplined the horse since he was six months old. He knew the horse well, making it difficult to believe what he just heard.

'The horse is ready,' he piped. 'He shows a lot of promise for a middle-distance runner.'

Bubbles was just over three years old, so in the racing world, the age was ideal. 'Bill, the horse has never displayed any power or stamina in the final stretch in any race so far.'

Bill huffed. 'He's a swooper, and he will fool everyone and stay at the back unleashing a fast-finishing burst on the outside. The other riders won't see him coming.'

'What you call the perfect race eh?' Jimmy tried to assure himself.

'That's right Jimbo. Start fast but save the energy for the homestretch. That's what we have bred the horse to do. He is well prepared. Mark will put the blinkers on him so he won't be distracted. Come on Jimbo. Let's do it. Don't give up now.' Bill was getting agitated. Jim had displayed these same apprehensions every week for the past month and his patience was wearing thin.

Jenny was listening to the conversation. 'No Daddy, don't pull him out. Mum and I have purchased our outfits. We picked the same colours as Mark's silks. I have a purple dress and Mum chose pink. Besides, I can legally drink this year.'

Bill gave her a worrying look, just as Bubbles trotted by. Mark, his jockey, tilted his helmet to the men and gave Jenny a wink. They all followed the horse over to the stables. Bubbles was already getting a brush down by the time they reached the stall.

Bubbles

'So, Mark, how did he do this morning?' Bill asked.

'He went great. No trouble at all. I even held him back on the final turn because he just wanted to go.' This was Mark's first race. He had always been a small kid and had inherited his mother's genes, that being very short. He was only five foot and weighed a mere forty kilograms, despite being seen to always be eating. Jenny would put on five kilograms just by looking at food.

'How can you be so skinny when you always eat bread?'

'Born different, Jens,' he said. His family owned an equestrian school on a neighbouring property, so he was always around horses. Being a jockey was the likely career choice.

'Hey Mark, Jimbo wants to scratch the horse,' Bill declared.

'You can't Jim. He's a winner. I can see victory already.' Everyone surrounded Jim, giving their opinions. After lots of badgering, Jim relented and decided to give in.

'All right, enough. Stop. We'll race him.'

After being attended to by the stable hands Gary, the farrier, checked over Bubbles hoofs. 'The horse is good to go from my point of view, Bill. He's in great shape and certainly ready to race.'

Jim was still dubious about racing Bubbles, but he had been overruled.

Jenny applied the woollen horse blanket and walked Bubbles to the adjacent field. She gave him a carrot.

'Good boy. Go and have a frolic.' Bubbles galloped off to his favourite tree at the far end of the paddock.

...

Race day had arrived, and the house was abuzz of excitement. Bubbles had already been loaded onto the float and on his way to the racetrack. Jenny and her mother, Eileen, were having their hair and makeup done by their friends, Beck and Kristy, from the local hairdressers. Everyone was enjoying a glass of champagne. Jim had been up early to see Bubbles loaded, and after a restless sleep, he was short tempered. He was pacing, hands deep in his pockets.

'How long are you going to be?' he snapped at Eileen. 'Don't have too many glasses of champagne.'

Eileen just smiled. 'We won't be much longer. Go and chill on the veranda. Maybe you should have a scotch or two, it'll calm you down. We'll be ready by ten-thirty.'

Jim left the giggling women and paced the veranda. Within an hour, they were on their way. The gates were opening at eleven-thirty, so they went to the stables first to check on Bubbles. Jenny was looking forward to seeing Mark. They had been dating for over a year and she wanted to show off her new dress. He saw her coming from afar and gave her several wolf whistles.

'Whoa … Wow … just look at you. You look amazing.' He held her hand, gave her a spin then tilted her, before giving her a long passionate kiss. Jenny was blushing. 'Here's my wallet, use the hundred dollars and go and see Old Bluey. He'll be the first bookie you see on the left as you enter the quadrangle. You can't miss him. He's tall, well overweight, got a thick mop of grey hair and he's always chewing a pencil. Oh, and he's very, very loud.' He gave her a wink as she headed off. 'Make sure you back him on the nose,' he called after her. She nodded and blew him a kiss.

Not only did Jenny put Mark's bet on, but she also went to the other nine bookies and placed bets.

She put fifty dollars to win at each stand. Most of them were paying 14 to 1, but Old Bluey had 20 to 1.

'He's a lay girlie. He'll probable come stone motherless last.' Jenny just smiled and left him laughing. 'Easiest money I'll make today,' he bellowed.

'You'll see,' she muttered under her breath.

Bill, Jim, Eileen and Jenny settled themselves up in the clubhouse. Each had a pair of binoculars, both restless and gulping their drinks. Eileen and Jenny had nearly finished a bottle of champagne.

'Here's to Bubbles,' they exclaimed as they lifted their glasses and joyfully clinked them together.

Finally, the announcement came. "Race One. Open Trial."

'Here we go Jimbo.' Bill gave Jim a firm handshake and a pat on the back.

The starting gate opened and the race caller yelled into the speaker. "They're off."

Bill was riding the race. Jim was speechless, and both Eileen and Jenny were screaming. Bubbles rounded the clubhouse turn. 'Bring him on the inside, not the outside,' Bill yelled. Bubbles was coming last. Jim was mortified.

Bubbles

'How humiliating, I told them he wasn't ready,' he whispered to Eileen.

As the race continued, Mark held the horse back. Bill kept yelling, 'Go … go…go. Let him go.'

The girls were out of control and squealing, 'Come on Bubbles, go.'

Then, as the horse rounded the far turn, it happened. Out of nowhere, Bubbles picked up speed, passing the field. In the final stages, he powered forward, winning the race by a nose.

Jenny and Eileen were crying and jumping up and down with excitement.

Jim was in shock and couldn't speak.

Bill just kept repeating over and over, 'I knew he could do it.'

They all rushed down to the enclosure to clap and cheer as Bubbles came into view. Mark was covered in dirt, his grin stretched wide across his face, easily visible from a distance. Jim shook his hand.

'You ran the perfect race Mark, well done.'

Jenny gave Mark a quick hug before he had to go and get weighed in. Bubbles was adorned with a blanket of red roses and then taken back to the stables. Once the formalities were over, everyone celebrated the afternoon away.

'This has been the best day,' Jenny said on the drive home.

'Wow, we made a killing today. Did you see Old Bluey's face when he had to part with all that cash,' laughed Mark. They all joined in the laughter.

'Now I can get that convertible,' Jenny sang out. She wound down the window and shouted, 'Yippee!'

Author Biographies

Carolyn Williams

Carolyn was born in the UK, where she trained and worked as a Registered Nurse and Midwife.

In 1988 the family left England to make their home in Australia. After retiring from a long and successful career in the health sector Carolyn now dedicates her time volunteering for animal rescue organisations.

Carolyn developed her passion for creative writing when she joined the Wauchope Friday Writers Group two years ago, and in 2022 saw her first stories in print in the book, Stories Around the Kitchen Table. This year Carolyn has published her first Childrens Book, which will be released prior to Christmas.

With the continued support of her wonderful family and mentor Desley Polmear, Carolyn is continuing her writing journey and is delighted to contribute to The Wauchope Friday Writers book, 2023.

Janette Cooke

Janette's life is filled with love for her husband, children and grandchildren. She is a long-time proud local who was born in Taree and is now a retired Administration Officer.

Janette has recently re-discovered an almost forgotten love of putting pen to paper.

The Wauchope Friday Writers Group reignited her passion to write fictionalised stories, based on people and events she witnessed with Australians she met during extended travels in the outback.

Desley Polmear

Desley was born in Brisbane and since retiring and moving to NSW, she has been writing fiction. Desley has at least one murder in her novels. She began painting in oils in the 80's while living on the Sunshine coast and watercolours in 2003 while working in an art gallery in NZ. In 2022, she turned to painting again. She spent the whole year painting in acrylics and graduated in December the same year.

In early 2023, she has had two exhibitions and three commissions in that short time. Her two loves are painting and writing, which keeps her busy. Her greatest joy is to help and inspire others who want to write.

Monica Hales

Monica Hales is a Registered Nurse, Midwife and mother of five. Realising the need to search for a hobby that delved into her own interests, she joined the Wauchope Friday Writers Group. This experience has been eye-opening, as it showed her that anyone has the potential to write a book. It was a proud moment for Monica when she took a leap and tested her writing abilities, resulting in her first short story, "The Power of Resilience."

Writing has become a surprising and delightful skill for Monica, one she never knew she possessed. This newfound passion for storytelling, has aspired her to keep writing.

Julie Deegan

Julie was born in Sydney. For many years she worked for P & O as a secretary in Sydney, and later, she worked at Media Monitors in Canberra as a broadcast editor. She is now retired and living in Port Macquarie. Julie loves swimming in the ocean, writing, and card making. One of her loves is listening to a variety of music.

Nola Turnbull

Nola was born in Kempsey and grew up in Warrell Creek.

She founded Fredo Pies in 1993. Following the sale of the business she gained employment in the aged care industry, as an Aged Care Advisor. Nola found this role fulfilling and compelling,

She now works from home, while also offering some voluntary assistance to those in need. She plans to expand her commercial involvement in aged care later this year.

It appears that retirement and Nola are not good bedfellows.

She is happily involved with family, who all live with her.

www.ingramcontent.com/pod-product-compliance
Lightning Source LLC
Chambersburg PA
CBHW070156120726
47909CB00001B/135